DAUGHTER
OF THE
REVOLUTION

DAUGHTER
OF THE
REVOLUTION

A Novel

Peter Hargitai

iUniverse, Inc.
New York Lincoln Shanghai

DAUGHTER OF THE REVOLUTION
A Novel

iUniverse books may be ordered through booksellers or by contacting:

iUniverse
2021 Pine Lake Road, Suite 100
Lincoln, NE 68512
www.iuniverse.com
1-800-Authors (1-800-288-4677)

This is a work of fiction. All of the characters, names, incidents, organizations and dialogue in this novel are either the products of the author's imagination or are used fictitiously.

ISBN-13: 978-0-595-41444-4 (pbk)
ISBN-13: 978-0-595-85828-6 (cloth)
ISBN-13: 978-0-595-85794-4 (ebk)
ISBN-10: 0-595-41444-3 (pbk)
ISBN-10: 0-595-85828-7 (cloth)
ISBN-10: 0-595-85794-9 (ebk)

Printed in the United States of America

Although the events described in this book are true insofar as they are based on the Hungarian Revolution of 1956, it is a work of fiction, and any resemblance to real persons is merely coincidental.

Photo Credits:
Cover: László Toth (mod.); Chapter 1: Árpád Hazafi, *Life*. Chapter 2: Pictorial Parade, Inc. Chapter 3: Eric Lessing, *Magnum*. Chapter 4: Eric Lessing, *Magnum*. Chapter 5: Hulton Press, Ltd. Chapter 6: Rolf Gillhausen, *Stern*. Chapter 7: Eric Lessing, *Magnum*. Chapter 8: Imre Balassa. Chapter 9: Rolf Gillhausen, *Stern*. Chapter 10: *Keystone Press*. Inserts: Courtesy of the American Hungarian Federation's 1956 Portal, with the exception of "Budapest, 1956" and "Péter's poem," which are from the author's private collection, and "Map of Central Budapest," which is courtesy of Opera Mundi, Paris.

The publication of this book was made possible
by support from the American Hungarian Federation, Inc.
www.americanhungarianfederation.org

This book is dedicated to the "kids" of Budapest,
who fought so bravely against overwhelming Soviet armor,
and to our grandkids, so they never forget.

My name is Izabella Barna. I'm fourteen years old. Yesterday, I was an average schoolgirl. Today, I killed a man. I wasn't born a killer. I had a loving mother and father. It all started in front of the Radio Building in Budapest, on October 23, 1956. Now, I have no mother and no father. Now, the closest thing to my heart is the submachine gun slung around my neck. I am the daughter of the Revolution now.

Chapter One

1

I was really in for it now. I stood at attention in front of Principal Aczél's desk staring at my handiwork, a poster that said, "DOWN WITH CUMPOLSORY RUSSIAN." I spent most of last night writing the same words in big bold letters on thirty sheets of art paper, made sure I got to school before it opened and tacked them on every door, including Principal Aczél's forbidding oak door. I didn't think anyone saw me. I guess I was wrong. Someone snitched on me. But who?

I had to say something in my defense. I told Comrade Aczél I was interested in learning other languages. "Why aren't we allowed to learn other languages besides Russian? Like English and—"

He cut me off sharply: "I don't remember saying you had permission to speak." Comrade Aczél was furious, and when he was furious, his sarcasm had an edge. "I can guess who put this in that fourteen-year-old head of yours. Who else, but your reactionary father. Oh, I beg your pardon. He couldn't have been the one, could he now? He's in prison, isn't he? For anti-Communist activities, I believe. Well, well, it seems to me you're doing everything in your power to make sure you follow in his footsteps."

I didn't react, and this made him so angry his breathing became uneven. Still, I had this feeling he was enjoying himself. He stubbed out his cigarette in its amber-colored holder and said, "I must warn you, Izabella Barna, this is not a game. Of course you realize you'll be kicked off the track squad. And, if I have my way, you'll be kicked out of school. You know where you belong? A youth brigade, like the old Stalin Work Brigade. Far away from anyone who would rather have you speak the language of our enemies that the language of our friends. You *will* learn to respect the language of our Soviet liberators, yes? And you will start tomorrow, yes? You are to report to this office at seven-thirty sharp, yes? The disciplinary committee will decide then what to do with you."

I hated school. But the thought of being away from my mother and my sister and my aunt made my mouth dry. "I'm sorry, Comrade."

"I don't think you know what the word sorry means. But you will. You will. Tomorrow, seven-thirty sharp, yes?" And that was it. The oak door closed behind me.

What was I going to tell my mother? She would kill me. Maybe I could talk my aunt into coming with me when I face the disciplinary committee. She was always good at talking to people. She was very charming when she wanted to be, and very persuasive. Maybe she could talk them into letting me stay in school.

Like any fourteen-year-old, I loved and hated school. I loved gymnastics because when it came to the balance beam and the parallel bars I was the best in the whole school. I was also the fastest in the 100 meters, even faster than the boys, except for Guszti Pálréti. My friends kept teasing me about him until my face was beet red and my freckles disappeared. They said I liked him and let him beat me every time we raced. Sometimes I pretended they were right, though I sure would've liked to beat him. Just once.

I didn't tell a soul, but I had this secret dream of becoming an Olympic champion one day and winning a gold medal for Hungary. When it came to sports, I was very proud to be Hungarian. Two years ago, in 1954, our soccer team almost won the World Cup in Switzerland, and we were third in the whole world in the 1952 Summer Olympics in Helsinki. Not bad for a small country of ten million.

Now that I was going to be kicked off the track team, my dream of ever making the Olympic team was shattered.

Track and field was my favorite event. I just loved to race. My hair was usually in braids except when I raced. Then, my long hair fluttered behind me like a banner in the wind. My classmates said I ran like a cheetah. I didn't mind being compared to the swiftest animal on the face of the earth, and it wasn't long before it became my nickname—especially when I beat Guszti in the city finals in Budapest.

It was something, crossing the finish line with hundreds of spectators cheering me on, including my mother and my little sister who shouted, "Go, Cheetah, go!"

I wished my father could've been there to see me win my big race. My little sister caught on to my new nickname in a hurry, but my mother didn't like it. To her, it wasn't very lady-like. I don't think my father would've minded. His nickname for me wasn't that far off. Ever since I can remember, he called me Kitty. He said as a toddler I'd leap on the furniture and bounce up and down on the couch like I was possessed. I was always a bouncer. I loved jumping. The higher the better, the farther the better. That was another thing I liked about school. The high jump and the broad jump. So, I guess you could say I liked gym.

I wasn't a slacker at schoolwork either. My grades were really good, especially in Art and in Hungarian. Now Russian was another story.

What I hated most about school was being forced to study Russian. It's such a hard language with their different alphabet and everything. I was pretty good at memorizing the grammar rules and some of the vocabulary, but to speak it or write it was near impossible and not just for me. My Russian language teacher was as strict as a boot camp commandant. We had to sit straight, with our hands folded behind our backs and stare ahead. Not that there was anything interesting on the wall, unless you were crazy about larger than life portraits of Stalin, Lenin and Marx.

A few years ago, the school took down all the pictures of Stalin. I guess it looked odd to have a blank space on the wall where the paint was a lot lighter. We joked about it, calling it Stalin's ghost. Our strict principal put Stalin's picture back. As far as old Comrade Aczél was concerned, Stalin, the great father and liberator, was back.

A great dictator is what my father called him. I really missed my father. They dragged him off to prison a little more than a year ago. My mother said it was because of Stalin. Because of what my father said against Stalin.

I wasn't very fond of Stalin. Ever since kindergarten, we were taught about Joseph Vissarionovich Stalin. I didn't mind the parades on May Day or singing the "International," but being fed all that stuff about Stalin being the great father and liberator, day in and day out, in just about every class was like stuffing geese. And we were the geese.

When I told my art teacher about what happened to me in the principal's office, she said Comrade Aczél was just trying to scare me.

If only I could believe her.

"Let me talk to him," she said.

Art was my last period class and, after gym, my second favorite. My art teacher never talked about politics except to say that propaganda art was a great waste of red paint. We were all afraid that somebody was going to report her, but no one did. I was glad about that because I liked her. She may have been old and poor, but she was full of life. She liked her students, and I think she like me.

One day she put a pair of tennis shoes on her desk. We all thought she wanted us to draw them. She had this habit of putting objects on her desk for us to draw, but this time the worn pair of tennis shoes were not part of our art lesson. She wanted us to buy them. We knew they were used, and that they were hers, even though she went out of her way to tell us the shoes belonged to a relative. We also knew how desperately poor she must be to have to do that. I felt sorry for her and offered to buy them from her. I tried them on after class, and they fit me fine. The problem was I didn't have nearly enough money so I told her I'd pay her the rest later. She let me take the shoes home anyway. To this day, I have not had a chance to pay her what I owed her. The funny thing is, she never once brought it up.

She was very serious about art. I remember the last class I had with her. She took her glasses off and placed them on her desk at an angle so they picked up the light from the windows. She wanted us to paint her glasses that way, with all the colors reflected in the lenses. Outside our second-story windows, the trees were turning not yellow so much but a rusty brown. The sky was blue with blotches of gray. I found myself staring out the window thinking about all sorts of things, mostly my father. When I didn't have school, he'd let me go with him on his job as a mailman. Once his mailbag got lighter, he let me carry it. How I loved the feel of the leather strap on my shoulder.

"Izabella Barna! Izabella Barna! Are we lost in reverie again? I know there's a lot on your mind, but would you kindly tell the class what is so interesting outside? You haven't even started on your water-color!"

Our teacher went to a window herself. She opened it to a blast of noise. A chorus of voices chanted, "Russians go home!"

She leaned out to see what was going on. "What on earth?" she said. "What day is it, children?"

Now that was strange. She never called us children before. It was always class this, or class that, or she'd address us by our last names.

We told her it was Tuesday. October 23. Like she didn't know.

It was one day I would never forget.

"As far as I know, there's no parade scheduled. Where are all those people going?" She went back to her desk, snatched up her glasses, and marched back to the window.

We jumped from our seats to see for ourselves. Suddenly it was chaos in our little classroom. Our teacher who was strict about discipline said nothing. We were amazed at the sheer number of people pouring down the street. Some were carrying Hungarian flags. One person held up a sign that said, "FREEDOM NOW!"

Our teacher clapped her hands twice. It was her usual signal to get our attention. "Everybody! Get back to your seats. Pack up your things and go home. I don't like the looks of this. You are all to go straight home, do you hear me?"

I didn't feel like going straight home. I wanted to see for myself what all this excitement was about. I was going to get it anyhow. Might as well do something to deserve it.

Putting on my pullover and backpack, I skipped down the stairs with my noisy classmates. It wasn't every day we were let out early. We sounded like swarming birds.

The air was dry and cool outside, as it should be on a late October day. I felt like I stepped out of a dark dungeon straight into a carnival. Before I caught on what was happening, I was swept into the crowd.

Most were students who attended college right here in the city. Two young men wearing sport coats and ties carried a placard that said Eötvős Loránd University. Another group was from the Technical University of Budapest across the Danube. A group of older girls walked arm in arm, taking up the whole street. I decided to walk alongside them. A car behind us honked trying to get through. We didn't budge. The girls were singing a song, but I couldn't make out the words.

People streamed in from side streets to join the swelling crowd. I had no idea where all this was headed. There was so much excitement in the air, enough for sparks to start flying. I figured this was some kind of spur-of-the-moment thing, not some official parade.

I asked the girl next to me where we were going. She didn't hear me. She simply locked her arm into mine and before I knew it, I was marching with them past the law school and the University Church where my family used to go before the Communists locked it up.

Our art teacher took us on field trips to show us some examples of beautiful architecture, and on one of these outings, she pointed out this church on the corner with its twin spires. She said we were looking at the finest baroque church in the whole city. We couldn't go inside, but she raved about the wood carvings on the altar and the choir.

The crowd crossed the street by the University Library with its corner copula. We poured into a square and stopped to let a yellow streetcar pass. I looked around to get my bearings.

The buildings were four or five stories high, like in most of Budapest. I now recognized the square as Felszabadulás Square with its ornate doorways of bearded gods or the heads of lions holding up an arch. Some doorways had strong women carved in stone holding up entire buildings. They were a signal, our teacher told us, that women were coming out through the portal to be part of city life. She said they were in the style of Art Nouveau, the French words meaning "new art." The other teachers thought our art teacher was off her rocker, that she was a *petit bourgeois*, but I could listen to her prattle on for hours.

Where I lived, the doorways were more old-fashioned. A half-naked Atlas crouched above one doorway. Our apartment was a lot scarier. A woman's head with squirming snakes for hair guarded our gate. It was Medusa, my father told me. If you looked at her, you stood a good chance you'd turn into stone yourself. Or maybe it was salt. He said it warded off evil spirits from the streets of Budapest.

I loved my city. I loved its ornate buildings, its squares, the tree-lined boulevards, the public gardens, like the one behind Heroes' Square. The dome-shaped Turkish baths, the Chain Bridge, the elegant Opera House, courtyards ringed with galleries of cast-iron railings. The story-book Fishermen's Bastion overlooking the Danube and the star-tipped dome and rising spires of Parliament.

Long before my art teacher, it was my father who inspired in me a special love for the city's architecture. You see, before the Communists came along, he used to be an architect. I was just a little girl when he'd take me around to see his favorite doorways and scrolled balconies. Old statues with broken noses. Mosaics that turned gold from the setting sun. He said he especially liked buildings that were modern expressions of Hungarian folk art, like frescoes of stylized Kalocsay tulips or mosaics made to look like embroidery.

My favorite was the Museum of Applied Arts on Üllői Avenue. Its bright green and yellow ceramic tiles and the multicolored copula with the Moorish design spoke to me of a fantasy palace somewhere in the lands of Araby.

I figured if I got kicked out of school, I could easily spend my time just walking the streets and ogling the buildings.

At the next intersection, the crowd was swallowed up by an even greater mob of people heading toward the Danube on Kossuth Boulevard, one our busiest thoroughfares.

After that last streetcar, the traffic came to a halt. I've never seen anything like it. All these people! I now wished my father were with me so he could see all this, be part of all this, whatever *this* was. It was crazy. Buses, cars, red trolleys at a standstill in the middle of the street. The passengers had no other choice but to get off and become part of the growing crowd.

I could see the Liberation Monument high on top of Gellért Hill, on the other side of the Danube. No way to cross the river. We were either going to have to stop or make a turn somewhere, because the bridge connecting Pest and Buda was blown up by the Germans during World War II. All that remained were the rusted towers with their severed arms.

The last field trip our teacher took us was to the top of Gellért Hill to see the colossal statue of a woman holding a palm leaf up to the sky. After we had eaten our lunch on the grass, she gave us a history lesson. Originally, she said, the monument was to honor Admiral Horthy's son whose plane was shot down by the Russians during a dogfight. After the war, the Russians turned it into a Liberation Monument for their soldiers. The Russian letters on it said that the monument was erected by the grateful Hungarian people in honor of the liberating Soviet heroes. She said it appeared our liberators must like it here since they have been with us now for the last eleven years.

At the base of the monument, they added a cast-iron statue of a Russian soldier with a submachine gun looking out over the city.

Gellért Hill had the best view of Budapest. You could see how the Danube divided the twin cities of Buda and Pest before winding westward by the Houses of Parliament.

Our art teacher had us walk around the old fortress in back of the Liberation Monument. We gawked at the massive walls pock-marked with bullet holes and shell marks that looked like craters.

By this time, the jostling crowd had grown so thick, we were shoulder to shoulder and closing ranks. I could feel the breath of the person behind me.

Something told me that our art teacher would not be taking us on field trips for a very long time.

The crowd was swept along the Danube, slowed down and finally came to a halt once it got to Petőfi Square, already overflowing with what must've been thousands and thousands of demonstrators milling around the statue of the poet Sándor Petőfi. I knew from studying Hungarian history that Petőfi was our most famous poet.

Because I was short, I had to strain my neck and tried standing on my toes. I was shocked when a lanky young college student behind me scooped me up and propped me on his shoulder. The girls around me twittered. I wasn't sure if I like it or not. I wanted to see, but I didn't care for being picked up like a little kid. Once I sized up what was going on, I asked the student to put me down, thank you.

It was enough for me to catch a glimpse of a man, probably an actor, who stood on a makeshift platform in front of the statue. He started to recite a poem by Petőfi that every Hungarian immediately recognized. "Stand Up Hungarians!" This patriotic poem started a revolution in 1848 against the Austrians. Imagine a single poem doing that! The man didn't have a microphone or anything like that, but he didn't need one. We knew the words by heart.

The fiery verses challenged Hungarians to stand up for freedom. "Now or never, let it be," the poem kept repeating, "Shall we be slaves or shall we be free?!" It wasn't long before the crowd joined in:

"Free!" the crowd roared. "Free!" I heard myself shout at the top of my lungs.

University students passed out posters with a list of demands. I took one from a young man wearing a coat with an armband of Hungarian colors. Because of all the excitement around me, I wasn't going give the poster more than a quick glance. Then I couldn't take my eyes off it. *One demand was for the release of all political prisoners.* The paper shook in my hand. My father. All I could think of was my father. That my father would come home to us. Then something else caught my eye. The last demand. It called for the withdrawal of all Russian troops from Hungary.

I looked around the crowd of demonstrators. They meant business, all right. What if the Russians had no intention of going home? What would happen then? What would happen to my father? What would happen to the demonstrators? Suddenly, I got scared. I stuffed the poster into my backpack and as soon as I wormed my way through the crowd, I ran all the way home to our apartment building on Sándor Bródy Street. I was breathless when I opened the gate under Medusa's gaze.

My mother met me in the foyer. She was angry. "Where have you been all this time?"

"The demonstrations," I said as we headed into the kitchen where my aunt was busy pedaling her sewing machine. My aunt sized me up over the rims of her glasses. "There are people everywhere," I plowed on. "Traffic is blocked and everything. They're passing out posters. They're demanding the release of political prisoners."

"What?" My aunt took off her glasses.

By this time I had my backpack off and I pulled out the poster with the demands. "Here." I handed it to my mother. I waited for her reaction.

Although my mother was some twenty years younger than my aunt, she was so much more serious and a lot more strict with me. I never knew whether this was because my father was gone or because she was disappointed in me. Like me, she was short, but that's as far as it went. She had this smooth, porcelain-like skin, not one freckle. She almost never used make-up or lipstick.

Raised in a village in southern Hungary, she was a bit old-fashioned in her ways about what good girls should be doing with their time. She liked to give me chores, and, if she had her way, I'd either be in church praying or in the kitchen cleaning and cooking and baking. She did have these dreams for me of playing the accordion one day. Thank the Lord we had no money to buy one. She said I spent all my time on the streets gawking at the buildings like I had never seen them before. I had better look where I was going before I walked in front of a streetcar. She had no patience with what she called my "nonsense."

My mother sat down on one of the kitchen chairs, glanced at the poster, shook her head in that impatient way of hers and passed it on to my aunt, who held it under her sewing machine's little light.

My aunt read what was on the paper but didn't say anything. Instead, she reached for a cigarette, lit it, and blew smoke out of her nostrils. "Interesting," she said. She told my mother to turn on the radio.

Nothing on but stupid music. My mother fooled with the dials but nothing was said about the demonstration. Nothing. I couldn't believe it.

I let them know the demonstration was going to continue on the other side of the Danube. By the statue of the Polish General Bem. "Can we go? Please?"

My mother shook her head slowly and said that I was insane. That the demands were insane. "Did you read all of them? Do you think the Russians will sit back and let a bunch of idealistic students run the country? You better think twice before getting your hopes too high."

I told her about all the people in the streets. The posters, the chanting. Petőfi's poem.

"Uhum. And look where he got us in 1848. It was the Russians then, too. The great Russian Empire. Don't they teach you that in your school? They may have changed their name to the Soviet Union, but it's still an empire. And here we are, a tiny country, challenging the great Soviet Empire. How smart is that?"

"Not very," my aunt said, lighting another cigarette. She was a real chain-smoker.

I was on the verge of tears and fought with my mother. "You just don't want Papa out."

"I won't be lectured by you about your father. He was irresponsible." She turned to my aunt. "Well, wasn't he?"

My aunt, who was my father's sister, pretended she was busy with the suit she was making for my mother.

"What about your sick sister?" my mother turned on me. "Who's going to take care of her when I'm out shopping? Your aunt? God knows how busy she is working for all of us. I told you about your father a hundred times already. Your dear father had to mouth off and get himself arrested so he could be carted off to God-only-knows-where. That's a fine way to run away from your family problems. By blaming the government. What about your poor sister? You expect me to drag her through a mob so you can pretend your father's coming back. Sorry, Kitty. I have to be responsible for all of us now. What you did today was very foolish. Very stupid. Just like your father!"

I loved my seven-year-old sister, and I loved her dearly, but I hated it when my mother tried making me guilty about her. Just because Krisztina had a bad heart and I didn't. "Where is Krisztina?" I asked.

"Yeah, where is Krisztina? You forgot about her, didn't you?"

"She's at the neighbors, playing," my aunt said. "Wait a minute. The radio. Turn it up. They're saying something."

My mother turned up the volume to hear a special bulletin from Radio Budapest:

> "This afternoon a vast youth demonstration took place in our capital. Although at noon today the Ministry of the Interior banned all demonstrations, the Politburo changed the decision. Scholars, students of the technological faculties, students of philosophy, law, economics, together with students from other university branches took part in the march led by their professors and leaders of the university Party organizations…At first there were only thousands but they were joined by young workers, passersby, soldiers, old people, secondary-school students and motorists…"

"See, I told you. Secondary-school students," I said.

"Hush," my aunt said.

"Can I go back out, just for a little bit?"

My mother turned off the radio and looked right at me. "No! And you can take that pullover off."

My aunt shook her head.

I started for the door, saying I was going to get Krisztina.

"You're staying right here," my mother said. "I'll get Krisztina."

I headed for the door anyway. One thing I knew was how to be defiant. I said I had to do homework. One of my friends in our building had this big Hungarian-Russian dictionary. I needed to use it. Just in case we had school tomorrow.

"Kitty," my mother said. "I know what you're up to, and I don't like it. I don't like it one bit. Now take off that pullover and wash your hands so we can sit down and eat."

"Oh, let the girl go. I can watch Krisztina," my aunt said. She went to her purse, took out a ten-forint bill and handed it to me. "You can fetch us two double espressos before you go out on your scouting mission. And get yourself a sweet. But do me a favor, take Michelangelo with you. Otherwise, you're going to have to stay behind on that skinny rump of yours."

Michelangelo was a neighbor on the ground floor. He was a bachelor in his early twenties, who worked at a tire factory. In his spare time he locked himself in his apartment doing God knows what. My aunt had him run a few errands for her now and then. I looked at my aunt pleadingly, "Do I have to?" Michelangelo was such an odd man. He was supposed to be in the air force but he was never on a plane in his life.

He was an artist type, my aunt said, as if that explained everything. Thought of himself as a painter who was going to be famous one day. That's why everybody called him Michelangelo.

Once I asked him to help me do a drawing for class and it turned out to be a disaster, but the worst part was he always whined, and he wouldn't shut up. I let them know I'd rather go with my friend Mariska.

My aunt took off the measuring tape she constantly wore around her neck. This time her tone was stern. "You'll do as I say or you don't go at all. *Kapish?*"

"Are you listening, Kitty?" my mother said.

"And you," my aunt said to my mother, "you can turn the radio back on. I wouldn't mind knowing what the hell's going on, if you don't mind."

And that was that. My aunt liked having the last word. Not this time, though. Unlike my aunt, my mother never swore. But she did go on and on about how someone will have to do some serious shopping, and soon. "We're out of bread and potatoes. We're out of the basics. What if there's a work stoppage or something like that? I guess I'll have no choice but to go out myself. And I'm tired of Kitty always getting what Kitty wants. And you're no help."

"Relax. We have all this work to do on your suit. The waist still isn't right. You'll have to try it on again. That is, if you don't mind."

This would be my mother's first suit. She had worn blouses, skirts, summer dresses, but never a suit. My aunt had been working on my mother's English tweed suit for I don't know how long. But tomorrow was the deadline. We had an appointment for Krisztina with a new heart specialist, and my mother wanted to make a good impression. She didn't want the doctor to think she's some village bumpkin.

"All right," my mother relented. "Can I at least worry about my daughter? She's just a kid, for God's sake. And she's a girl who does nothing but court danger. I'm sick of it."

"She's a big girl now. Aren't you a big girl, darling?"

I knew enough that now was the time to keep my mouth shut. My aunt looked at me. Our eyes met. This was my chance to talk to her about school. I signaled to her to follow me into the sewing room.

Once we were alone, I told her I was in big trouble. A lot bigger than coming home late. I recounted my meeting with Comrade Aczél. "He wants to send me packing to the Stalin Brigade as punishment," I said.

I was surprised by my aunt's reaction. "Oh, that old die-hard Stalinist! I'll tell you what, you stay home tomorrow, and your aunt will go to school and put that old fart in his place. The Stalin Brigade, my God!"

"No, Auntie. You'll get in trouble."

"You let me worry about that. I have friends in high places, myself. I once sewed a gown for Mária Gyurkovics, the famous opera singer. Wait till your stuffy Comrade Aczél hears of that!"

I gave my aunt a peck on the cheek and slinked to the door. I was already halfway out, when my mother shouted after me, "But you haven't eaten anything!"

I closed the door behind me. Our second floor, like the other four floors, was ringed by an open gallery with a wrought-iron railing. I looked up at the top tier, two floors above us, to see if Krisztina and her friend were playing there. Sometimes she rode her tricycle on the landing while her friend followed her in her wheelchair.

They weren't there. I pushed the red elevator button and waited for the birdcage elevator to take me up to the fourth floor so I could say hi to my little sister.

She was very happy to see me. I gave her a kiss on the cheek. Because of her heart, Krisztina's skin always felt warm, like she had a flush. Her color wasn't red but more bluish. That meant her heart didn't have enough oxygen. Maybe the specialist could fix the hole in her heart.

When I asked Krisztina what kind of sweet she wanted from the coffee shop, she said she'd like some *Krémes*, a vanilla-cream pastry. She looked up at me with those big, shiny, brown eyes that said she'd like to go with me. She knew she couldn't. I gave her a hug and promised her that when I got back we were going to do all sorts of fun things.

The truth of it was, poor Krisztina couldn't keep up with me. I was such a speed-demon. But I'd slow down for her. We spent hours one afternoon playing on the rug with my aunt's big magnet, the one she used to collect all the sewing pins that fell on the floor.

Krisztina liked playing with her little friend. She and her nine-year-old friend in the wheel chair got along real well together. Most of the time they played with this old raggedy doll, dressing her and undressing her, using my aunt's leftover fabrics. I'd cut out some patterns for them to look like little dresses.

My next stop was Mariska, my friend from school, who wasn't in school today. I wanted Mariska to tag along, but her mother said I was crazy. This morning she had a fever. And there was a mob out there! It was on the radio, she said. Mariska was not allowed out. Period. I was crushed. Then I had an idea. I asked if Mariska could go down to the coffee shop with me. She knew it was just downstairs. I told her I had to pick up some espresso, and cake for my little sister.

"Please?" Mariska pleaded with her mother.

Her mother relented, but we had to be right back or else. On the way, I let Mariska in on my school troubles. She was horrified, almost in tears. "Oh, my God!"

"It isn't that bad," I said. "My aunt will talk to Comrade Aczél tomorrow."

The empty coffee shop smelled of black coffee overloaded with sugar. I asked Mariska if she would do me a favor. If she'd take the cake up to my sister and a double espresso to my mother and aunt. "Tell them I'm looking for Michelangelo. And here," I gave her the ten forint-bill, "get yourself something, too." Mariska's eyes lit up like a Christmas candle. They were very poor and she hardly ever had sweets like the kind you could get here.

I had no intention of hooking up with that maniac Michelangelo. I wanted to go alone and be swept up with the excitement of it all when I caught up with the demonstration on Bem Square.

I got as far as József Boulevard around the corner when I felt a hand on my shoulder. It was him. Michelangelo. He sprouted the beginnings of a mustache and goatee. I wanted to tell him he looked like one of the Three Musketeers.

"And where do you think you're going, little girl?" he said, stroking the flyaway hairs of his new goatee.

He was wearing a trench coat and one of those stupid berets pulled down over his forehead. He said my aunt talked to him. I was not to go anywhere without him. "You're lucky I spotted you. Look at all these people!"

They were everywhere. On the sidewalk, on the street, streaming toward the Margit Bridge. The ones that weren't on the street stood on their balconies, waving to the crowd. One young woman waved a Hungarian flag from her window. I noticed that the red star had been cut out from its center.

A sign in the crowd said, FREEDOM, in huge letters.

I started to tell Michelangelo about the demonstration on Petőfi Square. He said he was there, too. I asked him if he got any posters about political prisoners. He didn't. He said *he* had been a political prisoner. For a week. Then he narrated a long story about how he was supposed to paint a giant poster of Stalin for a May Day parade some years back. The authorities didn't like it. He had made Stalin's mustache so droopy, he looked more like Genghis Khan than our great father and liberator.

"They put you in jail for that?"

"No. But that was just the beginning. They made me go back and retouch the painting. I had to shorten his moustache to make him look friendlier. Lots of work. The poster was huge. The size of a truck. We had a cable going from one rooftop to another. The poster hung from it like an oversized bed sheet, except it wasn't flapping in the wind. I had ten to fifteen minutes. And I had to stand on a fireman's ladder in the middle of traffic on Rákóczy Boulevard. I could've been easily knocked off my perch. I'm afraid of heights anyway. That's why I live on the ground floor."

"Is that why you never flew a plane?"

"The Hungarian air force only has so many planes. The Russians don't exactly trust us. But the real reason was because I was too talented as an artist. They had other plans for me."

Michelangelo was nearly breathless, not because we were walking too fast, but because he was getting himself worked up. About himself.

"Oh, yeah, they had other plans for me. I was supposed to be a great cog in their wheel of propaganda. That's what they said at the Party meeting."

"You're a member of the Communist Party?"

"You have to be if you're in the air force. The problem they had with me is that I wasn't enthusiastic. That's how they put it. I didn't have the right kind of enthusiasm or revolutionary spirit, whatever that is. So, I made a wisecrack during one of their propaganda jam sessions. After the fallout about my portrait of Stalin, we got into it. I felt they had violated my sense of artistic freedom and said so. They laughed and jeered and kept baiting me until I punched one of them in the mouth."

"So, they hauled you off to jail because of that?"

"You got it, kid."

I hated it when he called me kid or little girl.

I told him about my posters and the Stalin Brigade.

"The Stalin Brigade, huh? Maybe they're trying to make a soldier out of you," he said with a laugh.

"Our principal's an old fart," I said, borrowing my aunt's expression. "He said I'm following my father's footsteps straight into prison. Did you know my father's in prison?"

He said he knew about it. Michelangelo knew about everything, and he was talking up a storm like I feared he would. He whined about how artists have to serve the system instead of their personal muse. Stuff like that.

He did say something funny, though. It was a little off-color, but it was funny just the same. "It's crappy here in this country," he said. He had this friend of his who tried to escape by the border, but by nightfall, the border guards caught up with him. "The poor fellow," Michelangelo said, "didn't know what to do, so he squatted over a pile of dog kaka. You know, like it was nature's calling. The border guard directed his flashlight at the dog turd and said, 'Why, you scoundrel! That's dog shit.' In his defense, the man said: 'We have a dog's life. So we shit dog shit.'"

I cracked up. He said he read it in *Ludas Matyi*, a humorous magazine filled with political jokes. It was the only way people could blow off steam, he said. Then he added: "I wonder how many years he got for that little morsel."

Michelangelo kept up his drone whether I listened or not. After a while I stopped listening. Huge crowds came from all directions on the Pest side to cross the Margit Bridge which was now filled with a moving mass of people. Far off I could see that the Chain Bridge was also jam-packed with demonstrators going in the same direction.

Once we were part of the moiling mob in Bem Square, Michelangelo said: "My God, look at that sea of humanity. This is big," he said. "This is big. Look!" He pointed to a man who was using his pocket knife to slash away at a Hungarian flag. He was cutting out the Communist emblem at its center.

The statue of General Bem towered above the crowd. He was a Polish general who had become our national hero because he fought with the Hungarians in the War of Independence against Austrian domination.

The demonstrators were laying a wreath at the foot of the statue. Michelangelo explained that the Poles had a big protest only recently. We were showing solidarity with the Polish people.

We got here in the nick of time. I heard a microphone being tested. Soon a man who was introduced as the head of the Writers Union recited a 16-point demand against the government. The first one was a demand for all Soviet troops to withdraw from Hungary. Another demanded the election of new leaders by secret ballot. Another demanded that Imre Nagy be put in charge of the new government.

"That's stupid," Michelangelo said. "If they want free elections why do they insist on Imre Nagy. Why can't we vote by secret ballot like civilized countries?"

I didn't know who Imre Nagy was, so I asked.

"He's an old Communist dog, like the rest of them."

I was sorry I asked. I was anxious to hear something, anything about political prisoners. The man was already on Demand Number 10 and still nothing. Then he read off Demand Number 11:

"We demand that all political and economic lawsuits be revisited by an independent judiciary, and all unjustly convicted prisoners be freed and rehabilitated."

I though my heart was going to jump out of my rib cage. A chill ran up and down my arms. I knew what it all meant. The people demanded the release of political prisoners. I looked at Michelangelo. He heard it, too. He was nodding. My eyes got watery and so did his. "If the government gives in to these demands, your father is coming home, kid," he said. I gave Michelangelo a big hug. By now, my tears were flowing like crazy. I laughed and blew my nose. I was going to get my Papa back.

Suddenly the crowd got noisy. I glanced up. Some people on a second-story balcony were burning a red flag. We saw the Russian flag with the hammer and sickle go up in flames. Thousands cheered the rising smoke.

The crowd chanted, "RUSSIANS GO HOME!"

Michelangelo and I chanted right along. The chant came in waves. It would start with just a few people, then reach a loud, feverish pitch. My throat became hoarse from all the shouting, but I was ready for more.

From an open window overlooking the balcony, a man was taking one picture after another of the flag burning and the clamoring crowd.

"I bet you that cameraman is with the ÁVO," Michelangelo said.

"The what?"

"The secret police. If the government decides to crack down on the demonstrators, these guys will eventually catch up with our flag burners, arrest them, lock them up and throw away the key. You can count on it. The bastards."

"How can they? Look at all these people."

We must've been in the thousands.

The crowd started moving again, and we headed back across the Danube and into the heart of the city. We were chanting, singing old

Hungarian patriotic songs from the time of the Hungarian War of Independence in 1848.

A girl who I swear was younger than me was passing out little Hungarian rosettes and boutonnieres to pin to our collars or button holes. I pinned mine to the V neck of my pullover. I have never experienced so much brotherhood and camaraderie, so much good will.

It was getting cooler outside as the sun was going down, but I don't think anyone felt the chill. We were all fired up, that was for sure. And when you get fired up, you forget about time.

When we got to the end of Margit Bridge, word got out that other demonstrations were either going on or were starting up in other parts of Budapest. Workers from the factory district of Csepel were on their way to Heroes' Square to join thousands of protesters. The crowd was buzzing with rumors that they would topple the monstrously large Stalin statue there. Others were hurrying toward Parliament to demand independence for Hungary. Another group, mostly students, had these plans to go to the building of Radio Budapest to broadcast the 16-point list of demands to the people.

For Michelangelo and me it was snap decision. For different reasons, both of us wanted to see Stalin, the great father and liberator, topple from his high perch. But Heroes' Square was far away. And it would take some time for the Csepel workers to get there with their heavy equipment. We were already late. My mother would kill me for sure. We were maybe a block from the Parliament Building, so we decided to flow with the crowd, stop to see what was going on by Parliament, then head for home.

The square by Parliament had the most demonstrators yet. I'd say hundreds of thousands. This crowd was not as tame as the one by the Bem Statue. They wanted the red star on top of Parliament to come down, and they wanted the puppet Communist leader tossed into the Danube. Some of the protestors had bullhorns. They began to chant and the crowd would take up their chant. One chant after another:

> "Throw the tyrant in the River.
> All good Hungarians band together.
> Imre Nagy is our leader."

It was getting dark. Michelangelo glanced at his watch, and we shouldered our way through the crowd and picked up our steps to get home as soon as possible. I didn't want my head to end up on a platter.

Our building on Sándor Bródy Street was just a block from the Radio Station. I reminded Michelangelo that we were already in hot water, so we might as well go.

"It's your hide, kiddo, not mine. Not that I relish your aunt kicking me in the pants. She's done it before and she'll do it again. Maybe we better go home. Come on, I better take you home."

"Then you'll have to carry me, because I'm not going."

Michelangelo rolled his eyes. "Suit yourself. You'll be sorry. I have a feeling I will be, too." We both laughed.

But not for long. The scene in front of the Radio Building was already chaotic. Someone said a truck-full of armed soldiers tried to get through the crowd earlier, but the crowd closed ranks and wouldn't let them pass. They gave up and left.

By the Radio Building's entrance, a scuffle erupted between an angry mob of students and the police. A few windows were already broken.

Michelangelo asked the college student standing next to us what was going on. He said a delegation of students had gone in earlier but they didn't come out. They were probably detained by the secret police without being heard. "It may even be worse," he said. "Those closer to the building said they thought shots were fired. There's nothing left to do but to storm the building." Saying this, he elbowed his way toward the main gate.

The crowd was growing in size. They had become agitated. A rock sailed through the air and broke another window.

Finally, two officials from the Radio Station appeared on a balcony and shouted at the crowd to disperse. That only made things worse. Someone with a bullhorn hurled obscenities at the officials.

A student heaved a bottle which shattered near the balcony. Michelangelo and I laughed, seeing the officials scurry like rats back into the building, close the door, and turn off the lights. Then, one by one, each lighted window went dark.

The total blackout made the angry crowd even bolder. The protestors cleared enough of a path to let a car through. It looked like the car was going to ram the gate. I saw enough to know it was a Czech car, one of those little Skodas.

The crowd grew silent.

The Skoda's first impact was deafening. The little car spun its wheels till they smoked. The engine roared. Then the blunt sound of steel on steel. The Skoda's fenders were twisted like a pretzel, but it backed up for another running start. "Again!" the crowd roared. The Skoda rammed the heavy gate again. This time its hood crunched up and steam hissed out of its engine. The driver had trouble backing up. The front fenders rubbed against the tires. When it was about ten meters from the gate, the car gave up its ghost. The motor was dead.

I thought it was funny. But then, the gate flared open and these uniformed men with bayonets came charging out.

All I saw was one crackling flash after another, followed by the sound of gunfire. The intense volley from their guns pierced the darkness.

Michelangelo snatched me by the hand, ready to run for it. I froze. Another volley. Then another. The ÁVO men sprayed the Skoda's windshield with bullets, killing the driver. I saw a student go down, squirming in pain. We should've run, but I couldn't move. "Oh, my God," Michelangelo said. Then he let go of my hand. He lurched forward, grasping his leg in agony. Blood seeped from between his fingers. "My leg," he groaned.

I kneeled next to him. I had to do something to stop the bleeding, but first I had to get him out of here. "Bastards!" Michelangelo hissed.

Strangers bent over us. One said an ambulance was on its way. A blond woman in a long raincoat helped me get Michelangelo on the sidewalk and into a store doorway.

We were only a block from my apartment. I didn't want to leave Michelangelo, so I gave the address to the woman in the raincoat who helped drag Michelangelo out of the line of fire. "Tell them to get help. A doctor. Anything. Hurry."

Thanks to my days at Pioneer camp, I knew how to make a tourniquet. I took my pullover off, wrapped a sleeve tightly around Michelangelo's leg, just above the wound. I made a knot and kept tightening it and tightening it until the bleeding stopped.

Michelangelo was still groaning, shivering, his hand glued to his wound. In minutes my mother arrived in her English tweed suit. She looked horrified. I took the blanket from her and covered Michelangelo.

"Jesus! My God! Are you all right?"

"I'm all right, but Michelangelo isn't."

"I know," she said, "The woman told me about the shooting."

My mother took Michelangelo's bloody hand and gently pulled it from his leg so she could see how bad it was. "I can't see here. We have to get him to where I can see."

My mother and I each took an arm and pulled Michelangelo under a street lamp. There, my mother went to work. She patted around the bloody wound and wiped away at it with her handkerchief till she saw the torn skin where the bullet sheared it. Then she fished out a large sewing needle and a spool of thread from her half-finished pocket. "Oh, my God!" Michelangelo said. "Have you done this before?"

My mother didn't look up. "Never," my mother said. I sewed up a goose a few times in my life. After I stuffed it."

"God!" Michelangelo said.

"Leave God in heaven. It's only a flesh wound," my mother said as she started to stitch Michelangelo's wound. Michelangelo gritted his teeth.

The ambulance arrived as she finished up. The white vehicle, with a Red Cross emblazoned on its side, rolled right past us and continued toward the gate.

"Look where they're going!" Michelangelo said.

"You don't need an ambulance," my mother said to Michelangelo. "Now, see if you can stand up."

We hoisted Michelangelo up and propped him against the bakery door. He said he could use a cigarette. "Not good for you," my mother said. "Can you walk?"

"I don't think so."

"I'll go to the ambulance and get some bandages and see if they have anything for pain."

"No, mother, it's dangerous."

"You're going to tell me about dangerous? You? You stay with Michelangelo, you hear me?"

She tried threading herself through the crowd milling around the ambulance. We heard one of the protestors shout that the ambulance only came to help the ÁVO injured. The crowd blocked the ambulance from going further.

A burly student grabbed the ambulance's door handle. Someone smashed the passenger window with a cobblestone. "Guns!" they shouted. "They got guns! They're trying to sneak them in to the ÁVO! Seize the guns!"

The crowd swarmed around the ambulance. Its doors swung open. They pulled out the driver and the crowd pounced on him. It was a free-for-all. For the man. For the guns.

I couldn't see my mother.

Was she still trying to get bandages? God! A young man held a rifle high in the air. Suddenly, a flare shot from the roof lit up the building and the street. I heard a burst of machine gun fire. I didn't know where it was coming from. Then I saw him. The man in the ÁVO uniform. Between the Skoda and the ambulance. He was the shooter. His bullets ricochet off the ambulance with a tinny sound. Another burst, this one close, very close, chipping stone right in front of me, shattering the bakery window. I fell back like rag doll.

I was dazed. Michelangelo was gone. Where was he? Where was my mother?

I spotted Michelangelo. He was screaming, limping toward the ambulance when a fresh volley pinned me down. I crawled on my belly toward the ambulance.

My mother! Oh, my God! My mother lay on the ground in a pool of blood.

I knelt by my mother and tried cradling her. Michelangelo was unbuttoning the few buttons on her half-finished suit.

My mother clutched her neck. Blood soaked her suit, the English tweed absorbing her blood like a sponge.

She nodded to me that it was all right. I knew it wasn't. My poor mother had run out of the apartment without giving a second thought about anything except me, her daughter. The buttons weren't properly sewn on yet. Here she was bleeding to death in front of me in the only suit she ever wore in her life. And even that unfinished. I heard myself bawling. "Mother, please! Please don't."

Gunfire. Then an explosion. When I opened my eyes, I was on the other side of the street. I must've been thrown there by the blast. All I could see was the overturned ambulance on fire and my mother burning beside it.

Michelangelo had to use all his strength to drag me to safety behind a tree. I was choking, coughing from the black, oily smoke. Oh, my God! Mother!

I ran a trembling hand through my hair.

Another flare went up from the roof. People in the crowd were returning fire.

Michelangelo was suddenly next to me, dumbly staring at the sub-machine gun someone had thrust at him. He looked scared, confused. I saw the ropes working in his jaw. Before I knew what I was doing, I grabbed the gun, pointed it at the shooter and pulled the trigger. A burst, then a jolt. The sound was deafening. I felt powder on my face but I didn't care. "Killer! You killed my mother!" I cried as my throat burned with rage.

Riddled with bullets, the man fell backwards. Michelangelo said, "My God, you got him. Was that you?"

"I don't know." But I did know. I just killed a man. And I kept firing away, spraying the uniformed ÁVO man—until I ran out of bullets. Until I was numb enough not to have to feel.

There was a lull in the shooting. A dead silence.

Michelangelo tried taking the gun from me, but I had a death-grip on it. He said he had to take me home. Now. That was enough shooting for one night.

I told him I couldn't go home. Not now. I couldn't face my little sister after all I've done.

"It's not your fault." Michelangelo said. He pointed to the blood-soaked body of the ÁVO man. "It's his. It's theirs. They're the killers. They killed your mother. They're killing innocent civilians. They started it!"

"I swear to God," I said to Michelangelo, "they're going to pay."

"You don't know what you're saying. You're just a kid. What about your sister? Your poor aunt? She loves you like a mother."

"I have no mother."

Michelangelo's forehead tightened. For a long time nothing was said. He nodded to himself as if acknowledging something. He held out his hand for the gun. "All right," he said. "Let me show you something." He showed me how the round magazine of the submachine gun was loaded. Then he did something I didn't expect. He took the gun and slung the leather strap around my neck. "It's yours," he said. "You've earned it. Now, let's go."

"No," I said, my jaw set. "I will not leave my mother."

Chapter Two

2

What was sporadic gunfire now intensified. We were pinned down behind a huge chestnut tree in front of the shot-up bakery. The dead and the dying were all around us. Michelangelo kept trying to get me to make a run for it, but I refused to budge. The woman in the long raincoat dodged bullets to get to us. She was breathless, her eyes liquid. "They're murderers," she barked.

We ducked our heads and scurried for the safety of the bakery doorway.

I took a good look at the woman in the raincoat. Her nerve surprised me. She seemed too soft and too delicate to be fighting anybody.

"They killed her mother," Michelangelo said to her. "And she won't leave. We don't have enough guns. Enough bullets."

The woman, who was maybe in her twenties, said she knew. That's why she came back. She heard the protestors, workers mostly from Csepel, took over the Killián Barracks before the ÁVO could send in reinforcements. People were raiding the armory for guns right now. A truck-full of armed civilians was heading this way. "We may have a chance," she said. "My God, we just may."

Instead of armed civilians, two heavy tanks rumbled into the street. We couldn't figure out whether they were Russian or Hungarian. No flag, no insignia, just these numbers in white painted on their turrets. They didn't fire. They just stood there. Dark. Bulky. Motionless. A group of gutsy students surrounded them, shouting, "Shoot at the ÁVO! They're killing innocent people!"

The tank hatches remained shut.

It was eerily quiet.

One of the tanks was moving its turret. Sounding like a giant sprocket and chain, the turret ticked into firing position, taking aim at the balcony where the shooting came from only minutes before. The turret swung around again. For a terrifying moment, its cannon took aim at the milling crowd, before revolving back to its original position. The tank crews couldn't decide whose side they were on.

The crowd swelled again. People came crawling out from behind trees, side streets, gateways and alleyways. I saw the lid of a manhole being pushed up in front of me. A young man with slanted eyes and wearing army fatigues emerged from the sewer. An unlit cigarette dangled from his mouth. He had a gun like mine slung around his shoulder, and he smelled like a toilet.

Out of nowhere, smoking canisters sailed through the air. "Tear gas!" the man from the sewer shouted.

The shooting erupted again. We hunkered down. The man from the sewer returned fire, shattering windows around the Radio Building balcony.

The ÁVO was lobbing tear gas at the demonstrators while the tanks stood by.

A canister rolled near us. I had an instant coughing fit. My throat felt like it was on fire. My eyes stung and blurred. Michelangelo rubbed his eyes and said he couldn't see. The woman, and the man from the sewer, wiped their eyes and clutched their throats. Nowhere for us to go except inside the bakery building.

I knew from helping my father deliver mail here that a courtyard opened on the other side of the back door. "This way," I said to the others. They followed, coughing behind me.

The open air let us catch our breath. I sat with my back against the stone wall, wiping my eyes with my sleeve. The man from the sewer was crouched down next to me. He started reloading his submachine gun. I cleared my throat long enough to ask him if he was a soldier.

He nodded. "I'm a Sewer Rat," he said. "Took a short cut. From the armory." He lit his cigarette and said those tanks were manned by Hungarian soldiers. "They don't know what to do, the dumb asses!" he sneered.

"Who are you?" the woman in the long raincoat asked. "I mean what is your name?"

"Sewer Rat will do for now."

The woman said she was Sister Ágnes.

"A nurse, huh? You better stick around," Sewer Rat said.

"I'm not that kind of sister. I used to be a nun. Now, I'm a trolley driver."

The soldier laughed so hard, his belly shook, then he cut himself short.

Sister Ágnes said she was not a bad shot either. All she needed was a gun.

We left the bakery's back door open, so we could see what was going on in the street. Each tear gas canister was followed by gunfire. Bullets were chipping stone right by the doorway.

Sewer Rat looked at my gun and me, and asked how old I was.

I lied. I don't know why, but I lied. I told him I was seventeen.

Michelangelo didn't betray me. He did tell the man that my mother was killed.

"Sorry," Sewer Rat said. He asked Michelangelo if he was a soldier.

Michelangelo shifted his weight from one leg to the other, then gritted his teeth. "Used to be," he said.

"Don't worry. You'll be back." Sewer Rat then turned to Sister Ágnes: "Listen, Sister, take these two home and then come back. We need you here. See if you can get some bandages, anything."

Sewer Rat finished reloading his gun, darted back to the doorway and started firing away.

Sister Ágnes and I helped Michelangelo hobble across the courtyard. I knew of another door which would lead us outside to the next block. We were only a city block from our building.

I had to leave. I had to leave my mother. I had to think of my sister and my aunt.

What would I tell them?

I opened the gate with the key my aunt had given me. The other key on my chain was to the cellar. I ditched my submachine gun there, inside an empty wine barrel. Before we went up, I tried to clean the caked soot and tears from my face, but it was a lost cause.

When my aunt opened the door in her bathrobe in the half-lit foyer, she had black circles around her eyes. The cigarette in her hand trembled. "What's this?"

"Michelangelo got hurt. But he's all right," I blurted, avoiding her eyes.

My aunt led us into the kitchen and switched on the light. "Where's your mother?"

"Down there. By the ambulance."

"Why isn't she with you? Where is she?"

I couldn't hold it back any longer and broke down. I was crying too hard to make sense. My chest was heaving, and I could barely get the words out. "She's dead. Mother's dead."

"Almighty God, no!" my aunt said.

Her face turned chalky and her hand shook like it did when she was very nervous. She poured something into an espresso cup and ordered me to sit down and drink it.

I tried sipping it.

"No. Not like that. Down it in one gulp."

I knew what it was. That horrible *pálinka* adults drank. It smelled and tasted like rubbing alcohol. I hated it, but I downed it even though it burned my throat.

"Now, tell me where your mother is. I need to know. We have to bury her."

I was trembling so bad, half the drink dribbled down my chin. I was shaking my head, crying. I moved my mouth but no words came out.

"Were you hurt? Are you all right?"

"She's all right," Michelangelo said.

"Were you two there?" she asked Michelangelo and Sister Ágnes.

"I was," Michelangelo nodded. He explained what happened.

"God Almighty! My poor sister-in-law! I told you to bring Kitty home! Didn't I?"

Michelangelo looked down.

My elbows were on the table. My hands were propping up my head. I wished it was me instead of my mother.

"What are we going to tell Krisztina?" I sniffled.

"We're going to lie. You can lie to her, but not to me. Is that understood?"

I nodded. What else could I do?

"We're going to tell her just what you told me. That your mother is out trying to get your father back. She overheard us talk about your father and political prisoners and all that. We'll make her believe it. Because, in the condition she's in, the truth would kill her."

My aunt gave some *pálinka* to Michelangelo and Sister Ágnes. They had to drink it whether they wanted to or not, and they had to drink it bottoms up. Then my aunt excused herself, went into the bathroom and blew her nose over and over again. When she came out, her eyes were red. She tucked away the handkerchief into her bathrobe pocket and said in a calm voice, "I wish I could give you something to eat, but we don't have any bread."

"No, thank you," said Sister Ágnes.

Michelangelo wasn't hungry either.

"All right, then," my aunt said. "You two better get some rest. Now, off with you!"

Michelangelo said, "If you don't mind, I'd rather stay here and help out."

"And how are you going to that?"

"I can get some bread."

"But you're wounded. Or is it nothing? Because usually with you it's nothing."

My aunt was a strong woman. She had to be. Someone had to be. She lived through two wars, losing her husband in the last one.

"He's really wounded," I said in Michelangelo's defense.

"I'll take care of him," Sister Ágnes volunteered. "Once I get back from helping out by the Radio Building. They're still fighting out there. But I promise to come back. With some bread."

Michelangelo said Sister Ágnes used to be a nun before the Communists dissolved her order. Now she drove a trolley. Or did as of yesterday.

My aunt took a long pull on her cigarette, threw her head back and blew smoke out through pursed lips. "Oh yes," she said. "This world has turned upside down." A tear trembled in her eye. "I'm going to miss that woman. I was working on a dress for her. And now, this." She stubbed out her unfinished cigarette, poured herself another shot and told Sister Ágnes to go and help with the wounded. "Our people need you more than we do, God help them." She said, "Bottoms up!" and downed her *pálinka* in one gulp.

Sister Ágnes offered to help get my mother's body once the shooting stopped. For now, she had to worry about keeping the wounded alive. She asked if we had any bandages. My aunt said we didn't, but she did have this gauze-like material she uses when she reinforces brassieres. Maybe that would do. She went into her sewing chest and brought out a roll which she tucked under Sister Ágnes' arm. "Be careful. We'll pray for you, Sister. You pray for us, too."

With that, Sister Ágnes turned to go.

"Wait," Michelangelo said. "I may have some bandages. I'm on the ground floor. Corner apartment."

Once they left, my aunt embraced me and held me for a long time. Her eyes were moist. She said everything was going to be all right. Tomorrow, once things settled down, we were going to get my mother and give her a proper burial. "Now," my aunt said, "I want you to wash up and go to bed. No, on second thought, I better draw you a bath. You need to rest. We'll all feel better in the morning."

I lay on the living-room couch and stared dully at the ceiling. My aunt came to me to say that I should stay clear of the window.

The sounds of gunfire wouldn't let me sleep, even if I wanted to. All I could think of was my mother. Her half-finished tweed suit. The terrible explosion. The gunfire. Her charred body.

My arms and legs felt heavy, my eyes burned like I hadn't slept for days. My thoughts drifted to the coal cellar and the gun I hid there. I killed a man. I know I did. I had this strange, restless feeling in me that wouldn't let go. I sat up, then lay down again. I went to the clothes closet to feel for my mother's clothes, shuddered and stumbled back to my couch.

After a few minutes I got up again and went to my aunt's bedroom where Krisztina was sleeping. I tiptoed to her bed and gave her a light kiss on the forehead. Her skin was warm. She was so calm and beautiful as she slept. In the darkness, you couldn't tell her skin was bluish because of her bad heart.

I barely lay down again when the phone rang. I leaped out of bed and got it before the second ring. It was Michelangelo. He said Sister Ágnes had some bread and stuff. She told him the demonstrators seized control of the radio, but only for a short time. Something must've happened. Michelangelo asked if he could come by and drop off the bread in the morning. He was feeling much better. After he removed a piece of metal still lodged in his leg. It must've pressed on a nerve or something, he said.

I went back to bed and tried to get some sleep as the first light of dawn filtered through the window. Images from the night before kept returning with a fury. The gunfire. The shooter's face. His uniform with the shoulder straps. My mother in a pool of blood. All that blood. The explosion. Her blackened body. How were we going to give her a proper burial?

I was sitting up on the couch hugging my pillow, rocking back and forth, when Krisztina entered the room. She came to me, I opened my arms and gave her a squeeze. "I can't sleep," she said. "Why are those people shooting. Can you hear them?"

"They're far away," I said. "You're safe. The good people are fighting the bad people so Papa can come home. Mama is on her way right now to bring Papa home?"

"Will she be all right with all the shooting?"

"God is with her," I said. "You know how He watches after us. Go back to bed and say your prayers for Mama and Papa."

Mama. That's what I called my mother when I was little. When I was innocent. Mama. The word had such a sweet sound to it. I felt terrible for lying about something like this to my little sister, but my aunt was right. Knowing she would never see her mother again would send her into a downward spiral. She was too frail, too sick for such a shock. Her heart would give out.

I gave up on sleep and went into the kitchen to drink some water. My mouth was very dry. As I rummaged around for a glass, I heard a knock on the door. I glanced at the clock on the wall. It was six in the morning. Probably Michelangelo.

When I opened the door, I was surprised to see Sewer Rat with him. They had several loaves of bread with them and two huge, bulging flour sacks. They spoke in whispers. Michelangelo asked if he could have my cellar key. They needed to put some things in the coal cellar.

I didn't realize it, but my aunt was behind me, in the dark foyer.

"What is this?"

"Bread," I said. "They have some bread for us."

Michelangelo showed her all the bread.

"What did you do? Break into the bakery?"

"We didn't have to. The ÁVO did that for us. The storefront's been blown to smithereens. I think we took the last of it. We left some money on the counter."

My aunt had them wait. She'd be right back. She took me by my pajama collar into the kitchen and closed the door. "You stay put," she said. She grabbed her purse from the table, marched off and slammed the door behind her. I panicked. She probably overheard everything that was said. A little window opened from the kitchen into the outer hallway. I unlatched it just enough to be able to hear them.

My aunt tried giving them money for the bread, but they wouldn't take it.

"I see," my aunt said. "And what is it that you want my cellar for?"

"Nothing," Michelangelo said.

"I see you recovered enough to try to hoodwink me. Be careful, Michelangelo. Be very careful. You have guns in that sack, don't you?"

"No, madam," Sewer Rat answered."

"Madam? And who is this?"

"The name is Sewer Rat."

"Mr. Sewer Rat, may I take a peek into those sacks. I'd like to know what you plan on hiding in my cellar, if you don't mind?"

My heart was beating hard and fast inside my chest.

"My God," my aunt said. "There's enough in there to feed an army."

"It's not for an army," Sewer Rat said. "It's for you and the kids."

"My aunt's voice broke. "You don't need to do this, you know. Are you sure you don't need any money?"

"We're sure."

I heard my aunt's footsteps, closed the window and sat down.

She came in with all this bread. She instructed me to give them the cellar key. "And here," she said, "take this money and give it to them. They won't take it from me. Go on, scoot. Show them where our cellar is. You better put on a robe or coat or something."

I put on my winter jacket and took Michelangelo and Sewer Rat down the narrow, spiral stairs to the cellar. I opened the cellar door to a gust of mildew and darkness. Sewer Rat switched on his flashlight. No one said anything. They leaned the two flour sacks against the wall. I pointed to the empty wine barrels. Sewer Rat had no trouble prying the lid open. He saw my gun.

We heard footsteps.

The door creaked open. Sister Ágnes and a boy about sixteen or seventeen wearing a derby hat stepped into the cellar. They had three more bulging flour sacks with them.

Sewer Rat closed the door and latched it. They pulled out one gun after another and placed them in the empty barrels. Hand grenades, pistols, carbines, guns I've never seen before. And boxes of ammunition. Sewer Rat made quick work of resealing the barrels. He looked around to make sure we didn't miss anything.

We shuffled out, and I locked the cellar door.

I tried giving them my aunt's money, but they wouldn't hear of it. The reason they were doing this, they whispered, was because Michelangelo was already under suspicion because of his conduct in the air force. And Sewer Rat had recently defected on the side of the people. Their places would be the first ones to be searched.

I told them we better go back up. My aunt was expecting them. She had some leftover meat loaf and some margarine to put on the bread.

Sister Ágnes and the young man with the derby hat vanished. The rest of us hurried upstairs.

My aunt had already set the table in the kitchen. On a huge plate she had sliced some cold meat loaf, bread and green peppers. A bottle of *pálinka* sat in the middle of the table. She had made hot tea with lemon. "What took you so long?" she asked.

I described to her how I dropped the key and how it fell all the way down. We were lucky to have found it. So dark down there by the cellar.

"Well, let's eat," my aunt said to the company. "You can wash your hands here by the sink. Sit down." She was ranting about the ÁVO and government as she poured some *pálinka* into their tea. She cursed the Communists. They were assassins. Butchers.

We ate and drank silently in quick gulps.

My aunt had a few questions. Like, what was going on out there in the streets. Now.

"Russian tanks are all over the city," Sewer Rat said, an unlit cigarette moving in his mouth. "Every bridge, every public building. All the major intersections."

My aunt wanted to know if it was safe enough out there to pick up my mother.

Sewer Rat said: "There's no shooting for now. As far as I know, the victims are still there where they fell. The radio is saying we're allowed to move about the city to get food supplies and to pick up the dead. After that it's curfew, and anyone who's out and about could be arrested." His cigarette was still unlit and moving like crazy in his mouth.

My aunt struck a match and said, "Let me give you a light before you eat that cigarette. What is your name again?"

Sewer Rat blew thick smoke into the air. "Sewer Rat, madam."

"You're very outspoken for a Sewer Rat."

"Thank you, madam."

"What were you before you joined the army?"

"I didn't join. They took me. Before that, I worked for the city sewer works."

"But you talk like you had some schooling."

"I couldn't go to the university, because my father was an officer in the old Hungarian Army."

"I see."

My aunt now turned her attention to Michelangelo. "Michelangelo, dear!" my aunt said in a hushed voice. "Can you and your friend here, can you, could you please help us with Kitty's mother. I mean her body. I'll go with you."

"No, Auntie," I cut in. "It's too dangerous. Look what happened to Mama. I'll go."

"No!"

"I'm the only one who knows where she is."

Michelangelo stroked his goatee and kept quiet. He knew I'd seen too much and done too much for a kid my age.

My aunt sighed. She put down her fork. It was time for her to fire up another cigarette.

Sewer Rat suggested we turn on the radio for the latest bulletin. Things were changing like crazy from one moment to the next. There was only so much time.

My aunt brought in the radio from the living room, put it on the kitchen table and plugged in the cord. The first bulletin came on at 8:00 a.m.

"Attention! Attention! The dastardly armed attacks of counter-revolutionary gangs during the night have created an extremely serious situation. The bandits have penetrated into factories and public buildings and have murdered many civilians, members of the national defense forces, and fighters of the State security organs. The government was unprepared for these dastardly bloody attacks and therefore applied for help, in accordance with terms of the Warsaw Treaty, to the Soviet formations stationed in Hungary. The Soviet formations, in compliance with the government's request, are taking part in restoration of order."

"Liars," I shouted. "We were there." I could still see the face of the monster who shot my mother.

Michelangelo was outraged: "They started it. They fired on innocent civilians and they're blaming it on us, the bastards."

"What d'you expect? It's propaganda," Sewer Rat said. They're just buying time till they're good and ready to exterminate any semblance of free speech. All the people did was to demonstrate, for Chrissake!"

My aunt was already getting her coat and walking stick ready. She made sure I'd keep an eye on my little sister. Tell her we're going out to get some supplies before all the stores close. Before this martial law, or whatever the hell it is, takes effect."

Sewer Rat spoke up again. "I don't recommend it. It's best that you stay here with the little girl. What if we have to make a run for it? You'd never make it. It's not far, we should be back in no time at all. All we need is a heavy blanket to carry the—

"Shhh!" my aunt interrupted.

Krisztina was up. "All right," she said in a whisper. "Go. But please be careful. I'll get you the blanket."

In less than a minute, she was back with a rolled up felt blanket.

Three Soviet tanks were parked bumper to bumper by the Radio Building. I noticed the burnt-out ambulance had been moved. I had this fear they moved my mother's body.

People walked around corpses dusted with white powder. Sewer Rat said it was lime. To keep them from decomposing so they didn't spread disease. Some of the bodies had flowers heaped on them.

I saw mound after mound of flowers. A boy's body lay in the street. His eyes were wide open like a doll's eyes. His stomach bloated. The bouquet of flowers had slid off the body. On his forehead was a wet brown leaf. Or was it blood? Michelangelo bent down and tried closing the eyes but couldn't. I put the flowers back on the boy's chest.

We continued looking for my mother. I knew it was not far from the Radio Building's doorway, where the ambulance had been. The tanks blocked the entrance.

As we approached one of the tanks, the hatch creaked open. The soldier yelled at us in Russian and motioned for us to get back. My face contorted and a pain rose to my throat, but no tears and no words. It was like I couldn't get them out. We turned around.

But I was not about to give up. We looked at every body, even the ones far off, on the sidewalk. I didn't see my mother anywhere.

"They must've moved some of the bodies or their remains," Sewer Rat said.

I kept walking around the mounds of flowers. One body had a piece of paper with writing on it pinned on the coat. I had to bend down to read it. "Our beloved son, age 17." Then I saw something I recognized. The pain in my throat was back in an instant. A piece of English tweed burned around the edges lay on the cobblestone. The wind must've blown it beside the boy's body. I picked it up and studied the bodies near it. My mother wasn't any of them. I showed it to Michelangelo and he nodded. It was from my mother's half-finished suit. I put it in my coat pocket and held it there, feeling its texture.

A truck pulled up and they started loading the corpses. The bodies landed with a terrible thud on the bed of the truck. I was breathing hard. My muscles tensed up like never before. These were human beings, patriots, not "dastardly gangs" like the radio said. Liars!

A man and a woman were screaming at the truckers who were doing the loading. The man was pushed out of the way. His wife tried holding her husband back. He wouldn't back down until another man went up to him and struck him in the face so his glasses flew off. His wife picked up his glasses. They came right to where we were standing. This was the couple who had lost their son. The man, who looked like he was too old to have a son 17, was seething. His glasses were broken. His wife knelt by her son, took her tricolor boutonniere from her lapel and pinned it on her son's bullet-riddled coat. The man's face twisted into an anguished cry. I held what I had left of my mother in my clenched fist.

The mother dabbed her eyes with a soaked handkerchief as she spoke to us. Their son had been accepted as an electrical engineering student at the Technical University of Budapest. His whole life was ahead of him. Her husband shook his head violently. "No," he said. "We're not going to stand for this." He said he and his wife and their families were going to march on Parliament tomorrow. The whole city is going to be there, he said. "What kind of government lets something like this happen. Cut down peaceful demonstrators. Children! We're not going to let this go. They have no respect for the dead. They're tossing the bodies on the truck like they were animal carcasses. Barbarians, that's what they are!" The man spit. His chest was heaving.

I told them about my mother and showed them the piece of English tweed, frayed and burnt around the edges. "This is all I have left of my mother," I cried. "She was killed yesterday. Right here. She died in my arms, but I couldn't stay with her."

Michelangelo put his arm around me.

All the couple could do was to shake their heads in disbelief. "They didn't die for nothing," the father raged. "We'll be at the Parliament tomorrow, I don't care how many Russian tanks they got protecting these cowards!"

We had to go and break the news to my aunt. She would be devastated, too.

We saw nothing like the crowds we saw yesterday. There was a pall in the air. And fear. Fear of the tanks that kept rolling into the city.

Once we got to Sándor Bródy Street where my apartment was, I slowed my pace. I asked Sewer Rat if he thought most of the Hungarian Army would go over on the side of the people. He said he didn't know. It was too early to tell. It all depended what would happen in the next few days. The Russian tanks were not a good sign.

We made plans to meet the next day to take part in the mass demonstration by Parliament.

"You think your aunt will let you out?" Michelangelo asked.

"I'll think of something."

Sewer Rat grinned. "You're a pretty feisty kid, you know that? When I was 17, I was hitting the books. Not that it helped me any. My name was already on the shit list, so to speak."

I clued Sewer Rat in on how I protested against compulsory Russian. "If we go back to school, I stand a good chance of being booted out. Someone snitched on me."

"I swear, every other person in this godforsaken country is an informer. I thought differently yesterday seeing all those people. For a while there, I thought we would pull together."

Sándor Bródy Street was empty and gray. The windows that had shutters were rolled down. I was about to unlock our gate when a man on a motorcycle roared down our street, coming to a screeching halt by us.

"Hey, Sewer Rat," the man said. He didn't get off his bike.

We walked over to the curb. The man had a shock of chestnut brown hair and a thick mustache. His bushy eyebrows met by the bridge of his nose. He wore a long brown leather coat and a red, white and green armband. He scrutinized Michelangelo and me. Sewer Rat said, "It's okay. They're with us."

The motorcyclist spoke rapidly, telling Sewer Rat that armored cars were going up and down Üllői Avenue near the Killián Barracks. No one would be able to get in and out once the curfew started. The Russians were setting up checkpoints all over the place.

He pulled out a ream of fliers from a satchel and handed it to Sewer Rat. His words came out of his mouth in rapid fire. Sewer Rat was to take his "sewer subway" to the Hungarian soldiers inside the barracks and hand out the fliers. There was no other way to get information to them. They knew the radio broadcasts were full of crap, the man said. What they didn't know was that nineteen civilians were killed last night. They had no idea about the pockets of resistance, and not only in Budapest.

There were mass demonstrations all over the country. News had already leaked to the West. Radio Free Europe was rallying all Hungarians to make a stand for democracy.

The man said he just wanted to make sure that Hungarian soldiers acted like Hungarian soldiers when it came down to the wire.

Sewer Rat took the fliers.

"You may also want to check the manhole covers in and around the Corvin area. Are you armed?" the man asked.

Sewer Rat opened his coat. The shiny handle of a pistol stuck out of his belt.

"You better have more than that."

Sewer Rat nodded.

"All right. Take care," the cyclist said, his engine still running. "Oh, one more thing. Some of my men stashed some rifles in the Corvin Theater."

"Got it," Sewer Rat said.

"Good." The cyclist revved his engine and roared off, leaving a trail of bluish smoke behind him.

"Who was that?" I asked.

"Pongrátz. He's a sergeant. Or was. We were in boot camp together. He's a good guy. A real patriot. We call him Mustache for short."

I asked him if anyone had real names in this man's army.

The reply was a laugh and a quick no. When I asked him if he was coming up, he said he would, but just for a short time. He wanted my aunt to know he had kept his word and brought me home safe. Then he had work to do. He'd be by tomorrow. In the early afternoon.

The elevator wasn't working, so Michelangelo and I had to take the stairs. As I turned the key to the apartment, my aunt opened the door, stepped out, and closed it behind her. She said Krisztina was taking a nap. My little sister got sick from all the excitement about her father coming home, she said. And then they heard some shooting a few streets down. "It scared her and it scared me. I had to put a cold compress on her chest to slow down her heart. You know how breathless she gets when she's excited. All right. Where did you put your mother's body?"

I was about to cry but checked myself. Instead of saying anything, I took out the burnt tweed and gave it to my aunt. "That's all we have of her. We couldn't find her. We looked all over. They were throwing dead bodies on this truck. It was awful."

"Calm down. I'm glad you're in one piece. I was worried about you. You took so long."

My aunt held the burnt English tweed in her hand, as if she were weighing it. Then she closed her eyes, her eyelids pressing down hard. She had to hold on to the door to steady herself.

Sewer Rat and Michelangelo helped her into the kitchen where she collapsed on a chair. She placed the burnt tweed on the table and kept smoothing it while she stared straight ahead. I asked her if she would like some *pálinka*. "No, dear," she said.

Sewer Rat said he was sorry. And that he had to go. Michelangelo, too. They looked exhausted.

My aunt didn't answer.

They left quietly. I closed the door behind them.

I went into the living room, sagged down on the couch and stared into space. After five minutes I was up again. I went to check on Krisztina. She was sleeping soundly. I sat on the edge of her bed. Krisztina sighed in her sleep and lay very still. Too still. I bent over her and put my ear by hear heart. It was knocking and galloping all over the place. That's how her heart sounded. For Krisztina, it was normal.

For what must've been an hour, I was watching her breathing. When I thought her chest didn't move, I panicked. When she moved, when she turned on her side, I relaxed. I thought that if I wasn't watching her, she'd stop breathing. I was afraid for Krisztina and I was afraid for my aunt. I wished my father were here. He would know what to do.

Eventually, I wore myself out. I took my clothes off, put on my pajamas and lay down next to her. Soon I was fast asleep.

When I awoke, it was already dark out. Krisztina was not in bed. I rubbed my eyes. Somehow they got glued together while I slept. I had to strain to open them.

In the bathroom, I looked into the mirror and saw that the grit in the corners of my eyes had turned gooey. All the rubbing and washing made my eyes red.

My sister was on the floor combing out the fringes of my aunt's old Persian rug. The radio was on. Some stupid music, as if nothing had happened.

Krisztina looked up at me. "You've been crying," she said.

I told her I got something in my eye.

My aunt was busy with her sewing machine, pedaling her old Singer as if her life depended on it. She had an ashtray full of cigarette butts on her sewing table, one still burning. She looked up at me above the rim of her glasses. "Are you hungry?"

I wasn't and said as much.

I was not to worry, she said. She had everything under control. She said she can't say the same thing about the government. They were scrambling. "They keep offering amnesty to the people to lay down their arms. They say the same goes for all soldiers who defected. They keep making the same announcement every half hour. They keep extending the deadline. Now they're saying that the counter-revolutionaries have 15 minutes to surrender their guns to escape execution. Ridiculous! You know what I think? I think they're running scared. And then between broadcasts they have the nerve to play this insipid music."

I turned to go and play with my sister, but my aunt wanted me to stick around. She asked me about what I saw out there this morning. I let her know about the bodies and the couple who lost their 17-year-old boy. And the Hungarian rosette the mother pinned on her son's coat. "Tomorrow," I said, "there's going to be a huge demonstration by Parliament. To protest the brutal actions of the secret police."

"You're not going, if that's what you're gearing up for."

"Auntie, I think I should go. For Mama's sake."

"You haven't called her Mama in years."

"I know. It's different now."

"Come here," my aunt said.

She cut the thread with her teeth, put everything down and gave me a hug. "When everything settles down, we'll all go to church and light a candle for your Mama."

"I'd like that," I said. "But I'm not a child anymore, Auntie. I really want to be there at the Parliament Building. I think we can make a difference. There's going to be zillions of people there. Students, workers, soldiers. Everybody's going. I'll be going with Michelangelo and Sewer Rat. Sister Ágnes is coming, too."

"We'll see."

"Thank you." I gave her a kiss on the cheek.

"Go on, play with your sister. She misses you."

"Some of the protestors are wearing Hungarian-colored armbands," I said.

"That's nice," she said. "Now scoot. I have work to do."

I got on the floor with Krisztina. We drew pictures. I had a way of animating a cartoon by drawing a figure on a half sheet, folding it over, and drawing the same figure again, this time with her arm up. Then I took a pencil, rolled the sheets together and flicked the pencil back and forth. When you looked at it, the little figure was lifting her arm up and down. Krisztina got a huge kick out of it.

Krisztina drew a cat. I asked her what kind of cat it was. She said it was me. "Cheetah." But we couldn't animate her or make her run. I rolled down the blinds and pinned Krisztina's drawing on the curtain. I turned the lights off and held my aunt's flashlight so it lit up the picture. We pretended we were seeing a movie.

"I told you," my aunt scolded us from the other room, "get away from the window!"

"But there's no shooting now."

"I don't care. Stay away from the window till I tell you otherwise. *Kapish?*"

I turned the lights back on.

"When are Papa and Mama coming home?" Krisztina asked.

"Oh, not for a while," I said. "Papa is very far. Mama had to take a train."

That answer seemed to pacify her for a while.

"Want to play with magnets?" she asked.

"Sure."

The radio was at it again with the amnesty for guns and surrender program. I quit listening. Music came on, this time a waltz.

Krisztina wanted to dance.

I held her little waist and hands, and we twirled around lightly. She loved to dance, but she couldn't overdo it.

My aunt marched out of her room and turned off the radio. "You know better than that, Kitty. You want to make her sick? Just think of what your mother would say."

I ran into the bedroom, threw myself on the bed, and sobbed into the pillow.

My aunt came in and sat down by me. She stroked my back. She said she was sorry. It was just that Krisztina was already sick once today. "God, I miss your mother," she said.

I turned around and put my head by her chest. "Me, too. And I miss Papa."

"Don't cry, dear," she said. "Don't let your sister see you cry. Why don't we eat something? We'll feel better."

We had the last of the leftover meat loaf and bread with the stale margarine I hated. No complaining this time from me. My sister ate like a bird. I never saw her hungry. After we ate, my aunt told me to give Krisztina a bath. "Make sure the water's not hot. It has to be lukewarm. Hot water makes her dizzy."

I said I knew.

"Okay. I know you know."

We went to bed earlier than usual. I couldn't sleep. The catnap I took in the afternoon was enough. I got up, waited till my aunt's sleeping pill took effect and for my sister to be sound asleep so I could turn on the radio to see if I could find Radio Free Europe. The station was jammed as usual. All you could hear were beeps and static. The government had banned it. You could end up in jail if you got caught listening.

I went into my aunt's sewing room with the radio, turned it on and lowered the volume just in case something got through. That's when I noticed the four armbands on the sewing machine. And the four safety pins. Tears welled up in my eyes. My aunt sewed each of us an armband of Hungarian colors, just like the one Mustache wore when he roared into our street on his motorcycle. One for Sewer Rat, one for Michelangelo, one for Sister Ágnes. And one for me. I put one on. I tiptoed into the bathroom, turned on the lights and looked at myself with my patriotic armband. I liked what I saw.

Chapter
Three

3

The next day was bright and sunny. We were part of a huge crowd that had gathered on the city's west bank, the Buda side, all geared up to cross the Danube and march on Parliament. Our spirits were high. Michelangelo said his injured leg was fine. He felt better than ever. He really liked the armband my aunt made for us. We were all wearing them, me, Michelangelo, Sewer Rat and Sister Ágnes. My friend Mariska tagged along, and I was happy about that. She was the only one among us without a Hungarian armband, so I ended up giving her mine. She was so excited, she was ready to jump out of her skin. She had never seen so many people before.

Sewer Rat said he had left his gun behind. This was going to be a peaceful protest. We didn't want the radio to accuse us of being "armed counter-revolutionary gangs."

There was one obstacle to the peaceful demonstration. Make that two. Two Soviet T-34 tanks blocked the entrance to the bridge that led to the Pest side and Parliament.

"How's your Russian?" Michelangelo asked me.

"Lousy. I can say good day, Comrade, but that's about it. Mariska's is a lot better."

"Ask the soldiers if they'd be kind enough to let us through," Sewer Rat said to my friend.

Mariska was shy. She told *me* what to say to the Russians. It was an earful, and I had to repeat it several times before I got it. I guess I should've taken the language more seriously in school. Served me right for having been a pain in the butt.

I went up to the tank and looked up at the young Russian who was waist deep in the turret. "*Zratste davarish*," I said in his language. "*Proposti nas.*"

The young soldier grinned. He didn't understand or he didn't want to. I looked back at Mariska lamely. She chickened out. I tried again, with some sign language this time. I tried convincing them to let the crowd cross the Danube.

The soldier's grin widened. "*Da, da,*" he said. "Yes. Yes." He understood. Soon they were fraternizing with us. A group of demonstrators surrounded the tanks. Some were trying to explain to them in Hungarian that the ÁVO killed many civilians in cold blood.

The Russians shook their heads. "*Nyet. Nyet.*" They didn't speak Hungarian.

It was stale-mate for about thirty long minutes. Then it was their turn to use sign language. It meant we were too close for comfort. They started their motors, and the heavy treads made a move. We stepped back. One person fell back and had to be helped up. The tanks turned and slowly rolled ahead of us. The young gunners motioned for us to follow. "*Eddee za nami!*" they shouted. Come on! Come on!

The crowd cheered. Many hoisted their flags and homemade signs high in the air, even the ones that said *RUSZKIK HAZA!* Russians go home! As unbelievable as it was, it looked like the Russians were going to escort the protestors over the bridge to Parliament. Some brave souls, mostly kids, climbed on the tanks for a free ride.

We closed our ranks. There must've been thousands pouring onto the bridge, marching behind the clattering T-34's. We were shouting the slogans of the French Revolution. Liberty! Equality! Fraternity!

Once they got to the Pest side, the tanks made a turn and rumbled along the east bank toward the neo-gothic spires of the Parliament Building. Our march was as peaceful and as orderly as any May Day parade.

The Hungarian Parliament faced the Danube and formed a spacious square called Kossuth Square that held as many people as the People's Stadium. This was where the tanks came to a stop. One of the demonstrators draped a Hungarian flag on the Russian tank.

The crowd filled the square and overflowed into the nearby streets. People stood shoulder to shoulder all the way to the Ministry of Agriculture across the square.

Sewer Rat spotted his friend. Mustache was parking his motorcycle against a lamp post by the equestrian statue of Rákóczy. He didn't lock it. No one thought about things like that now. Sewer Rat didn't bother with introductions. All eyes were on Parliament and the Russian tanks. The crowd was filled with anticipation. I had no idea what would happen next. Then all at once, as if on cue, everyone started to sing our National Anthem. *Isten Áld Meg a Magyart.* God Bless the Hungarians. We were a chorus of thousands. Mariska and I were standing at attention, holding hands. It gave me chills just to be part of the protest.

Then: Gunfire! The distinct crackle of machine gun fire. Screams. The shots were coming from the direction of the Agriculture Ministry across the street. We were packed into the square with no cover, no place to run.

I pulled Mariska down to the ground. The blood-curdling screams continued.

One of the Russian tanks opened fire. I thought at first it was a warning shot over the heads of the civilians. But it wasn't.

The tank was aiming at the snipers on the roof of the Agriculture Ministry. The shell took out a piece of wall on the upper floors.

The shooting stopped.

Mariska was curled up on the pavement, crying

"Get up. We've got to get out of here."

The tank fired again and again.

A blast of air sent us flying. I lost my grip on Mariska.

When I turned toward her, bright blood was drooling from her mouth and the back of her head.

Mustache snatched her up in his arms and we fought our way around the bloodied bodies of the dead and wounded to his motorcycle.

I held on to Mariska and Mustache's waist. He kicked his motorbike in gear and we were off, honking, weaving, racing to the nearest hospital.

He carried Mariska into Rokus Hospital. She looked like a limp white doll in his arms. The hospital was already in chaos, and by the time we got a doctor, Mariska had no pulse. The doctor could not revive her. The X-ray showed that it was a fragment from a tank shell. It tore into Mariska's brain, killing her instantly. I couldn't believe it. That she could go so fast. I stood by her side stroking her hair and arm. The Hungarian armband I had given her was speckled with blood. I slipped it off her arm and put it away. She paid for it with her blood.

I felt a pain in my chest and an urge to cry. I couldn't cry. I only felt anger welling up inside me in waves.

Mustache asked if her family owned a telephone. I said no. I didn't tell him *we* had a phone. Or that we were neighbors. I just didn't have the heart and the guts to break the news to her mother, because then I would break down. I didn't want to break down. I couldn't. I wanted to fight.

I said goodbye to my friend Mariska. Her face was frozen from the shock of the blast. I kissed her on the forehead. Her skin was still warm.

Mustache asked me where my father was. When I told him he was a political prisoner, he asked me if he was at the Vác prison. If so, he stood a good chance of getting out. There was a plan afoot to free all political prisoners. But first we would have to deal with the Russians.

I got on the back of Mustache's motorcycle. He had to weave around angry, shouting crowds to get me home. "Death to the ÁVO!" they were screaming. "Death to the Russians!"

Mustache wanted me to tell the others that he would be at the Corvin Theater. "Tell them to use the back entrance, and to come when it's dark, and to bring weapons. We need all the help we can get."

When I got home, I pushed on our doorbell and waited.

My aunt opened the door. "Dear God, now what? Look at you!"

I just stood there, unable to cross the threshold. I was a mess. Blood on my clothes, on my hands. "They shot at us!" I babbled angrily. "It was a peaceful demonstration! No one was armed! How could they? We were mowed down! No protection, no nothing. It was a massacre!"

My aunt pulled me into the apartment. "Calm down. You're not hurt, are you? Who got shot? Where are your friends?"

"I don't know. We lost each other in the crowd. Blood everywhere. Look at my clothes!"

"Whose blood is that?"

"I don't know," I screamed hysterically.

"All right, calm down. Sit."

I couldn't. I couldn't do anything. I could tell my aunt about Mariska later. I would tell her later. And I couldn't face Mariska's mother, not now. Later. I would do it later.

My aunt led me into the bathroom and turned on the faucet in the tub. She helped me off with my bloody clothes. I told her about the tanks. How could they fire on the crowd like that? Just kids!

"What did I tell you? You think you'd listen to me by now. But, no!" My aunt waved her hand in the air. She was nervous and getting angrier by the minute.

After a long hot bath, I put on my pajamas and checked in on my sleeping sister. I hoped all the commotion didn't wake her. The medication Krisztina was getting for her heart made her sleepy all the time. She was out as usual.

Although I didn't feel like talking to anybody, I went back to the kitchen to keep my aunt company.

She was hunched over the radio. The volume was up. From what I could hear, they said nothing about the massacre at the Parliament Building. It was the same old drone.

My aunt lowered the volume and said the government dumped the hard-line Stalinist Ernő Gerő and replaced him with János Kádár. He was now the Communist Party's new First Secretary.

I couldn't care less who was in charge. They refused to admit that people were getting killed. The liars! What about all those bodies? How were they going to explain all those bodies?!

My aunt upped the volume again and listened intently:

"Hungarian workers, dear Comrades! The Politburo of our Party has entrusted to me the post of First Secretary in a grave and difficult situation. The demonstration march of a section of our youth, which started peaceably in accordance with aims of an overwhelming majority of participants, degenerated after a few hours, in accordance with the intentions of anti-democratic and counter-revolutionary elements which joined them, into an

armed attack against the State power of the people's democracy..."

"Hogwash!" my aunt said.

I headed back to the bedroom to lie next to Krisztina.

"Where you going?"

I told my aunt I wasn't feeling well. I wasn't. My body was hot
and cold all at the same time. I lay down and slept till one in the
morning, when I was awakened by gunfire. More gunfire than I
heard the last three days. I was surprised my aunt and Krisztina were
able to sleep through it all.

I got up, went into the kitchen and made myself some tea. Then I
headed to the living room and looked out the window. Our street
was dark. What must've been explosions in the distance lit up the
low-hanging clouds.

On my aunt's sewing table, I found a pencil and looked for a piece
of paper. When I couldn't find any, I saw Krisztina's drawing of the
cat. I decided to write the note on the back of it.

> Please forgive me for leaving you, but I have to fight. I have to
> fight for Mama, for Papa, and for you. And for Mariska. She was
> killed at the Parliament Building by a Russian tank. Please don't
> come looking for me. I promise to find Papa and bring him
> home.
> Love Always,
> *Cheetah*

I put on the tennis shoes my art teacher gave me for next to nothing. I donned my heavy jacket and looked for a pair of gloves but
couldn't find any.

I went back to the bedroom and took a last look at them, mouthed a silent goodbye and slipped out the door. I scurried down the spiral stairs and went straight to the cellar to retrieve my gun.

It wasn't there. The wine barrels were empty. Nothing in the flour sacks, either. All the guns and ammunition we had stashed in the coal cellar were gone. I was angry. I had this urge, this need to hold the gun, just to touch it and to hold it, so I could feel whole again. I couldn't explain it, but I was not going to be left out of the fight.

I took the elevator up to Mariska's floor, and rang her doorbell over and over until her mother came out, her face a mask of red lines. I told her what happened and all she could do was gasp, fight for air. "She's at the Rokus Hospital," I said. I didn't tell her she was dead. I couldn't.

A man who I recognized as Mariska's uncle came to the door and looked at me as if I were some ghost out of a bad dream. He led his sister back inside. Without going in, I told them I was sorry for everything. For waiting so long to tell them. I don't know if they heard me. "I'm sorry," I said again. "Mariska was my best friend."

I was left standing at the door with nothing to do but to leave them to their grieving. I couldn't grieve, and I hated myself for it, all the while knowing it would eventually catch up with me, and with a vengeance.

In spite of the nonstop gunfire, I felt better once I was out on the street. I took shortcuts through the open doorways and alleyways I knew so well. In no time at all, I found myself standing in front of the Corvin Theater.

The theater was a solid three-story structure encircled by an eight-story building which seemed to hug it. An arcade ran through the larger building from Üllői Avenue to the narrow, winding street known as the Corvin passage.

Plastered on the walls were posters advertising the latest attraction. Inside, the theater was not exactly a beehive of activity. Most of the two hundred or so seats were empty. A small group of armed civilians stood close to the stage littered with maps and newspapers. The few men who sat in the front row looked impatient as if they were about to watch an exciting movie. Except they had guns in their laps.

Sister Ágnes was the first one to spot me. She came up to where I was standing and embraced me. She took me to Michelangelo who was sitting in one of the aisle chairs in the back, and, next to him, my gun. He stood up and said he was sorry about Mariska. He had been at our apartment, but my aunt said I was sleeping. She wouldn't let him in. "In a way, I was glad," he said. "I was hoping she talked some sense into that head of yours. But, and this may sound selfish, I'm glad you're here. You give people like me courage."

Sewer Rat joined us. He said things were all screwed up. Mustache wasn't here. Until he showed up, we were on our own. We could set up tank barricades, and then look around for an empty apartment close by. Something overlooking the street.

"What are we supposed to do? Look in the newspaper?" Michelangelo said.

"Very funny," Sewer Rat said.

"I know of a few places," I said.

They looked at me quizzically. I explained to them that I knew the area pretty well, because it was on my father's old mail route. I knew of some apartments that had been empty for years. Although the housing shortage in Budapest was critical, no one reported them. They were afraid the authorities would move in one of their own, like some snitch.

I knew for a fact some of the high school students had parties in these abandoned places. All they had to do was to pick the lock. The ones with broken windows were inhabited by pigeons.

"Good enough for me," Sewer Rat said, patting me on the shoulder. "I'm glad you're here, kid. You can show us where these apartments are. We'll even have a choice, eh?"

"I'd like one with a shower," Michelangelo said.

"I'd like one with a view," Sister Ágnes said. "A view of Russians climbing out of tanks."

"You said that right, Sister," Sewer Rat said. "The only showering we'll be doing is with bullets. From a window. The higher, the better."

Michelangelo said he was afraid of heights.

"Okay, then," Sewer Rat replied. "You'll be on the roof. Now, let's go."

We dawdled around for another half an hour. Michelangelo said he had to use the washroom, and so did I.

On my way out of the washroom, I ran into a young man wearing tortoise-shell glasses. He looked like a university student. He said he couldn't help but to overhear what we said about apartments. He had been sitting right behind us. He said he and his friends had this huge party once at the very place I was describing. "The one with the pigeon shit. On the corner of Üllői, right?"

"That's the one," I said.

"Is that where you're headed?"

"You just gave me an idea," I said.

He wished me luck. He was very good-looking, even with his glasses.

We were off, finally. The curfew was on, so we had to be careful. The sporadic gunfire never let up. We slinked along the walls and used the cover of darkness and anything and everything we could get our hands on to set up tank barricades on the streets around the Corvin Theater and the Killián Barracks.

Most of these streets were narrow and easy to block. All it took was a couple of park benches and a kiosk, a boulder or two or ten thousand cobblestones. We must've spent the first hour unearthing cobblestones and heaping them into small mountains.

We used trash, debris, anything we could find. Near the intersection of Üllői Avenue and Raday Street, we found an abandoned Skoda, missing a wheel. We had no trouble rolling it into the middle of the street and turning it on its side.

But the big chestnut tree on Práter Street gave us plenty of trouble. It was already torn from the ground, roots and all, thanks to a Russian tank. We worked up a sweat angling it to block the street.

We built another cobblestone mountain before we went hunting for apartments.

The first place I showed them was the one on Üllői Avenue. I took us through a back entrance of an abandoned store. We climbed the five flights in total darkness. At the top, Sewer Rat had to resort to his flashlight so I could find the door. The apartment was in a dark corner overlooking the street and an inner courtyard. We leaned on the wrought iron railing and looked down. Five floors below, the courtyard was pitch black.

The door was locked. I asked Sewer Rat if he could pick the lock. As an answer, he took out the handgun from his belt.

"God, no," I said.

"Relax," he said. He broke the glass with the handle of his gun, reached in and undid the lock.

We opened the door to a fluttering of wings. This was the apartment of pigeons. It smelled like it, too. Sewer Rat's flashlight ran along the floor and the walls. Everything was covered with pigeon droppings. We went to the double windows to check out the view. Only a few glass fragments were left in the frames. Sewer Rat seemed pleased. "Perfect!" he said. "My kind of place."

"What next?" Michelangelo asked.

"Tank barricade time," Sewer Rat said, poking his head out the window. "The street is pretty empty. Except for all those cobble stones."

"Not again," Michelangelo said.

We laughed. I felt surprise and guilt for being able to laugh at all.

We built another cobblestone mountain. Right under the apartment window.

"Now what?" It was Michelangelo again.

I know what I wanted to do. I wanted to go back upstairs, pigeon crap and all, and wait for a tank. But it was not going to happen.

Sewer Rat said it was time we headed back to headquarters.

"Headquarters? You mean the Corvin Theater."

Sewer Rat said that's what he meant.

This time the theater was packed with people and guns. I was amazed at how young everybody was. It kind of made me feel good. I wouldn't be standing out like some oddball. Mustache was still not there, but he was expected shortly.

We spent the time going over the basics of my Soviet submachine gun. Sewer Rat showed me the proper way to hold it and aim it. How to do a quick load, how to clean the barrel.

How to pull the pin on a grenade, how to throw it, how to put it between the cast-iron wheels of a tank.

At last, Mustache appeared on the stage. The auditorium got suddenly quiet. He spoke in a soft voice and some in the back had trouble hearing him and said so. Mustache bounded down from the stage and stood in the aisle. "All right," he said. "My name is Gergely Pongrátz. I'm not a politician or a preacher. And I'm not much of a speaker, either. I'm a soldier. I'm twenty-four years old and I'm the Commander of this strike force."

Strike force? I looked around at the ragtag army of volunteers. One boy held a gun that was bigger then he was. The kids were dressed like they were going hiking. Scuffed street shoes, worn jackets, oversized raincoats, leather coats so faded they had the texture of erasures. Hats of all shapes and sizes, mostly the beret or a felt cap. The one that stood out from the others was a derby hat. It was worn by the only person I had seen before. He was the kid who came by with Sister Ágnes when we hid the guns in the cellar.

A pretty Gypsy girl in her late teens wore a fur hat, the kind you'd see in a fashion magazine. I guessed most of them to be in their teens and some, like our Commander, in their twenties. Ex-soldiers or students probably. The studious type with the tortoise-shell glasses I spoke to earlier was here.

Five or six soldiers with their Soviet-style insignias torn from their uniforms stood close to the stage. An older man with a wooden leg and a wide grin chain-smoked as he spoke with them. I was told his name was Peg Leg. Peg Leg's shirt had seen better days. Some strike force, I thought. Of course, who was I to talk? I was part of this ragtag army.

The Commander said: "Many of you call me Mustache. I don't mind. In fact, I prefer it."

Mustache took a deep breath and continued, "Yesterday, the Soviets massacred some one hundred and fifty peaceful civilians. I personally witnessed the murder of one such civilian, a young student, a female, brutally cut down in front of my eyes. By a fragment from a Russian tank shell.

"We all have our personal reasons for being here. But whatever the reason, we are more effective as a force if we are organized. I saw a young man, a mere kid, with a BB gun strapped to his shoulder, get shot in the back by trigger-happy Russian gunners. That is not the way to drive out the Russians from Budapest. As I said, we all have our personal reasons to want to fight. Let me give you another. This poor country of ours, this small country, has not had a taste of real freedom for a long, long time. First it was the Mongols, then the Turks, then the Hapsburgs, the Germans, and now the Russians. A lot of Hungarian blood has been spilled in the name of freedom, and, don't fool yourself, there's going to be more blood spilled."

"And he said he wasn't a speaker," Michelangelo mumbled to me. "Once these guys get started, they can't stop."

"Quiet. I want to hear this."

Mustache said we all had one goal. To drive the Russians out of Budapest. "We will use hit and run guerilla tactics. We will harass the enemy. We will destroy or disable their armor with their own invention. A simple bottle filled with gasoline and corked with a rag. It was incredibly effective against German panzers in Stalingrad. The so-called Molotov cocktail. We will take the fight to the street, the rooftops, and the sewers, if we have to. We will lure their tanks and armored cars into a tight space and serve them a Molotov cocktail. Best served while hot. But make damn sure your fuse is long enough, otherwise Dr. Leocky will have to cut off your arm or leg, and you'll be knocking about like old Peg Leg here."

We laughed. I laughed.

"Oh, brother," Michelangelo muttered. "A comedian, he's not."

According to our Commander, the first order of business was to liquidate Russian armored cars and tanks in this part of the city. He had maps of central Budapest identifying the main roads the Russians used to enter Budapest. Üllői Avenue was one. It was a long road running all the way from the airport to the heart of the city, cutting through hundreds of intersection, including József Boulevard by the Killián Barracks on one corner, and the hidden Corvin Theater on the other. Because of my father's mail route, I was pretty familiar with this section of Üllői Avenue.

Mustache concluded by saying that we must strike swiftly and decisively, when and where we can. Our hit and run tactics could take us to Lenin Boulevard one minute and Múzeum Boulevard the next. He expected the fighting to spread to every part of the city. He said, "We can't afford to wait for the West and the Americans to bail us out. Our lives are on the line. We have no choice but to fight. The Russians are killing our people. I'm not going to stand around seeing kids 14, 15, 16 dying for our country. I'm a veteran soldier. I look around and feel nothing but shame, seeing how young some of you are."

Mustache paused to dry his eyes.

"What about the Hungarian Army?" Peg Leg asked. "Why are they still dilly-dallying in the barracks? Don't they have tanks?"

"The chain of command is a difficult thing. It always breaks down in a crisis, especially when the orders have usually come down from the Soviets. Some of our crack soldiers are devout Party members. Many have defected, and that will help us tremendously. Until then, we are it. We're young, but we're fast. And we're agile. And we're passionate. And we're not afraid to die," Mustache said, his voice faltering. "But get this, and get it straight, I don't want heroes. I don't want martyrs. I want young warriors, and I want that to be understood. Your team or group leader, or whatever you want to call him or her, will fill you in on the specifics. Are there any questions?"

Sister Ágnes asked about what to do with the wounded to which Mustache replied, "Pray for them, Sister. Actually, we do have a doctor on standby at the Üllői Avenue clinic. Her name is Dr. Judit Leocky. And her assistant is a student volunteer by the name of Pali Szilágyi. He's a chemistry student at the Budapest Technical University, and he's a good Hungarian. They will be making runs with that little truck of theirs to pick up the wounded. I hope you won't have to run into them."

Sister Ágnes nodded. Then she asked about Cardinal Mindszenty. If anyone knew where he was held prisoner.

Mustache replied: "Cardinal Mindszenty has been held in a remote location since his show trial in 1948. All we know is that he is not at Vác. We're going to be doing everything possible to liberate all our political prisoners. But first we have to liberate Budapest. The Soviets have shoot-to-kill orders. After curfew, they can fire on anything that moves. Questions."

A boy with the derby hat raised his hands. "When do we start?" he asked.

Laughter.

Mustache didn't laugh. His reaction was just the opposite. His eyes welled up, and he had to wipe them again.

So many other young kids in the theater. Too many. He looked at his watch and said there were a few hours of darkness left. It was time.

But first he had us all stand and take off our caps.

We sang our national anthem, "God Bless the Hungarians." The last verse brought tears to many eyes, including mine.

A people torn by wars for ages,
paid in blood and tears
for, oh, so many years.

Our group was ready to go. Sister Ágnes, Michelangelo, Sewer Rat and me. I was the Cheetah. That was my name here. Sewer Rat was in charge.

It wasn't until we got to the pigeon-crap apartment that Sewer Rat unfolded his plan. We brought beer bottles, gasoline, rags, hand grenades, and our guns.

Michelangelo and Sister Ágnes were to stay in the apartment as snipers. Their job was to take out the tank crew once they were exposed. Mine was to disable an armored car or a tank with a hand grenade and force the crew out so Michelangelo and Sister Ágnes could pick them off.

I was to sneak up on a tank on the crew's side, shove a grenade between the tread and the wheels and run like there was no tomorrow, because there was a chance there *would be no tomorrow*. Sewer Rat was to stay with me until I got the hang of it. Then he'd try getting near tanks from any manhole close enough to roll a bottle of gasoline under them.

He said hitting the tank's air vent was good, too. Even if the tank didn't catch on fire, the smoke alone would suffocate the crew. But for now, Sewer Rat said, his job was to turn the heat up under the Russians. Like lighting a burner under a frying pan. Mine was to wake them up. With a bang!

Sewer Rat and I positioned ourselves in a doorway held up by Egyptian stone figures, and like most doorways in Budapest, this one was an arched tunnel that extended all the way to the inner courtyard. We waited. And we waited.

Finally, an armored car rolled into the street, firing at anything that moved behind a window. Sewer Rat said the armored car was an older model. The newer ones were shaped like a boat. He told me not to waste my hand grenade. A cocktail should do the job.

I watched him make a Molotov cocktail. The beer bottle was already three quarters full with gasoline. He stuffed a long rag into it, leaving about fifteen centimeters out. Then he corked it. And gave it to me.

We waited for the armored car to make up its mind. It was impossible for it to get through our cobblestone mountain. It could always turn around.

This one didn't. The armored car came within ten meters of the cobblestones, then turned off its headlights. It inched forward slowly and was coming in our direction. It looked like the driver wanted to go around the pile of cobblestones by scraping the building. Were they crazy?

The armored car was now at an angle, its wheels spinning wildly against the cobblestones on the sidewalk. If it came any closer, I could reach out an arm and touch it.

Sewer Rat nodded for me to go ahead.

I lit the end of the rag. The flame was far away from the lip when I heaved the bottle at the armored car.

Instead of exploding, the bottle glanced off the armor and hit the building. The air reeked of gasoline.

Time had slowed down. I saw the flame go out before the bottle connected with the armor.

Sewer Rat lit a cigarette and tossed his match away at as calmly as if he were on an evening stroll.

A flash. A huge whoosh.

We fell back. The sidewalk and the armored car were on fire.

The screams coming from inside were terrible.

The vehicle started firing and jumped the curb in reverse, right into a parked car.

A flaming bottle sailed through the air from above. It hit near the wheels and exploded. Something creaked open. The hatch. Michelangelo and Sister Ágnes opened up with all they had.

The armored car was pinned down and burning.

We headed upstairs so Sewer Rat could finish his cigarette. As we turned the corner to take the stairs, all hell broke loose.

A blast ripped open the gate behind us. We spun around. Machine gun fire sprayed the inside of the doorway, ripping off the plaster. We heard a series of loud commands in Russian. A hand grenade rolled through the opening. The blast shook the entrance and shook us. We scrambled up the stairs to the top floor.

We heard voices in the apartment. Russian?!

Sewer Rat put a finger to his mouth. We sneaked up to the open door. The apartment smelled of gasoline. In the dim light, we saw that two men had Michelangelo and Sister Ágnes against the wall, their hands behind their heads.

One of the men was Russian, the other wore a Hungarian ÁVO uniform. Sister Ágnes had her blouse torn open. The Russian was signaling and yelling something outside the window.

Sewer Rat gave his own signals. He pointed to the Russian by the window. He was mine. His was the man holding a gun on Sister Ágnes and Michelangelo.

"Now!"

We stormed in. The Russian by the window turned around to fire. A burst from my gun ripped into his chest. He dropped his gun and collapsed on the floor.

Sewer Rat wounded the other, causing his weapon to fly from his hand. The bleeding man lunged at Sewer Rat who tried fending him off with the butt of his gun. The man was frantic and ferocious. Sister Ágnes jumped on his back. We fell on him like a pack of wild animals. Somehow we wrestled him to the window, but he still had Sewer Rat in a choke-hold. Sister Ágnes had herself wrapped around the man's waist. He arched his back to shake her off. For a second she hung outside the window. That's when she sank her teeth into the man's neck.

The man let go long enough for us to shove him out the window. He landed with a loud thud on the parked car next to the burning armored car—and a tank that seemed to have come out of nowhere.

"Damn!" Sewer Rat gasped. He was panting, massaging his neck, trying to get his breath back. "You all right, Sister."

Sister Ágnes was buttoning up as much as she could. The men had torn her blouse and tossed her gun and Michelangelo's gun out the window. They had poured the gasoline on the floor.

Sister Ágnes nodded that she was all right.

"I'm not," Michelangelo said.

"Not what?" Sewer Rat said.

"Not all right. She could've been raped. We could've been cremated without our consent. And it's not over. There's a damn tank down there. Now what?"

Michelangelo did have a point.

The damned tank had a heavy machine gun attached to the turret. And their gunner was turning the weapon on us. Sewer Rat and I returned fire. The gunner disappeared down the turret. The hatch went down with him.

The tank rolled back, crunching over stone, plaster, broken glass. Its armor-plated turret turned its cannon toward our window.

"We gotta get out of here!" Michelangelo said.

Another explosion. Unbelievably, the Russian tank's turret had blown off.

We heard a wild, eerie laugh below. Coming from a doorway on the other side. A cannon poked its smoking barrel into the street.

The cannon fired again. The shell slammed against the tank's side. The cannon rolled into the street and fired at what was left of the tank point blank. Oddly, not a soul near it.

Then a man with a wooden leg hobbled out from the doorway. I've never seen a cripple move so fast. He was running his hands along a string attached to the cannon. He rolled his little cannon back and disappeared through the doorway.

"Peg Leg!" Sewer Rat said. "The man's amazing. He lost his leg in the Second World War. Damn amazing, if you ask me."

We had to agree. He just saved our butts.

Peg Leg came out to show himself to us.

The coast was clear for now. Michelangelo said, "He might as well take a bow."

"Oh, you!" I said.

"Just kidding."

We took the Russian guns and hustled downstairs. The Egyptian figures were now part of the rubble on the sidewalk. Thick smoke billowed from the burning tank and the armored car.

We dashed across the street to thank Peg Leg. But he was already gone. Vanished into the building. Sewer Rat said the little 84mm cannon was pretty portable. Its barrel could fold into a vertical position. For all I knew, Peg Leg took it up in the elevator.

We waited a few minutes, then we beat it. "Time to go back to the movie house," Sewer Rat said.

We stuck to side streets. Something was eating at me about the Russian and the ÁVO man we killed. How did they know where we were? How did they get into the building in the first place? It wasn't through the gate. I asked the others about it.

Sewer Rat said it looked like I wasn't the only who knew the ins and outs of the building.

We started to talk about what just happened. Sewer Rat said to Sister Ágnes, "You really took a chunk out of that bastard's neck. I didn't know you had it in you, Sister."

Sister Ágnes said that one of these days she'd have to tell us why she could do something like that. Something to do with "Do unto others as others have done unto you."

We stopped talking. Straight ahead of us, we found ourselves face to face with the murky silhouette of a monstrously huge tank. This one also had a machine gun attached to its turret.

Now what?

I thought we could avoid it by cutting through another building. I took them through a maze that snaked around the elevator shaft and the courtyard. The alley was filled with glass, garbage, and empty bottles. A set of rusted spiral stairs led to the roof.

Sewer Rat found a manhole cover. He pried open the lid and slid it off. "All right, here's the plan," he said. He wanted Sister Ágnes and Michelangelo high up. We would we wait in the sewer.

"Throw us a stone once you get up there."

"Up where?" Michelangelo said.

"The roof."

"Jesus!"

Sewer Rat's flashlight zigzagged only for a moment. Long enough to pick up some of the unbroken beer bottles. Motioning for me to follow him, he lowered himself into the black abyss of the sewer.

The sewer smelled like a public toilet in a train station. Sewer Rat flicked on his flashlight. He said this was *his* sewer, one of many where he stockpiled gasoline. As he spoke, he took off his jacket and a shirt. He had another shirt underneath it. With a switchblade, he cut strips of cloth from the shirt.

From what I could see, the sewer was more like a cavernous underground tunnel. Sewer Rat turned off his flashlight, and we waited for the sound of stone hitting the manhole cover. That would be our signal that Michelangelo and Sister Ágnes were on the roof and ready. I made some Molotov cocktails myself. My fingers tingled from the gasoline.

We waited several long minutes in total darkness and ankle-deep muck when we heard the sound of a stone bounce off the metal lid. We pushed it up and looked out. It was still quiet around the tank. Keeping my head down, I crept toward the tank.

Sewer Rat aimed his machine gun at the tank to give me cover. The tank had its caterpillar treads on part of the sidewalk, only a few paces from me now. No noise, no sign of any activity inside. They were probably asleep. "Go and wake them up," Sewer Rat hissed.

I pulled the pin on my grenade, lurched forward and wedged the grenade between the wheels. Then I raced to Sewer Rat and the manhole. I dove into the black hole in the nick of time, because just then, the fiery explosion behind me lit up the alley.

We waited in the darkness of the sewer, listening to our quickened breathing, our guns at the ready. Soon we heard shouts in Russian, then gunfire. Single shots, then the quick rat-tat-tat of a machine gun. We heard the tank's engine rev up.

Sewer Rat sprang into action. He took a Molotov cocktail and climbed out. I was to stay put in the manhole with the cover on.

With the barrel of my gun, I lifted the lid to have a look for myself. Bullets from the roof were glancing off the armor. The tank was trying to go in reverse, but couldn't. Its machine gun was firing at the roof.

I heard Sewer Rat's cocktail hit. Then a flash. The Russian working the machine gun was on fire, screaming, climbing out of the tank.

I pulled the trigger.

The Russian was hurled onto the sidewalk, his sprawling body burning.

Sewer Rat raced back to the manhole. I had the lid up, waiting for him. He gave me his gun and I thought he'd follow, but he didn't get in. He was furious with me for not following his orders, for risking my life and for wasting ammunition. "What are you, crazy? This isn't a free for all. You do as I say!"

"Sorry," I mumbled.

"Armored car!" we heard Michelangelo shout from the roof.

No time for small talk now. A boat-shaped armored car with three wheels on each side screeched to a halt in front of the burning tank and started to spray the burning tank with some kind of chemical.

Sewer Rat rolled toward the wall and on his belly took aim at the armored car, but his gun jammed. "The tires! Shoot out the tires!" he snapped.

I fired round after round until the boat sank to the pavement at an angle. Soldiers were crawling out of it like cockroaches. I kept firing. Sewer Rat rolled back for another Molotov cocktail.

"Cover me," he said.

He hugged the wall till he got to the mouth of the alley before tossing his cocktail. In seconds the armored car was engulfed in flames. A blast of black, oily smoke smelling of rubber swept through the alley.

Sewer Rat crawled back. His blackened face made him look like a chimney sweep. "You're a hell of a shot, soldier. Another cocktail, please!"

We killed most of the crew, but two were still firing from behind the disabled tank. I handed Sewer Rat another cocktail.

He slithered back to the alley's entrance, lit the fuse and lobbed it high in the air so it landed on the other side of the tank. The Russians weren't hit, but they were flushed from their cover and had to scramble.

Our snipers on the rooftop took them out.

"All clear," came Michelangelo's booming voice from the roof.

For the time being, the fireworks were over. Cautiously, we emerged from the manhole to inspect what we've done. The armored car was still burning in the pink and gray light of dawn. We stepped over the bodies of the two scorched Russians. Their weapons were incinerated.

On the other side of the tank lay the sprawling bodies of four Russians. We took their weapons. One submachine gun was still hot. From the corner of my eye, I saw a squirming black figure hold up a pistol. I whipped around and landed a blow on the back of his neck with the butt of my gun. His helmet flew off. He stopped moving. I was either stronger than I thought, or I was lucky enough to have hit him where it counted.

Sewer Rat picked up the Russian's pistol, inspected it, and put it in his belt. "Way to go, kid!"

I didn't say anything back, but I felt the little hairs on my neck rise.

We rushed through the alley and dark, empty streets to get to the Corvin Theater.

Some of the fighters were already there. They got an espresso machine working. The entire auditorium smelled of coffee. They must've made a hundred liters, Sewer Rat said. The smell made me think of my aunt and Krisztina. I imagined my aunt reading my note, asking my little sister about the name Cheetah. Krisztina would know. I wanted to go back to the apartment and hug them, but I knew if I went back, I'd never be able to tear myself away from them again.

I drank the first cup of espresso in my life that morning. It tasted sweet and bitter. The student with the thick glasses offered me a cigarette. I told him I didn't smoke. A cool sweat beaded my forehead. I looked around for something to eat but there wasn't anything. Only coffee and cigarettes. I decided it was better not to say anything than to whine about my rumbling belly. So far, I was feeling pretty good about myself.

I was happy to see Michelangelo show up. He had bits of gravel and pigeon droppings all over his trench coat. He said Sister Ágnes had gone off to scrounge for food. "It may take a while," he said. "I saw one bread line snake all the way to József Boulevard. The tank had pulled in just about the same time as that armored car. Wasn't that something? We got all of them, though."

"Almost," I said. "I had to whack one with my gun. He was trying to take a shot at us. You want to see all the guns we got?" I took Michelangelo over to a seat in the front row, so he could see our take. The crushed velvet movie seat was bristling with guns.

"Nice," he said. "Whew, I could eat a horse."

"There's coffee and cigarettes."

"I'm a tea man. Caffeine upsets my stomach."

"How about your phobia about heights? Lying on your belly on the roof all that time?"

"I know. Weird, isn't it?"

I asked where Sewer Rat had disappeared to. He shrugged. Probably briefing the Commander. Michelangelo wanted to know if I was scared.

"Shitless."

Sister Ágnes was back with some goodies. Bread and prune jam. Enough for a regiment. The pruned jam looked like tar, but it never tasted better. I was famished. I haven't eaten much for days. I couldn't. Ever since the massacres. The suddenness of it all had me in a state of shock. Compared to that, fighting for my life, dodging Russian bullets was not half as bad, I guess because I was more in control of what was happening. It's not that I was shrugging things off. Something in me was hardening. Maybe it was a process all fighters had to go through.

As I looked around the auditorium, I noticed some new faces. A handful of fighters I remembered seeing when I first wandered in here were missing. Where was the pretty Gypsy girl? And the boy with the derby hat who was so anxious to fight?

We soon found out. The two were shot and killed off Üllői Avenue where they were setting up barricades, the soldier who was with them told us.

Sister Ágnes came over to me and gave me a hug. Her eyes were liquid. She said that was terrible about the two young people. Being cut down like that. She said she knew one of them. The boy with the derby hat. "My God," she sighed. "The girl who died with him was his girlfriend. The boy's family threw him out of the house because he was seeing a Gypsy. So sad."

After an awkward silence, Sister Ágnes changed the subject. She smiled. She wanted me to meet someone who may have interesting news for me.

We went over to a haggard man holding a cup of espresso and a cigarette in the same hand. When we shook hands, I noticed that the man's hand had a tremor. His other hand was in his pocket. His bony face had a fresh scar on it.

Without introducing himself, he said he remembered hearing my father's name at the Vác prison. He never saw him, but he remembered hearing his name. "After October 24th the guards changed their attitude toward us," he said. "They tore off the Communist emblems from their uniforms and started wearing Hungarian colors. We knew something big was happening on the outside. We wanted to break out in the worst way. Only a few of us succeeded, but there are more than a thousand prisoners there, about half serving life sentences for defying the government. Every day there was a near riot. Some of the prisoners used the bars from their metal bed frames as weapons."

The man took a sip from his coffee, which must've been cold by now. "Some of us were lucky enough to get out," he said. "The prison is heavily guarded on the outside by the ÁVO. I had to tunnel under a couple of gates only to face a barbed wire fence. It was my only chance. I climbed it. Got cut up in the process but I climbed it." He turned up his sleeve to his elbow to show me how he got his cuts. "Compared to what they did to us in there, this is kid's stuff."

He took the hand that had been in his pocket all this time and held it up to us. "Look what they did to my hand." Two of his fingers were missing.

"My God!" I said.

The man sighed and furrowed his sparse eyebrows. He said there was a chance my father could be one of the escapees or that he was still inside. "Maybe a dozen got out, I can't be sure," he said. "Everybody sort of scattered. We had a better chance that way."

I forgot I had told Sister Ágnes about my father. I think by now, everyone knew. They also knew about mother and best friend. People who were total strangers a few days ago were now shedding more tears for my loved ones than I was. It made me feel bad. What was wrong with me? I bit my lip. Here I was, having run away from home, risking my life, when my father could be at our apartment right now, hearing about my mother's death and looking for me. God!

I asked the man to tell me everything he knew. How long did it take him to get to Budapest? When did he arrive? And how? By train? Were the trains running? Were some prisoners still detained?

The man said many couldn't get out because they were too sick to leave or had nowhere to go. Some were in special high-security cells. They were not part of the group that got out. As far as the journey itself from Vác to Budapest, the 40 kilometers took less than an hour, the man said. Of course he was lucky enough to get a ride on a truck taking bread and food supplies to Budapest. "That's where we got the bread and jam," he said, glancing at Sister Ágnes.

The driver of the truck, he told us, was kind enough to get him some clothes so he could shed his prison garb. The truck driver was from Győr in northwestern Hungary, and he had all sorts of news. They had taken over the radio there and were able to broadcast to all of western Hungary. The same thing had taken place in Miskolc, another big Hungarian city. They now have a Radio Free Miskolc. Only Budapest seems to be in the dark.

I was taking all this in when Mustache, our Commander, indicated he wanted to speak to us. It took a while for everybody to settle down. Just about everyone had stories to tell about the fighting in the streets. What went right, what went wrong. How many of the enemy they killed or wounded. How many weapons they were able to confiscate.

We sat down in the movie chairs next to our pile of weapons. Sewer Rat had finished conferring with Mustache and came to join us. He winked at me as he sat down.

The Commander had good news. First, he told us that the Hungarian National Guard was finally mobilizing on the side of the freedom fighters. Colonel Pál Maléter was organizing a revolutionary team. "Yes," Mustache said, "it's the same Maléter who fought side by side with the Russians as a partisan. But he has come over to our side. He's a Hungarian first and foremost. This is great news. This is what we've been hoping for.

"Second. The larger cities and towns in the eastern and western parts of the country are now in the hands of the revolutionaries, including the radio and the print media.

"Third. Yesterday, a modest group of Hungarian political prisoners escaped or were released from Vác prison. We have just received information that the guards appear to be more conciliatory, but there is still a stubborn contingent of heavily armed ÁVO men guarding the perimeter.

"Fourth. We have found out the whereabouts of Cardinal Mindszenty. He is in Felsőpetény. We have information that the security there has been beefed up. In any event, we will be putting a team together to free the Cardinal in the coming days.

"Fifth. Our mission in Budapest remains unchanged. To drive Soviet forces from the city. We need to recruit more volunteers, take more weapons, confiscate, destroy or disable the enemy's military assets. We will continue using guerilla tactics to achieve these aims.

"Sixth. Two comrades in our unit have fallen fighting for our country. They had shown valor and spirit. And we'll miss them. I would like all of us to stand in silence for two minutes for our fallen comrades."

I said a quiet prayer, one my mother taught me. I also said a prayer for my father's safe return, for my little sister and for my aunt. I wondered seriously about going home to see if my father was there. I didn't want to abandon my comrades or to betray our fight for freedom. It was a cause that to me felt—it's hard to explain—sacred, I guess. Something like that.

I knew I couldn't leave. Maybe I could call them. As far as I knew, the telephone lines were still working.

Mustache wasn't done. He gave us what he called "an assessment" of our activities. Other than the two fighters who lost their lives in our unit, other units throughout the city reported heavy losses, as many as 300. The real number would be much higher. In our unit, three were nine wounded, suffering burns on their hands and arms from gasoline bombs. Pali Szilágy and Dr. Leocky picked up the wounded who were being treated at the Üllői Avenue clinic.

"Now," Mustache said, "here's what we know. We have destroyed or disabled 17 Soviet T-34 tanks and 21 armored cars. We killed or wounded a significant number of enemy troops. I don't have the exact numbers, but we estimate that the number killed to be upwards of 200. We have taken a substantial number of weapons and ammunition. We have disabled a T-54 tank. I'm told that the tank is now guarded by the Hungarian Army. Word is that they will be able to make the tank—one of the new Soviet models with the high turret and the mounted machine gun—serviceable as early as 24 hours. I want to commend those that were involved in capturing that tank for us. And a special commendation goes to Peg Leg and soldiers like Peg Leg who have risked their lives to save their comrades in arms. And to all of you for putting your lives on the line daily for a free and democratic Hungary."

I knew at that moment that I was not going to go home. I was needed here. I was still my father's daughter, but I was more than that now.

The words of our national anthem played itself over and over in my head about Hungarian blood and tears and atoning for past and future years. My place was here with my comrades. I placed my father and what was left of my family in God's hands.

Our Commander reminded us that, although the Corvin area was secured along a two block perimeter around the Killián Barracks, the government curfew meant that most of the fighting would have to be under the cover of darkness.

Sister Ágnes, Michelangelo and I went out into the safe zone to have a look around and maybe find the tank we were supposed to have captured.

It was a cool, clear October day. The branches on the trees were wet from a morning sprinkle. We saw two destroyed tanks with its cannon blown off. Russian soldiers burnt beyond recognition lay near the armor. Further down, a yellow streetcar had overturned, its wires in tangles, the words "Russians Go Home" scrawled on its side.

Hungarian flags hung from windows and balconies. We came to the old Killián Barracks and saw heavy machine guns in the upper windows. It felt good to know they were manned by Hungarian soldiers who were now committed to defending the city against the Soviets. Must've been hundreds in the barracks, maybe more.

We finally came to "our" tank. Michelangelo was so excited, he asked the Hungarian soldiers guarding it if he could paint the Hungarian crest on it.

He left us on the spot and told us to wait for him. In half an hour, he was back with some red, white and green paint and, in no time at all, he painted our Kossuth coat or arms on the tank's turret. He stood back a distance and went back for a little retouching.

The soldiers liked it. They offered us some hot tea from a canteen.

A journalist from some foreign country, I think America, took our picture. He had me and Sister Ágnes pose with our guns. He told us to smile.

Chapter four

4

The next night, we split the team up. Michelangelo and I went back to the overturned Skoda and set it on fire to lure a Russian jeep that reportedly fired into a group of civilians earlier, killing two. Once the jeep rolled into Raday Street, Sewer Rat opened fire from a doorway with a machine gun. The Russians never had a chance.

It went on like this till daybreak.

We alternated using hand grenades and Molotov cocktails. We tossed them from the roof or a doorway. Sometimes, we sneaked up behind the armored cars and heaved a gasoline bomb right at their air vent and choked off their air supply. They had no other choice but to climb out. Sewer Rat took care of the rest.

Once we got low on hand grenades and gasoline, we played chicken or, I should say, I played chicken. I fired at them from the middle of the street, then ran like a maniac around the corner where we had set a trap. Once we trapped a tank, we waited till the crew got out. They had to get out sometime. If they didn't, we set fire to them. The crew usually got out—under the hail of our bullets.

We got better and better and took more chances. Sewer Rat burned his hand when his sleeve caught on fire while tossing a Molotov cocktail. And when a T-34 tank came up against the big old chestnut tree and shut off its engine, I did something really stupid. I thought I'd save a step by sneaking up to it, climbing up to the hatch and dropping a grenade. I was trying to open the hatch when it opened on its own and slammed into my shoulder. I jumped off and ran like hell, dodging bullets and diving into a doorway. Idiot me.

We killed a jeep, no less than five armored cars and four tanks that night, and a good many Russians. By the time the sun came up, we were back at our headquarters at the Corvin Theater.

After a breakfast of stale bread and cold coffee (the machine broke from overuse), we talked seriously about a different way to lure and trap tanks. Running around like human bait was just too crazy. No more of that nonsense. Michelangelo gave me a good drilling: "As much as I like to see you run the 100 meter dash, why don't you do us all a favor and save it for the stadium. Mustache doesn't give gold medals to corpses. No heroes, remember?"

Michelangelo had an idea. Since we were low on hand grenades, and gasoline bombs were dangerous, he thought of another way to lure the Russians out of their tanks—without damaging the tank. He got the idea while he was on the rooftop. He had already told Sister Ágnes who suggested he run it by Sewer Rat.

Sewer Rat was all ears, listening to Michelangelo through his cigarette smoke.

Michelangelo said when he worked as a propaganda painter for the air force, they would string along these immense portraits of Stalin, Lenin and Marx and hoist them over the street by attaching the ends of the rope to the rooftops.

"It's too early for a parade," Sewer Rat said.

"Hear me out," Michelangelo said. "What if I take cardboard boxes, like the ones they brought the jam in, paint them black, and pull them along on a string in front of tanks? The crew would take them for mines."

"I say, give it a go. I'll get you some boxes and paint.

"I got all that," Michelangelo said. "The question is, who is going to be our runner?"

"You mean your cannon fodder."

"I'll do it," I said calmly.

They looked at me in shock. "You?"

"Yeah. I'm not going to be cannon fodder. I won a medal for the 100 meters."

Michelangelo threw his hands in the air. "You see, this is what I mean. Cheetah thinks this is a game."

"Tell me about the medal," said Sewer Rat. He was serious. He really wanted to know.

I filled him in on the citywide competition and my medal. And how I got my nickname. "Everybody in school calls me Cheetah. My little sister calls me Cheetah."

"Okay, Cheetah," Sewer Rat said. "It looks like you're on. But you know the risks. If they spot you, you're dead."

I said I could've been dead at the Radio Station or at the Parliament.

It was a done deal. Michelangelo and I got started on his "mines."

Mustache gave us another long-winded pep talk. He told us about the government's bogus offer of amnesty by reading from a transcript of a radio broadcast at 2042 hours today:

> "Another 18 minutes and the time limit set by the Central Committee for laying down of arms will expire. Another 18 minutes and we shall put an end to the bloodshed in Budapest. we can end this fratricidal fight. The fight which the young have begun, we may safely say, has triumphed. Further bloodshed is senseless…There may be some people who think the amnesty declaration is a sign of weakness on the part of the government. No, this is out of the question. We are not in the habit of using threats and we do not approve of the policy of intimidation, but we must declare that those who do not yield to conciliatory words and for whom the amnesty decree is not enough, will have to bear the full brunt of our concentrated forces."

The theater erupted with shouts and mocking laughter. "What bullshit!" someone sitting behind me barked. "What concentrated bullshit!" I turned around. It was Peg Leg, who else? "They say they don't want to make any threats," he said, "then a minute later they threaten us with annihilation." Peg Leg waved his hand in the air. "We heard it all before," he said.

Mustache quieted us down. He looked at his watch and said the 18 minutes were up three hours ago. "Is anyone here ready to surrender his or her arms?"

The auditorium reverberated with shouts of NO!

Mustache's take on the broadcast was that the government was scrambling. Apparently they believed we had a real chance we could actually succeed. "I agree with them about one thing and one thing only. That we owe our successes to the young. They're afraid of the kids of Budapest the most. You know why? Because the kids of Budapest know no fear."

Michelangelo had his dummy mine strung so we could test out our cat and mouse game with the tanks. He reshaped the original cardboard box with scissors and tape, then painted it brown and black. To me it looked like a kitchen kettle with the lid on. Maybe we should've just raided the kitchen and saved the trouble. The artist in Michelangelo took offense. It wasn't funny. Nor the idea of me being bait, he said.

I shrugged it off. I didn't like it when he got suddenly serious.

Mustache's scouts had reported on tank movements in the city, including Üllői Avenue. Our targets were three tanks positioned at the intersection of Üllői Avenue and Múzeum Boulevard. I wondered if that was where our comrades got killed. I don't know why, but it helped me to pretend that these tanks were somehow responsible for their death.

The four of us took dim back streets to get near the intersection. I found us a four-story warehouse for our stake-out. The ground floor housed several empty stores, including a shoe store that was now in shambles. I recalled my father and I taking a break from his mail route once, and we had come here to buy me a pair of sandals.

Now, the entire store front was blown away. A door in the back was off its hinges. Sewer Rat decided it would be good cover for me and Michelangelo. Sister Ágnes was to take up position on the roof.

Sewer Rat and Michelangelo exchanged weapons. Michelangelo got the heavy machine gun with the dipod and Sewer Rat the high-powered rifle. Sewer Rat also took my gun and gave me his handgun. He was going to be in a doorway across the street, at an angle, so we didn't end up shooting each other.

The tanks were lined up bumper to bumper a block east of us. Neither the traffic light nor the street lamps worked. Across the way stood a turn-of-the-century apartment building. A shell had apparently taken out the heavy doors, taking part of the wall with it. All the rubble in the street was going to be a problem.

I riveted my eyes on the gaping archway directly across from us. That was going to be my finish line. Once I made it into the inner courtyard, I was safe. From there I could hide anywhere in the building.

For the umpteenth time, Michelangelo went over every detail of his handiwork. He had tied a baton-like thing to the end of a 50-meter rope, more than enough to cover the length of the street. Tied to the other end was the dummy mine.

I held the baton in my right hand.

Once Sewer Rat and Sister Ágnes gave us the signal that they were in position, we were on. We listened intensely for the sound of stone hitting the sidewalk.

We heard one hit, then another. They were ready. Were we?

Michelangelo gave my shoulder a squeeze. I felt like I was at the starting gate, ready to break loose. "Ready?" Michelangelo said.

He picked up one of the shoes scattered all over the floor and threw it across the street. It was our signal that we were ready.

A second later, Sewer Rat and Sister Ágnes started sniping at the tanks. It was enough to get one tank's attention.

The first tank rumbled forward. The turret was turning in the direction of our building, and, as the tank advanced toward us, its cannon was angling at the roof. The cannon fired, ejecting a cloud of smoke as the barrel recoiled.

The roof came raining down with a blast of dust. More rubble.

Michelangelo hesitated. He didn't bank on an obstacle course, and asked if I wanted to call it off.

I shook my head no.

"All right. On your mark."

Before Michelangelo could say "Get set! Go!" I dashed across the street as if I were running the hurdles. I don't think the Russians saw me. I don't think anyone saw me. Until I got to the last hurdle a few feet from the finish line, where I got snagged by something sharp sticking out of a massive slab of concrete. Bullets ricocheted off the cement. I felt I was being sandblasted. I was down and couldn't get up. I jerked my leg hard but only slashed my leg above the ankle. I couldn't free myself. I heard Michelangelo screaming behind me, spun my head around and saw him lurching toward me. He dove on top of me.

Sewer Rat ran across the street and fired at the tank before diving into a doorway. It was enough to distract them. Michelangelo freed me and carried me to safety.

I had never let go of the baton. I had a death grip on it.

We were hunkered down in a broken elevator shaft, both of us panting. Between gasps, Michelangelo said, "This is not a stadium, damn it! It's a race with death here and you almost lost. Forget the grandstanding. You want to see your father alive? You'll be lucky if he sees *you* alive. What is the matter with you? I should've never given you that gun."

I started bawling. I told him that he saved my life. Not just now. But at the radio station, when he gave me my gun.

"Shhh!"

I swallowed and waited. The blood was pounding in my ears. Michelangelo took the baton from me, climbed out of the elevator shaft and edged toward the opening. Using the baton, he reeled his dummy mine in front of the first tank.

We waited.

The second tank advanced.

It was eerily quiet for another five minutes.

Then, a miracle. I heard one of the hatches creak open. Then another. I inched to the opening next to Michelangelo and pulled out Sewer Rat's handgun.

Weapons drawn, the Russians dismounted and approached Michelangelo's land mine with caution. That's when Sewer Rat and Sister Ágnes and Michelangelo opened up on them from all directions. The Russians went down.

We heard the third tank fire up its engine, its turret turning our way.

"Run!" Michelangelo shouted.

We made a beeline for the inner courtyard. By the time the tank fired shell after shell at our doorway and at the empty warehouse, we were long gone.

As usual after an assault like this, we fanned out in different directions. Michelangelo and I took a separate route back to the Corvin passage where we waited to link up with Sister Ágnes and Sewer Rat.

We got there first. The area in front of the theater bustled with activity. We wormed our way through the crowd and realized they had prisoners. Three uniformed ÁVO officers were lined up against a stone wall, their hands in the air. Two of our soldiers pointed their guns at them.

"No! No!" someone shouted. "String them up!"

I looked at the faces of the men. They looked terrified, like cornered animals. One man wore an officer's hat. A woman, I took to be a civilian, slapped him so hard his cap flew off. Then she spit at the decorations on his chest. The man had blond wavy hair. His eyes darted nervously from face to face.

I knew that if we didn't do anything, they would be executed on the spot. I told Michelangelo to do something. Michelangelo said in a firm voice: "Shouldn't we wait for the Commander?"

One of the soldiers said they'll wait 30 minutes, but that would be it. The Commander was with Colonel Maléter at the barracks. Who knew how long he would be tied up. They had more important things to worry about than the lives of vermin.

"Then let's at least wait for Sewer Rat," I heard myself blurt out.

"These are the real rats," the woman who had spit shouted.

I glanced at Michelangelo's watch. Where were Sewer Rat and Sister Ágnes? They ran an hour late already. I started to get antsy.

Another fifteen minutes went by as the crowd was trying to decide what to do with the prisoners.

"Everybody stand back," one of the soldiers ordered.

"No!" I shouted.

Too late.

The soldiers fired their automatic weapons. The last thing I saw was the officer with the wavy hair hold his arms in front of him. His eyes were pressed shut. The three ÁVO men crumpled to the ground to loud cheers.

Michelangelo and I had been powerless to stop them. The crowd was bent on revenge. The last thing we wanted was to stain our sacred Revolution. It was too late.

The journalist, who had taken a snapshot of Sister Ágnes and me, was now taking one picture after another of the sprawling bodies. His camera was clicking away at a furious clip. He had seen it all.

Some in the crowd were still spitting at the dead ÁVO men when we hurried into the theater. Maybe Sewer Rat and Sister Ágnes were inside.

They weren't.

I sat down with Michelangelo. My earlier high spirits had all but evaporated. I thanked Michelangelo for saving my life. He was right, I told him. I was an ass. This was no game.

It was already 0500 hours and still no sign of them.

Finally, they showed up.

Something was wrong with Sewer Rat. He had half of his head wrapped. He was shaking his head. He fished out one of his cigarettes, but this time he lit it right away.

"Where were you?" Michelangelo said. "We could've used you half an hour ago. The crowd just executed three ÁVO guys. No questions asked."

"What?" Sewer Rat tilted his head toward us.

"He's deaf in one ear," Sister Ágnes said. She went on to explain what happened.

Sewer Rat had hurt himself when he dove for cover during the fiasco on the street. Sister Ágnes didn't say, but I knew it was my fault for hamming it up out there. Sewer Rat didn't realize he was hit till he touched his ear and saw the blood. A bullet had smashed through his left ear. "He had to keep fighting, though," Sister Ágnes said. "Could've bled to death. Then he got it into that crazy head of his that he had to take out the third tank. Like there was a quota or something!"

I started to feel real bad. Now Sewer Rat had a gaping hole in his ear because of me. "I'm sorry, Sewer Rat," I said.

"He can't hear you," Sister Ágnes said. "Talk into his right ear."

I let it go. No way in the world could I make this right.

Sister Ágnes said that after we left, he hatched his crazy plan at the last minute. By that time, the bleeding by his ear stopped, but he wasn't hearing right."

Sewer Rat's plan was to have Sister Ágnes fire at the tank from the corner of Üllői and Múzeum to provoke it to move. That's pretty much what happened. The tank continued in reverse. Sewer Rat waited for it to get close enough so he could roll a couple of hand grenades under it.

"That's when things got out of hand," Sister Ágnes said. "The hatch opened and one of the Russian jumped out. I heard him but I couldn't see him. Their machine gun kept me pinned down. I didn't notice the soldier going to the manhole. And Sewer Rat couldn't hear him. And then this God-awful explosion. At first I thought it was Sewer Rat's hand grenades. What must've happened was, the Russian crept to the manhole, lifted the lid and tossed something into it. A grenade or something. By that time it went off, Sewer Rat had pulled back. He says it was more than a grenade."

"What?" Sewer Rat said.

Sister Ágnes repeated the words *"more than a grenade,"* this time louder.

"It had to be," Sewer Rat said. "Dynamite or something. I swear I smelled the fuse burning. I was thrown back on my ass. My ear is still ringing. But the bastard paid for it. The blast killed him."

Sister Ágnes said when she realized what was happening, she ran around the block, hoping to link up with Sewer Rat where he entered the sewer. "I didn't think he'd make it. I didn't think I'd make it. Let me tell you, I ran like hell."

"What?" Sewer Rat said.

"HELL!" Sister Ágnes shouted. "All right?! He can hear me. He just likes to have me say 'hell.' He must've gone to a Catholic school when they were still legal."

"What did she say?"

"She said 'hell'," Michelangelo said.

"Anyway," Sister Ágnes said. "I had to drag him to the Üllői Avenue clinic where Dr. Leocky sewed up his ear. Too bad! He could've worn such nice earrings."

They laughed. The cut on my leg where I got snagged started to smart. I forgot about it. Mustache had come in and he was ready to address us.

He apologized for the delay. He had some bad news. Seven young Hungarians were killed in action. They were ambushed by heavily armed Russian troops near the Astoria Hotel. It was as if they knew of our movements, the Commander said. Another group of fighters walked into a similar trap by the intersection of Lenin and Rákóczy Boulevards. He read off the names of the seven men and one woman killed by the enemy. Then we stood up for a moment of silence to remember our fallen heroes.

Mustache seemed to have the weight of the world on his shoulders. He said he heard about the execution of three ÁVO men in the Corvin passage and considered it not only regrettable but offensive. "Prisoners are to be taken alive, not shot in cold blood," he said. "Otherwise we're no better than they are. Actions like that will not be tolerated. I have taken the two soldiers involved and relieved them of duty. I also had a talk with Colonel Maléter about where to confine our prisoners and how to coordinate our assaults."

According to Colonel Maléter we had to stick to our role as guerilla fighters. "The Colonel did stress something which I think is extremely important," Mustache said. "That we keep tight-lipped about our plans. As distasteful as it is, I have to consider that one of us has been feeding information to the enemy."

We glanced around, shifting in our seats.

The Commander said eventually we would find out who the spy was among us. Eventually. Till then, each group was to act independently, as if they were cells. "I will help you to identify the targets and keep you abreast of Soviet and ÁVO movements. Early tomorrow morning, Colonel Maléter is planning a military action that may involve some of you. That is all I can tell you at the moment."

I had trouble focusing. I wasn't feeling very good. My stupidity could have cost Sewer Rat his life. I bent my head down and looked at my shoes. Something was wrong. The inside of my tennis shoe was caked with blood. I excused myself and rushed to the washroom under the mezzanine.

Finding a booth, I locked myself in to examine the leg.

I heard someone enter the washroom. Sister Ágnes had come after me. "Cheetah, are you in here?"

I didn't want to give myself away. Too late for that, I thought. She must've noticed my shoes. "Cheetah? Are you okay?"

She must've seen the blood. "You're not okay. Can I help?"

To my horror, I came close to whimpering. I clenched my teeth so I could speak without my voice shaking. What came out of my mouth was, "I'm all right. I just need a sewing pin and some thread."

"What on earth for?"

I told her I needed to sew the tear in my pants. That it was easier with my pants off.

She asked me again if I was all right. I assured her I was. She walked out and returned in a few minutes with a sewing pin and a spool of thread. I waited for her to leave. Then I started to sew up the gash in my calf. The blood had clotted around it, but when I poked it, blood dribbled out. I didn't want to let the others know how bad it was. I was afraid they would send me home.

Sister Ágnes waited for me by the door. She said she wanted to have a talk with me. Woman to woman.

We sat down by ourselves in one of the back rows. The first thing she asked was if I was bleeding. "Cheetah," she said in her soft voice, "it's time to tell the truth. You're hurt, aren't you?"

I lifted up my trouser leg.

She looked horrified and said, "*Jézus Mária!* You're going to have to show that to Pali Szilágyi. He should be here soon with Sewer Rat's antibiotic. I have a feeling you'll be going to the clinic today."

"Oh, no." I told her about my fears of being sent home.

"How old are you, Cheetah?"

I just turned eighteen, I told her.

"Listen, Cheetah, if you're eighteen, then I'm Pope Pius XII. You don't look a day over fourteen."

I felt my eyelid twitch. "Michelangelo told you."

"Michelangelo didn't tell me anything. That, I'll swear to. It's just that you remind me so much of myself. When I was fourteen."

I saw Sister Ágnes in a new light, as if for the first time. Here face was so white, it looked almost transparent, like porcelain, like strong sunshine would be too much for her. Her turned-up nose was delicate. Thank God for the hint of freckles across the bridge of her nose. It made her human.

Instead of scolding me, she gave me a hug. She said she knew how I felt. During the war, when she was about my age, she was brutally raped by a Russian soldier. She couldn't tell anyone, not her mother, not her friends. For the longest time, she had felt that something was wrong with her.

Sister Ágnes took out a white handkerchief and blew her nose into it. "A week later," she said, "the soldier returned. This time with two of his comrades. They did horrible things to us I can't even talk about to this day. All I know is that deep inside I'm angry, and the feeling won't go away. A part of me wants to forgive, but I just can't. I had hoped that joining the Sisters of the Sacred Heart would help me find peace. I had just declared my vows when the Communists dissolved the order. So, you see, I know how you must feel, having lost your mother and your friend the way you did."

"Will it ever go away, Sister? I mean the anger?"

"I don't know."

We kept on talking. No one ever shared so much of her life with me. I felt so, so grown up. And she wanted to know about me. About what I was feeling. I told her about how bad I felt for Sewer Rat. How my mistake almost cost him his life, how I was afraid they would send me away. How I missed my father.

Sister Ágnes listened to my every word. She said she was worried about me taking too many chances. Not being careful enough. Then she said something that felt like a stake through my heart. Sewer Rat wanted me to stay off the street. And it had nothing to do with his ear. Sister Ágnes went out of her way to reassure me on that score. He was afraid for me, that I'd get myself killed.

I asked her if she felt the same way.

She looked me in the eye and nodded.

I was crushed.

Sister Ágnes said, "Now, let's take care of that wound of yours! I see Pali's here."

It was turning out to be a very bad day for me. One glance at the haphazard stitches on my swollen, bloody calf was enough to convince Pali that he had to stuff me into his little truck and whisk me to the clinic. They would have to undo my bungled attempt at suturing my own skin. Pali said, "The good news is, it looks like you can tolerate pain pretty well. The bad news is, the clinic has run out of anesthetic."

I was too miserable to laugh at Pali's attempt at being funny. He wasn't kidding, though. The clinic had no anesthetic.

Once they gave me a shot of penicillin and some white pills, Pali drove me back to the Corvin passage where Michelangelo was the first one to break the news to me. Colonel Pál Maléter wanted to see me.

Instead of being excited, I was crestfallen. I was sure I was about to be given the boot.

Mustache himself took me over to the Killián Barracks. Because of the intense shooting in the street, he decided that we should take the tunnel that led from the theater to the barracks. I told him I had no idea they were connected.

"Doesn't Sewer Rat tell you these things?" He was genuinely surprised when I told him he didn't.

Unlike the dark, smelly sewer, this underground tunnel didn't smell of human waste. It was also well-lit.

Mustache knit his bushy eyebrows and asked if I minded if we talked while we walked? He wished we could've sat down somewhere and hashed things out, but he just didn't have the time. He had a hundred things to do before tomorrow's mission.

"No, it's fine," I said.

"I'm sorry, Cheetah. But I don't want you fighting in the streets anymore."

I nodded without saying anything. What was there left to say? This was it. I was dismissed and would have to go back to my former life as a schoolgirl. A schoolgirl who ruined the life of her sick sister and her crippled aunt. A schoolgirl who couldn't make things right. A schoolgirl who played chicken just to show the world how fast she was. A schoolgirl who almost cost her comrade's life. A schoolgirl who might yet have to face Comrade Aczél one day.

A schoolgirl!

By now, we had come to the end of the tunnel. Mustache swung open the thick metal door. On the other side, a man in a Hungarian soldier's uniform cradled a Russian-made burp gun. He and Mustache escorted me to Colonel Maléter's office. The soldier knocked on the door and was told to go in. He poked his head in just long enough to announce us, then waited by the door. Mustache took my arm as we walked in.

Colonel Maléter was sitting behind his desk, studying the papers in front of him.

Mustache said, "This is the young lady."

Without looking up, Colonel Maléter unscrewed his fountain pen and asked me my name.

"Cheetah," Mustache said.

"Her real name." The Colonel wanted my real name.

Mustache didn't know. He turned to me for help.

"Izabella Barna," I said.

Colonel Maléter stood up. That's when I noticed how tall he was. He was lean, very lean, so lean you saw the bones and muscles of his long, angular face, and he was so tall, he could easily make two of me. He was the tallest man I ever saw. He wore a decorated Hungarian officer's uniform, a wide leather belt and holster. "Izabella," he said. "An interesting name. Do you know what your name means?"

I didn't.

"It means queen of war."

Yeah, right, I said to myself.

"My spies tell me you're pretty handy with a submachine gun."

Right, again, I thought. Handy and cocky. I expected Colonel Maléter to give me a lecture right about now.

He didn't. He said, "My spies also tell me your father is a political prisoner, is that right?"

"Yes, he is."

Colonel Maléter strolled back to his desk and shuffled through some papers. "His name?"

"László Barna."

His fountain pen went down a list of names. "Barna. Barna," he said. "There it is." He looked up at me. "According to this list, which is not very reliable unfortunately, your father is being held at Vác."

The Colonel pushed himself back from his desk, stood up, and came up to me. Even as he stooped, he towered above me. He said, "How would you like to be part of a mission that liberates the prisoners at Vác?"

"I'd like that very much."

"Good," he said. "Consider it done."

I was stunned. I didn't know how to thank him. I didn't even know what to call him. Sir? Comrade? Colonel? Colonel Maléter? All I knew was that I wanted to kiss that monstrously large hand of his.

On our way back to the theater, I told Mustache that I'd bet he had known about this all along. He pretended like he hadn't, but I knew better.

My life suddenly looked a lot brighter. Not only were they sending a rescue party tomorrow to where my father could be, but I would be part of that rescue party. I wondered if Mustache did that intentionally and asked him. As usual, he was tight-lipped about it. He said he took his orders from Colonel Maléter.

"How do I address him, anyhow?"

"Colonel Maléter. But something tells me that soon he will be Major General Maléter."

I caught up with my group and the man from Vác prison by the broken espresso machine. Sewer Rat noticed my bandaged leg and said, "How you doing, kid?"

"Great," I said. "How about you?"

He said he'll live.

I asked him how big the hole was. In his ear.

"Like Sister Ágnes said, big enough for an earring. Maybe after we drive the Ruskies out, me and old Peg Leg can go on the road as pirates," Sewer Rat laughed like a hyena.

He put a cigarette into his mouth but didn't light it. "By the way," he said, "Mustache does everything intentionally. He doesn't like giving chance much of a chance. Hey, we even have a tour guide to take us through the prison."

We spent the next twenty minutes or so poring over a map of the prison compound the man from Vác had drawn up for us. He was going to be our guide.

I was about to get a piece of bread for myself when Sewer Rat said it was time for us to change and get our gear ready.

Sister Ágnes and I disappeared into the washroom and changed into peasant clothes, which meant long skirts over our regular clothes and polka-dot babushkas.

We met the others outside the theater where a canvas-top truck waited, its engine running. To my surprise, Sister Ágnes was going to do the driving. It was not a trolley, but it was close enough, she laughed. The rest of our party piled in, clambering over a mound of cabbage. Just in case anyone suspected otherwise, the truck was carrying cargo to the city from the countryside. Food was scarce in Budapest, and it was not unusual to see these canvas-covered trucks rolling in and out of the city. What they didn't know was that behind that pile of cabbage eleven fighters were armed to the teeth.

Budapest, 1956

Ornate stonework over windows and doorways

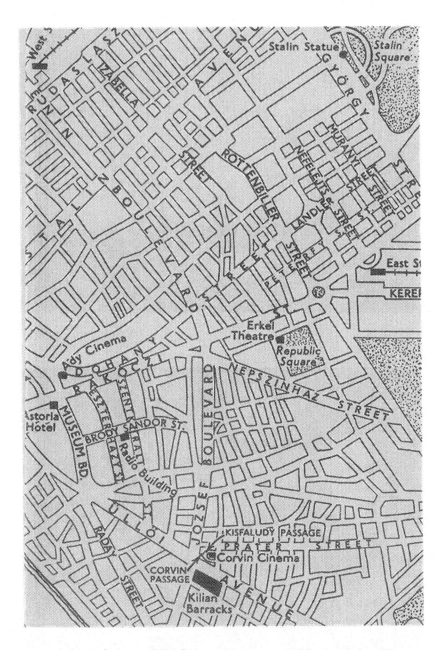

Map of Central Budapest (Courtesy of Opera Mundi)

Demonstrators on Petőfi and Bem Squares

Victims of ÁVO snipers

Firing on demonstrators

Russians Go Home!

The Corvin passage

Fighting back from doorways

Freedom fighters and destroyed Soviet tanks

The "kids" of Budapest

Killián Barracks after crushing Soviet offensive

Hungarian refugees flee toward Austria

FREEDOM FIGHTERS

We freedom fighters made a stand
To win back our Promised Land.
We fought and bled till we won,
Our only friend was the gun.
We fought the good fight,
Roamed the streets in the night,
Our machine guns closest to our hearts.
Stil, a bullet pierced our chest,
And we died a hero's death.
Poor Hungarians! Will we again be free?
Communist whips buckle our knees
To suffer in slavery.
To die for Hungarian liberty.

Nine-year-old Péter's poem (English translation by author)

Sister Ágnes settled behind the wheel, I sat in the middle, and our guide, who needed no change of clothes, sat by the window.

The traffic was nonexistent, the streetlights out, still it was slow going. Rubble, chunks of armor, overturned streetcars blocked the roads. It made for a ghoulish obstacle course.

We had to go around burnt-out cars, unearthed trees, tank carcasses, canyons of rubble and cobblestones. Sister Ágnes got off the main boulevard, and as she made a right hand turn, she noticed a truck in her mirror. She said she hoped we weren't being followed. She made another right turn to see if the truck would follow us. Not only did the truck follow, but it was tooting its horn like crazy, closing in on us.

"Tell Sewer Rat a truck is following us."

I turned my head around and looked through the cabin's rear window, a small opening without any glass. I told Sewer Rat we're being followed. I watched him stumble to the rear of the truck, climb over the mound of cabbage and open a flap in the canvas to have a look for himself.

"Shit," he said. Then he shouted: "Sister Ágnes, can you pick it up a little?"

Sister Ágnes shifted gears and stepped on the gas. A sudden jolt. We heard what must've been the cabbage bouncing around in the cabin.

The truck jumped the curve, took out a lamp post and came to a screeching stop.

The truck following us pulled up alongside. A man in civilian clothes rolled down his window and asked if we knew how to get to Bosnyák Square. He'd been circling around the city for hours. We sighed in relief. Sister Ágnes rattled off the directions.

Before he drove off, the man said, "Women drivers! God help us!"

"Damn," Sewer Rat was back, trying to stick his head into the cabin. "That driver doesn't know how close he came to having his head blown off. Now see if you can get us to Vác in one piece, Sister." Sewer Rat had his dressing changed. The new one looked a lot smaller and tidier. He said he was afraid the Commander was going to tell him that he wasn't fit enough to go. "But, hell," Sewer Rat said, "I wouldn't want to have to sit this one out. Imagine locked up in a hole like that year after year? I want to be there when those prisoners see the light of day for the first time in God-knows how many years. How many years were you in there?" he asked our guide.

"Four and a half," the guide said." "Make that three and a half. I was transferred there after a four-year stint at Csillag prison in Szeged. Sometimes, they transfer people back and forth. Some were sent to Recsk, some were shuffled back to Budapest. To Andrássy Street. To be interrogated and tortured. People who were unlucky enough to go there came back maimed or broken, if they came back at all."

I asked him if he had any family.

He shook his head. He started to speak in a low, trembling voice. "They were all deported. Every single one of them to Russia. Siberia probably. The government accused me of being a spy for the American CIA. Imagine that! I don't even speak English. Back in 1948. Me, a foreign agent! They wanted me to confess to something I didn't do. When I refused, they threatened to deport my family. Then they told me my wife remarried in Vladivostok. Imagine that! I didn't know what to believe. A lot of us couldn't take it. The torture, I mean. My cellmate hanged himself. The guards calmly took the rolled-up sheet from around his neck and gave it to me.

"The next day, they accused me of murdering him. This is how I got my life sentence. They kept asking me about my activities as an

American agent. I could've played along, but I knew next to nothing about America. True, I have a distant relative living in Cleveland, Ohio, but that's all I know. He never wrote to me, and I never wrote to him! To this day I have no idea how they got it in their heads that I was a spy."

I asked him if he wrote letters to his family.

"Tons of letters," he said. "Mostly to my wife. In the beginning I wrote a letter a week. In all these years she never answered. I don't know if they got to her or what. It's easy to get paranoid in prison."

Everybody huddled together by the cabin window to listen to our guide. It was a long and bumpy ride, and our guide kept us on our toes with one horror story after another.

I was afraid for my father. I wondered what horrors he had to endure. I tried not to think about it. Instead, I thought of the good times we had together, like the first time he took me sled riding. How we fell off the sled and rolled down in the snow. How much he liked to sing and dance. His favorite dance was the *csárdás*. I remembered the New Year's Eve celebration when he danced with me. I was all of six. I had my shoes off and in my stocking feet, I stood tiptoe on my father's shoes as he danced me around the room. I often wondered why he never wrote to us. I figured he couldn't.

I started listening again. They were talking about the demonstrations that started it all. Where they were at the time and all that. The student with the tortoise shell glasses said he was at Heroes' Square when the statue of Stalin was toppled.

On the evening of the 23rd, he and his friends took the subway to the square. Thousands of people thronged around the statue.

Sister Ágnes, who heard, said, "Tell him what was in that spot before they erected that monstrous statue.

I had no idea. I've been to Heroes' Square plenty of times. Usually on my way to the skating rink. I never just crossed the square. The statues of our ancient chiefs mounted on their proud horses always caught my eye. And the carved likeness of our kings, heroes and our patriots standing in a semicircular colonnade. In the center of it all rose a column of some thirty or so meters supporting the angel Gabriel with these immense wings. I remembered the angel, but I had no idea what stood on or near the square before they erected Stalin's huge statue.

"A church," Sister Ágnes said. "They deliberately tore down a beautiful Catholic church to make way for their atheist god. Tell the boy."

I did.

The student ignored me and plowed on with his story. "The protestors put a steel noose around Stalin's neck and tied it to a diesel truck. It wouldn't budge. Then some workers from Csepel took an acetylene torch to the knees. The truck tried again. The big bronze knees buckled and ripped at the knees. All that was left of the statue was a pair of hollow boots. The demonstrators had a lot of fun severing the head. Some chipped away at the torso with sledge hammers. Then they dragged Stalin's carcass down the boulevard that used to bear his name. Each time the big hulk banged against streetcars tracks, sparks flew all over the place. Where any of you there?"

Michelangelo said, "I wish I could've been. We went to the Radio Building instead."

"Oh," the student said. He took off his glasses and wiped them. "That's where all the shooting started."

"You're telling me," Michelangelo said.

"You mean you were there?"

"Don't get me started."

Yeah, I thought. Don't get Michelangelo started. Sewer Rat retreated to the back of the truck. I watched him make a nest for himself on top of the mound of cabbage. He was close enough to the tailgate to open the canvas. Blinding light lit up the heads of cabbage. They were pale green and wrinkled. He lit a cigarette and blew smoke out the opening.

The countryside got suddenly hilly along a line of tall poplar trees and white kilometer markers. The bare fields were interrupted now and then by rusty cornfields. Dilapidated farmhouses, ancient pole wells. A small flock of muddy geese tottered toward a ramshackle barnyard.

"Oh, oh. Trouble up ahead," Sister Ágnes said. Looks like a checkpoint. Tell Sewer Rat. Quick!"

Sewer Rat bounded to the cabin window and saw for himself. Up ahead about two kilometers an armored car guarded the tiny train station. "Shit!" Sewer Rat said. "Russians."

Sewer Rat turned around. "Everybody lie down. Get ready. Just in case."

We had phony papers. None of us looked anything like the pictures on our ID's. Sister Ágnes and I deliberately smudged the pictures to make them look fuzzy. We all knew that if the Russians got suspicious, looked inside, and saw more than cabbage, we'd have a firefight on our hands.

Chapter Five

5

A pudgy Russian officer in his square-shouldered uniform signaled for us to stop. Four Russian guards stood behind him. Sister Ágnes put the brakes on. Our front wheels were on the tracks. Beyond it, the open road. Other than the armored car and the five Russians, the station was deserted.

Sister Ágnes rolled down the window.

The pudgy officer wanted to see our papers. He used the word "Control."

We handed our papers over. My heart was pounding against my ribs. The Russian motioned for us to get out of the truck. Instead of doing that, Sister Ágnes stepped on the gas and ran the checkpoint, sideswiping one of the soldiers and the fat little officer.

We bounded over the tracks as the stunned soldiers shouted after us in Russian. They fired, first a single shot, then a volley from an automatic weapon.

Our guys returned fire from the back of the truck. "Two down," Sewer Rat shouted.

It wasn't long before the armored car was in hot pursuit. We had no doubts that they would radio ahead to the next checkpoint on the road to Vác.

Our guide said we were not far from the city. Maybe five kilometers. He advised we get off the road. And fast.

The armored car fired salvo after salvo, shredding most of the canvas. We knew we were in trouble. Our bullets bounced off their armor like pebbles, and because of the car's boat shape, it was impossible to shoot out the tires. Sewer Rat lobbed a hand grenade, but it exploded on the cobblestone.

Up ahead was a dirt path that cut through a dead cornfield. We whipped up dust as we made a sharp turn. Two members of our team leaped off. I couldn't make out who they were.

As the Russians made the turn after us, one of our grenades exploded under them. I saw the armored car lift off the ground.

Sister Ágnes slowed down, then stopped. She whipped the truck around to give the men cover. Two Russians, crouching by their wrecked vehicle, were shooting into the brown corn stalks. I yelled for Michelangelo to hand me my gun, when someone answered that he was off the truck. More of our team jumped off. The rest kept firing at the Russians pinned down by their armored car.

That's when a white flag went up. One of the Russians tied something white at the end of his gun and held it up. His comrade was down.

First Michelangelo, then Sewer Rat, then the others got up from the cornfield, their guns trained on the Russian.

The Russian threw down his weapon and held his arms high in the air.

Sewer Rat looked into the armored car. The others searched the soldier and bound his hands.

Then they dragged him to the truck.

"What are we going to do with him?" I heard someone say. "We can't take him along."

"Why not?" Michelangelo said.

"That's right," Sewer Rat said. "Our orders are clear. No executions. We take him with us. Maybe we'll lock him up in Vác. You know, in exchange for 1,200 of our prisoners."

That got a laugh. A laugh we really needed to break up the tension.

Sister Ágnes fired up the engine and we started our bumpy ride on the dirt road. Sewer Rat asked if anyone spoke Russian. I was not about to open my mouth and make an ass of myself. The college student said he spoke some.

Sewer Rat said, "Ask him if they radioed ahead?"

The student asked in Russian.

The Russian said, "*Nyet*. No radio."

We asked him why the Russians were occupying Hungary to which he said he didn't know about politics. But he liked Hungarians, he said. He said he liked Hungarian bread and Hungarian sausage.

"Ask him, if the Russians like us so much, why are they killing us?" Michelangelo said.

The Russian said, through our interpreter, that the Soviet Army was called in by the Hungarian government to restore order, so the old fascists don't take over the country. The Red Army lost twenty million people in a war against the fascists. He said his father was killed defending Stalingrad.

"Ask him if we look like old fascists to him," Sewer Rat pressed on.

"*Nyet*."

"What?"

"No. He said no," our interpreter said.

But Michelangelo wouldn't let it go so easily. He made the Russian look into the cabin at me. He asked the student to translate what he was about to say: "Does she look like an old fascist to you? She doesn't even know what fascist means. She's only fourteen, for Chrissake. Tell him that!"

"Fourteen?!" Sewer Rat said. "She told me she was seventeen."

"She lied."

"I'll be damned."

The cat was finally out of the bag.

"Tell him," Michelangelo said, "that her mother and teenage friend were killed by the Russians. Translate!"

"One was a Hungarian ÁVO man," I corrected him.

"Shut up," Michelangelo said. "I'm trying to make a point."

It went on like this till we got to the outskirts of Vác. an old town on the bank of the Danube. A range of low-lying hills rose behind it.

Our guide spotted the tall chimney and the spires of the prison chapel. He said the hundred-year-old spires reminded the inmates of a monstrously large organ. No services were ever held in the chapel, only assemblies. Orgies of brainwashing.

Were we in for a great surprise. The city was overrun with people. Huge crowds on the streets clustered around the prison. Hungarian flags everywhere.

Sister Ágnes rolled her window down. We were told that the prisoners were all coming out. Peacefully. Not a shot fired.

We parked the truck in the back of the prison complex, between the river bank and a thick row of trees. We left our heavy weapons hidden among the cabbage. "Handguns only," Sewer Rat said. I tucked mine into my belt. The university student with the tortoise shell glasses who spoke Russian stayed on the truck to guard our prisoner and our guns.

Thousands crowded around the prison. They cheered as one inmate after another, clad in prison garb, came through the heavy gates.

We shouldered our way through the crowd to get a closer look. I riveted my eyes on each and every prisoner, hoping to spot my father.

They staggered into the bright sunshine, pale, unshaven, rattle-boned, their cheeks sunken, their eyes squinting. Some in the crowd gave the men a coat or a jacket. A little boy even handed one man a comb. The prisoners filtered through the mass of people only to disappear into dark alleys or to jump fences and head for the nearby hills.

I asked as many prisoners as I could if they knew a László Barna. Most were in too much of a hurry and brushed past me. One man, who walked with a limp, said he was sorry, but he had not heard of that name.

I tried describing my father's dark hair and brown eyes, the scar by his heel where he was wounded by shrapnel on the Russian front. No, the man said, he had no memory of anyone like that.

My eyes darted to the next inmate emerging through the gates. He was too short to be my father. I wondered how many had already come out. If I had missed him. The short man kissed the ground. He stopped by us. He and our guide embraced. The man was crying. He said all he wanted was to go home. Someone thrust some money into his hands and the crowd swallowed him up.

The next man to walk out was overcome from excitement or exhaustion or both. His face was flushed. He was taking in air in quick gulps. "Have you heard the name László Barna?" I asked him. He didn't or couldn't answer. He looked at me with great fear.

A shiver ran through my body.

The inmates started coming out three or four at a time. It was impossible to keep up with the faces. Hundreds must have passed by me before an inmate missing most of his teeth said he knew my father but that was a year ago. He thought my father got out.

"He didn't come home," I said.

"The guards never told us anything," said the man. "Of course after October 23rd it was a different story. I didn't know your father well, but, sure, I'd seen him. He liked to sing. That man knew more songs!"

The man said there was a possibility my father was transferred to another facility. Maybe to another city. Kecskemét or Szeged. Only the Warden would know.

I made up my mind not to leave here without getting some information that would lead me to my father. Michelangelo and our guide both said they would help me.

I wanted to sit down with the man and talk to him, maybe take down his address, anything, but something in me kept asking the inmates who were now streaming through the gates if they heard of László Barna. One of them nodded: "Oh sure. He'll be one of the last ones out. The poor fellow's on crutches."

My heart was in my throat.

The inmates were swarming now to get through the gates. It was like the floodgates had opened. Some were running.

I heard machine gun fire and screams. I hit the ground instinctively. I strained to keep my eyes on the inmates charging through the gates. Some were going down.

"On the roof!" Michelangelo shouted.

I glanced up and saw puffs of smoke on the prison rooftop.

"To the truck!" Sewer Rat ordered. "Now!"

We raced toward the Danube, but a mob of terror stricken people prevented us from getting to the truck and our machine guns. Our only option was to squeeze through the crowd of inmates pouring through the gates.

Once inside, Michelangelo and I bounded up the first flight of stairs in attempt to get to the roof. All we had on us were our handguns.

I looked down from the staircase, scanning the faces of the prisoners jostling against each other in the corridor below. The loud bursts of the gun overhead didn't stop them from lunging toward the gates. My father was not among them. Some of the inmates shouted that the door to the roof was bolted. ÁVO guards had retreated to the roof. They were the ones doing the shooting.

Sewer Rat ran up behind us. He said Sister Ágnes stayed with our guide who was hit.

Sewer Rat had to pump two bullets into the bolt on the metal door before we could bust through. On the other side, a short set of spiraling stairs led to the roof. Michelangelo scanned the roof. "Nobody," he said. "They must be on the other side."

I looked for myself. The roof was empty, except for the brick chimney. The square building enclosed an inner courtyard and the organ-shaped chapel. Wire mesh covered the open courtyard. We realized the main building was really two separate buildings in the shape of an L. The catwalk that connected the two sections was down.

The crackle of guns and the puffs of smoke came from the other building. We figured the shooters must be on the other side of the roof where it slanted down.

We couldn't see the shooters and they couldn't see us. But we could hear their guns and the screams of the people below.

No way to get to them. The catwalk that had connected the two buildings was now hanging vertically by a single bolt. Below was a four-story drop to a bird-cage-like wire mesh top. What we heard next was an ear-piercing explosion. A plume of smoke rose between the prison and the Danube.

The ÁVO men kept sniping.

The wire mesh gaped under me like a circus net. Before Sewer Rat and Michelangelo could figure out what to do, I was already airborne. Taking a running start, I had leaped off the roof.

It was a longer distance than it looked. My legs bicycled in the air in slow motion. The ledge I was aiming at looked like it was a whole city block away.

I pressed my eyes shut as I crash landed on the clay tiles. My handgun fell from me and was bouncing down the steep incline toward the edge. I dove after it. I barely had the gun in my hand when I slipped. At the last moment my free hand grasped the catwalk which now dangled with my weight. I heard Sewer Rat shout, "Stay down!" I spun my head around. Bullets ripped into the tiles around a chimney where he and Michelangelo scrambled for cover. They returned fire but the sniper was out of range of their handguns.

I pulled myself up enough to see him and his scoped rifle. I took aim and pulled the trigger twice in quick succession.

The sniper rolled down and tumbled off the roof on top of the wire mesh.

"Cheetah, look out!"

I glanced up. Another shooter appeared by the hip of the roof. I don't think he saw me. He fired at Sewer Rat and Michelangelo who were returning fire from behind the chimney. Their bullets fell short, smashing into the clay tiles not far above me.

I strained to pull myself up to see if I could get a shot off. In the process, I made the catwalk swing from side to side. The metal hit against the wall.

The shooter heard it.

I ducked. I couldn't hold on much longer. All he had to do was wait till I dropped. But he didn't. When I heard something roll down the slope, I jerked myself up again. A hand grenade was coming my way. I waited for it. The grenade could blow up in my face or roll off the roof. I took my chances. I scooped it up and lobbed it back.

The explosion created an avalanche of shards, sweeping the man down with it. He was scraping on his belly, head first, his arms and legs spread to break his fall.

He came to a stop right in front of me. For a moment we were eye to eye. He was so close, I could've put the barrel of my gun between his blood-shot eyes and pulled the trigger. I don't know why I didn't. Maybe it was something Sister Ágnes said, I don't know. I just couldn't.

The man lunged at my neck. I ducked. He overshot. The momentum put him over the edge and he went flying off the roof.

I looked down. I thought he'd break his neck for sure, but he was only dazed. He grabbed the other man's gun.

Too late. Sewer Rat and Michelangelo sprayed his body with bullets.

My arms were burning. I felt like I had done a hundred pull-ups. I used the last bit of my strength to pull myself up. I was breathing hard, soaked to the skin in my own sweat. The inside of my hands swelled to bloody streaks.

I managed to crawl up the steep incline to the top and look down. Below, the dead and the wounded littered the street. I searched for a man on crutches. Most of the crowd had scattered. Smoke billowed from the river bank.

I crawled back to the catwalk on all fours.

Michelangelo asked if was able to get down. Should he get a ladder or a rope or something?

I couldn't leapfrog to the other side this time. The roof on this building was too steep for a running start.

I steadied the catwalk and lowered myself notch by burning notch. The rusty metal bit into my bloody hands. I didn't make it to the end of the catwalk before I let myself drop. The wire mesh bounced me around before I landed on my side.

I lay there for a long time, thinking less about the pain and more about how dumb my latest feat must've looked from the roof. I was a bouncer all right.

Michelangelo and Sewer Rat were shouting, asking if I was all right. They were on the edge of the roof looking down.

I raised myself. My arms felt like they were made out of rubber. The raw insides of my hands were on fire. I blew air out of my mouth.

Then I checked on the men. They were dead. I looked around, scanning the walls of the courtyard for a way out. Every window was covered with iron bars.

I discovered an air vent and decided that was my best chance. I yelled that I was climbing through.

"Go through their pockets first," Sewer Rat shouted.

I rifled through the dead men's pockets. Other than their ÁVO papers, nothing. One had a key-chain on his belt. I undid the belt, slid the keys off and into my pocket.

I pried the rifle from the man's hand. With the butt of the gun, I busted through the air vent. I tossed in the rifle and squirmed through the narrow opening. The last thing I heard was Michelangelo's yelling they'd be right there.

Wherever "there" was.

The first thing I smelled was smoke. I landed in some kind of office with a huge picture of Lenin and all sorts of file cabinets. Piles of paper lay scattered all over on the floor. I noticed the smoldering heap of ashes behind a desk. I stomped out whatever life it had left.

I slung the rifle over my shoulder, took out my handgun, and slipped out the door into a dark hall.

This part of the prison seemed deserted. The air was cold and dank. Hugging the wall, I found a door at the far end. I opened it. A single light bulb covered with wire mesh lit up a narrow staircase.

I headed down. On the ground floor, I opened the door to another empty corridor. This one smelled of urine and cigarette smoke.

"Here!"

Michelangelo and Sewer Rat rushed toward me. "You had to do it again, didn't you?" Sewer Rat scolded.

My eyelid twitched.

"Steal the show," Michelangelo said.

"You sure you're not hurt?"

"Just a few scrapes," I said. I didn't tell them that I left a nice layer of my skin on the catwalk.

I handed over the keys I took from the dead ÁVO man.

"You're incredible, you know that?" Sewer Rat said.

"She's part cat," Michelangelo said.

"She's all cat," Sewer Rat, said. "She's the Cheetah."

I don't know if I turned red or not. I had more important things to worry about. Like where was my father?

We rushed through the prison, cell block by cell block, looking for him. Not a soul anywhere. Then we hustled out through the gates.

The carnage outside was frightening. The wounded were squirming, howling in pain. Dead bodies everywhere. Sitting in the shadows, her back to the prison wall, Sister Ágnes was holding the head of our guide in her lap.

He was dead. A tiny hole no larger than the size of a coin above his eyebrow. His hand with the two missing fingers were still clutching Sister Ágnes' jacket.

The poor man just got out of prison and had come back to help his comrades escape only to be mowed down in a bloody massacre. And I didn't even know his name.

We told Sister Ágnes about the ÁVO snipers.

I asked her if she saw a man on crutches come out of the building. She didn't.

Some of our group spotted us and came over to say our truck had blown up. No one had any idea how it happened. Maybe the mob set it on fire or the retreating guards.

I asked them if anyone saw a man on crutches. A prisoner who seemed to know our guide said he saw someone on crutches hobble off toward the prison chapel.

"Are you sure?"

"Sure."

Michelangelo and I set right off for the prison courtyard and the chapel. Michelangelo wanted to stay outside. When I told him to come in, he said something to the effect that he didn't want to disturb a reunion.

I rushed through the ornate doors. The church was dark and empty, but once my eyes got used to the light I spotted a man in prison garb kneeling by the altar. His crutches lay on the floor next to him.

"Papa!" I yelled out as I ran toward him. He turned around. It was not a face I recognized. "László Barna?" I said.

"Varna," the man corrected, emphasizing the V.

My heart sank. "I'm sorry," I said. "I thought you were my father. His name is Barna with a B. Have you heard of him?"

He shook his head sadly.

I left the man and the chapel in tears.

I told Michelangelo.

"Oh, God."

"Where's Sewer Rat?"

Michelangelo said he went off with the rest of our team to see the truck for himself.

When we got back to Sister Ágnes, she was with one of the prisoners. The man's face contorted into pain as he pulled a blanket over our guide's head.

When I told them what happened, the prisoner wanted to help me find my father. He said that was the least he could do for someone who saved his life.

This time I asked the man what his name was.

"Imre Pálréti," he said. He'd been in for seven years, serving a life sentence for anticommunist activities.

"Did you say Pálréti?"

"Yes."

I was stunned. I asked him if he was any relation to a Guszti Pálréti, my schoolmate in Budapest.

"I don't think so. My nephew is only fourteen or so. He was maybe five or six when I started my sentence here."

It had to be Guszti. It had to be. Pálréti is a common name, but Hungary was a small country. Still, what a coincidence! I mean, what were the odds? I even remembered the words "anticommunist activities." I asked Imre Pálréti what the words meant.

He said they could mean anything they wanted them to mean, from badmouthing the government to spying. "We were eventually accused of spying for the Americans." He glanced at our guide's lifeless body and said, "Poor Gyuri."

Only now did I find out our guide's name.

A misty-eyed Imre Pálréti said, "Gyuri and I were trying to persuade the guards to come over to our side. That was the day after

October 23rd. By that time we figured out something huge must be happening in the country. Our guards were suddenly kinder. They gave us coffee, cigarettes. Poor Gyuri! It was his idea to break out. And he was one of the first ones to get out. Then, this morning the rest of us took our iron bed frames and hammered away at our cells. Most of the guards just stood by. Some disappeared. The two die-hards on the roof were the most sadistic. They were the torturers. Many inmates had their nails pulled out. They were the ones who cut off Gyuri's and Tibor Tollas' fingers. Monsters, that's what they were. Most of the other guards just beat us. But these guys? My God!"

It was painful listening to him. I didn't want to hear anymore and changed the subject to my father. "My father's name is László Barna. With a B. Have you heard of him?"

He said he had. As far as he knew, my father had been transferred to a prison in Kecskemét in southern Hungary, maybe a year ago, maybe less. "Time does crazy things to us in prison," he said. "But the Warden would know. Of course they're all gone now. All the guards fled except for the two sadists on the roof. We should've killed them when we had the chance. I never thought they would shoot at innocent people. I saw them shoot inmates before for the fun of it. The Warden, who was a Muscovite trained in Russia, would yell at them as if they were kids caught doing some mischief. But a massacre? Maybe I shouldn't be too surprised."

I asked him if the Warden's office had a portrait of Lenin to which he replied that he was sure it did. Every government office had a picture of Lenin.

"This one is about the size of a window with Cyrillic writing under it." I told him what I saw in the room, including the filing cab-inets and the heap of ashes.

Imre Pálréti offered to help me sift through whatever records were still up there.

Sewer Rat was back. His face was drawn. He said we lost our interpreter. "He was a good kid. Smart, too," he said. "Had everything to live for. He's burnt so bad, I couldn't even recognize him. Our prisoner is burnt to a crisp!"

Sewer Rat didn't feel right about the Russian losing his life while he was in our hands. The truck, he didn't worry about. He was certain the Russians at the checkpoint had radioed ahead, and it was just a matter of time before they'd come looking for the truck.

Sewer Rat took the keys I had taken from the ÁVO man and showed them to Imre Pálréti. Did he know what any of these keys were for.

As far as he knew, Imre Pálréti said, all the cells were open, even solitary confinement. He didn't know of any other place where they held prisoners.

"Did the ÁVO guard have a car? This shiny key here looks like a car key."

"I wouldn't know about that. I never drove a car. But I wouldn't be surprised. Those two ÁVO bastards had everything. Your best bet is to ask some of the locals."

Sewer Rat nodded and slipped the keys back in his pocket.

Part of our team fanned out to cover the entrances to the prison, others headed to the chapel with Sewer Rat to figure out our next move.

Imre Pálréti took me up to the Warden's office, the very office I had crawled into after I crash landed on the wire mesh. The dim room still smelled of burnt paper. I sat on the floor and went through the scattered papers, including those that were partially scorched. Imre Pálréti worked on the files, opening one drawer after another.

We spent most of an hour without any luck, when Imre Pálréti said, "Here it is. Barna, László, filed out of order, of course."

I stood up and went over to him. He had my father's dossier, dated March 11, 1955, to November 2, 1955. As he lifted out the bulky file, a stack of envelopes fell to the floor. They were letters bound by a shoestring. Must've been twenty or so.

"There's more," Imre Pálréti said. "They slipped to the bottom of the drawer."

These letters were loose, but the address was the same. Our address, bearing my mother's name, a few my aunt's. None of the envelopes had stamps on them.

Imre Pálréti glanced through the file's official documents which confirmed that, yes, my father had been transferred to a high-security prison in Kecskemét on November 3, 1955. That was last year.

I opened one of the letters with trembling fingers. I recognized my father's beautiful handwriting. The individual letters were carefully drawn, almost like calligraphy. The letter was dated March 14, 1952. I was ten at the time and Krisztina three.

> Dear Bella, Kitty, Little Krisztina!
> I am fine. God willing, I'll be back with you soon. I am sorry I couldn't write to you from where they first took me. But now they are letting us write letters home. I am very excited about that, because I can tell you how much I miss you and the children. Please don't worry about me. I am not sick. I feel strong. We get to exercise in the morning, and the food isn't all that bad. Nothing like the chicken *paprikás* you make, though, my sweetheart. How I miss being with you. Touching you. I miss hugging the children. I would give anything to see them now, how they must have grown. It hurts me that I will miss out on so much. Please, Bella, write to me about what is happening with you and

the children. I want you to know how much I care for all of you. I promise, we will see each other soon. God bless you, my angels. Your Papa sends you hugs and kissed. I have to go now. They are turning out the lights.

I wiped my eyes. I didn't want anything to fall on the paper and smudge the ink. "They never sent any of these letters home. We had no idea where they took him," I said to Imre Pálréti.

He let out a long sigh. He said he didn't think any of the letters were ever sent, including his letters to his wife. It was a travesty.

Michelangelo came into the room. I told him what we found. I showed him the letter I just read. There were at least a hundred here. The prison officials never sent them!

"It's torture, that's what it is," Michelangelo said. "Pure and simple torture."

"Just another way too keep us in line," Imre Pálréti said. "Even the strongest among us had become emotional wrecks. We thought everyone had abandoned us. Can you imagine? Not a single letter from home. I know my wife. If she could, she would write. I don't know if she's alive or dead. That's what eats at you. Everyday it eats at you. It never lets you go. Physical torture was a lot easier to handle. They cut two of Gyuri's fingers off, but that didn't hurt him half as much as when they told him his wife remarried. To a man in Russia of all places. I told him it was nothing more than psychological manipulation, but he wasn't so sure. It ate away at him till he broke down. Before he busted out of this hellhole, Gyuri said all he wanted to do was to get out and bring these bastards to justice for ruining our lives."

I thought about how my mother felt about my father. At first she grieved, then she hardened, grew angry, impatient. After a while she started blaming him for getting himself arrested. How could she blame him? He didn't abandon us. He stood up for what he believed in? He was a patriot. My mother said family was more important than all this political mumbo jumbo. It was different with my aunt, who told my mother: "That's your husband. He is what he is. You knew that when you married him."

What my aunt meant was that my father was not a follower. Not because he had trouble with authority, but because if he saw an injustice he couldn't keep quiet. I wondered if my father did anything here at Vác to cause him to be transferred to a hard-core detention place like the prison in Kecskemét.

I gathered all my father's letters and bound them with the shoestring I took from a pair of shoes the Warden left behind.

We walked down a half-lit corridor along a row of cells. I stopped to look inside. Flush against the bare cement floor was a flimsy cot. On the ceiling a lone bulb covered by wire mesh. The cell itself was tiny and smelled of mildew and human waste. I asked Imre Pálréti if he knew what kind of prisoner my father was. Why he was moved to another prison.

Imre Pálréti didn't know. My father wasn't here that long. Many inmates got into trouble for refusing to snitch on their cellmates. Interrogations were a matter of course here, even if a prisoner was already serving his sentence. In Imre Pálréti's case it was a life sentence. Still they were after him. Either they wanted information or to plant information to make a case against someone he didn't even know.

Once we got outside, we noticed that Gyuri's body was gone. The townspeople had trickled back to take care for the wounded and to take away the dead.

Rolling toward us was a private car, light-brown in color. The Russian-made Pobeda stopped right in front of us. The door opened and Sister Ágnes stepped out. Sewer Rat stayed in the passenger seat checking out the inside of the car.

With the help of a local official sympathetic to our cause, Sewer Rat and Sister Ágnes located the ÁVO officer's car. Sewer Rat rolled down the window and said that for now we had a wire cutter, a pick ax, and guns and ammunition in the trunk. Compliments of their armory.

We were invited to get in the car. Sewer Rat had an unlit cigarette in his mouth. "We got lucky," he said. The others on our team were heading back to Budapest, taking different routes. Some were hitching rides in delivery trucks. A group already left on the back of a horse-drawn wagon. They had our dead interpreter's personal things with them, like his wallet and glasses.

Dusk was settling in when we piled into the back seat. Since I was the smallest, I squeezed between Sewer Rat and Imre Pálréti. With his long legs, Michelangelo sat up front. As before, Sister Ágnes did the driving. No one else knew how to drive.

Sewer Rat asked Imre Pálréti where he was headed. He said, before he was arrested, he lived in Balástya, a little town 25 kilometers from Szeged. His family had been living there since the last century.

"Good," Sewer Rat said. "We'll drop you off. It's not that far from Kecskemét."

"We're not going back to Budapest?" I asked.

"Change of plans," Sewer Rat," said. "We're going to free your father. I have specific orders from Mustache himself to get your father out of prison. So, we take a little detour."

"Like 200 kilometers," Michelangelo said. "Why not?"

I lowered my head, put a hand over my eyes, because I was going to cry. My father's letters were in my other hand. I wanted to read one out loud, the one I opened in the Warden's office, but I didn't think I could do it. My voice would crack and I'd bawl through the whole letter.

But throughout the long ride I kept reading one letter after another to myself, shedding silent tears. Papa really missed us. He never once complained about how miserable he was in prison. Said nothing about all the humiliation and cruelty he must have endured. I was sure it was because he didn't want us to worry. That's the kind of man my father was. That's how I remembered him. To us he never complained about anything, even when he was sick. Of course Stalin was a different story. As was our puppet premier Rákosi.

I told everyone in the car how my father worked day and night for us. On top of being a postman, he had these extra jobs, menial jobs, like being a night watchman at an orchard or cleaning toilets in a factory at night, all because he refused to join the Communist party. And he was an educated man. Maybe that's what bugged the Communists the most, that he had more education than they had. The more I talked about him, the more Sewer Rat liked him.

When Sewer Rat lit up his cigarette, he rolled down the window. The air was cool outside and dark. He rolled it right back up because it started to rain.

It was safer driving at night, less chance of getting caught. Our forged papers had been taken from us at the Russian checkpoint. Now we were on our own. In a stolen car.

I held on to my father's letters with both hands as I glanced around the Pobeda's plush interior. I had never been inside a car before. This one even had a radio with dials and everything. We were afraid to turn it on. What if it was more than just a radio? What if it was connected to ÁVO headquarters? They could trace us for sure. We were anxious to find out what was going on in Budapest, but it was too risky.

The cobblestone National Highway that ran south was nearly deserted, with an occasional canvas-covered truck zooming past us in the rain. Our windshield wipers were barely keeping up with the downpour. In the darkness there was little to see except for the pelting rain and the occasional kilometer marker caught in the headlights.

Sister Ágnes had to slow down to keep from running off the road. She was a great driver. Before driving a trolley she drove a Skoda taxicab for a short time. She told us about the time these tourists from Holland gave her a hundred forint bill as a tip. With more and more of her receipts going to the State and with fewer and fewer Western tourists like her passengers from Holland, it just wasn't worth her while.

Sewer Rat took out a round loaf of bread and a huge slab of salt pork wrapped in newspaper. With his switchblade he cut up some bite-size chunks of pork and bread, and passed them back. We were hungry, and ate like starving wolves. The salt pork had a nice and smoky taste. We washed it down with some homemade red wine we passed around in a long-necked bottle.

I had wine before at one of our family's New Year's Eve celebrations, but I don't remember it tasting this sour. Imre Pálréti said it was the best meal he had in seven years.

The rain let up once we neared Budapest. What we saw ahead of us made my heart sink. An endless column of Soviet tanks rolled toward the city from the east. In the distance, we could see fires lighting up the night sky. I shuddered to think of what those tanks could do to a defenseless city.

To avoid the tanks, we made a quick turn and took a roundabout route that, after a detour of several kilometers, eventually put us back on a southerly course down the National Highway.

Hardly had we gone twenty kilometers when we spotted another column of Russian tanks heading in the direction of Budapest. "Dear God," Sister Ágnes said. "They're going in for the kill."

Again, we had to turn off the main road, this time finding cover behind a haystack. We got out of the car to stretch our legs and to watch the hundred or so heavy Russian tanks rumble past us on the cobblestone highway.

Back in the car, we kept our lights off for a stretch to avoid the Russians spotting us. We were in the dark in more ways than one. Michelangelo said he just didn't get it. Why wasn't the West doing anything to intervene? How long could our rag-tag army last against such overwhelming armor?

Imre Pálréti spoke up: "Ah, the West. They had their chance in 1945. Patton was going to come in and save us from the Russians. But the Big Three made sure that didn't happen."

"The Big Three?" I said.

"Stalin, Churchill and Roosevelt," Sewer Rat explained. "They did a nice job carving up the world. Us included."

Michelangelo said, "That's what we get for siding with the Germans."

"What about Austria?" Imre Pálréti put in. "They got to pull out of the Warsaw Pact, didn't they? The word got out even in prison. It was big news, all right. They're a neutral country now, aren't they?"

"Just our luck," Sewer Rat said. "Or destiny. I guess without any friends in high places, we'll just have to do our own fighting."

We were far enough away now, so that Sister Ágnes could safely turn on the headlights and we could pick up speed.

"We have to hold out and hope," I said.

"Amen," Sister Ágnes said.

For a long time we were quiet. One thing that really stayed with me was our Commander's words: We had no other choice but to fight. They were going to kill us anyway. "God willing," he had said, "the West will come to our aid. All we have to do is to hold out and hope. For a week or two."

"The Cheetah's right," Sewer Rat said. "All it takes for the West is a show of force, and the Russians would back down. All they have to do is to fly overhead. A hundred American planes, nice and low."

"Why not a thousand?" Michelangelo said.

Sewer Rat answered Michelangelo's gibe with one of his own: "The reason they won't send a thousand is because we don't have enough uranium or oil or aluminum. We have some but not enough."

"What about humanitarian reasons?" Sister Ágnes said.

"Oh, that!" Michelangelo said. "They'll send us butter, so we can butter our bread for our last meal."

"It's just us, isn't it?" Imre Pálréti said.

"Hasn't it always been?" Sewer Rat said.

"That's why we lost every war," Michelangelo said.

"No, it's because we're a country of poets. And artists, like you!" Sewer Rat said.

"One of our inmates was a poet," Imre Pálréti said. "He'd pass his poems around in the prison chapel when we had our assemblies. When the guards got wind of it, they tortured him by taking away his pen and paper. When that didn't work, they cut off his index and middle fingers, so he wouldn't be able to write again. You think that stopped him? Not on your life. Not Tibor Tollas. He'd recite his poems to us and we'd memorize them. Now that really ticked off the guards. Those two bastards you took care of? They talked the Warden into putting him into solitary. This was around 1953. You won't believe what he did then.

"By that time he had learned how to use his left hand. But he had no paper and pen, right? And no one around to memorize his poems. So, what he did was take his socks, extract the dye from them, and with a safety pin write his poems on toilet paper. He wrote in painstakingly tiny letters. He rolled the poem into a little ball the size of a thimble. The he melted plastic on it from his glass frames. Soon he befriended a guard who swallowed the 'capsules'. The guard passed it during a bowel movement. That's how he had his poems smuggled out of prison. Imagine that! The first poem that was passed on like this was my favorite. The first line goes something like this: *They have walled up every window with tin*."

"Why tin?" Michelangelo said.

"For heaven's sake, Michelangelo! It's tin because it's tin," Sister Ágnes said from behind the wheel. "What difference does it make?"

"Who is this man?" Imre Pálréti asked, referring to Michelangelo.

"Oh, don't mind him. He's just a killjoy."

Michelangelo grunted. "So now I'm a killjoy."

An uneasy silence followed. Michelangelo kept looking out his window to avert his face from us. I've never seen him this upset.

Hardly anything was said until we got to the outer fringes of Kecskemét, and Sewer Rat unfolded his plan. He had learned from one of the inmates that the prison itself was in the basement of a relatively small government building manned by the secret police. Only one watchtower, but armed sentries, three at the most, were posted round the clock. All the windows had bars on them, and the entire perimeter was surrounded by a barbed wire fence.

"Now, here's the plan," Sewer Rat said. "I'll cut the wires on the blind side of the tower, sneak up on the guard in the tower and take him out with my switchblade. Then, on my signal, you follow under the barbed wire. Find cover, a bush, a tree, a wheelbarrow, anything. The building inside may be crawling with ÁVO men. We'll have to do everything we can to avoid alerting them. We'll have to use the bayonets in the trunk. Sorry, I thought I'd save the best for last. Any questions?"

I didn't know if Sewer Rat was on the level or just saying things for Imre Pálréti's benefit. Either way, it sounded like a cruel game.

Imre Pálréti had a question. Did we have a weapon for him? He said he was raring to go.

"Sorry," Sewer Rat said. "I already lost one prisoner. Two would be too many. We want to get you home alive. If we don't make it out of there, you'll have to drive yourself. You know how to drive a car?"

"I rather drive a mule than this Russian piece of crap," Imre Pálréti replied.

We had a good belly laugh at that. Then, suddenly, things got weird again. Sewer Rat's eyes flitted from me to Sister Ágnes. "What about you two? You sure you have the stomach for it?"

Sister Ágnes looked Sewer Rat in the eye through her rearview. "It's not so much a question of whether we women have the stomach for it or not. It's more a question of brains."

"Yeah?" Sewer Rat said. "You have a better idea?"

"I may. You have any more of that wine left? Why don't you give us the bottle and we'll lure the boys to the gate. And once we give you the signal, you can get on all fours doggie-style, burrow your way under the barbed wire and do what you have to."

"You're not getting soft on me, are you, Sister?"

"You'll be amazed at what a little softness can do, soldier boy."

"All right. All right."

Imre Pálréti said: "Why does he keep calling you Sister?"

"I'm a Sister of the Sacred Heart of Mary."

"Mother of God, help us," Imre Pálréti said.

I put myself into Imre Pálréti's shoes for a second and winced. We weren't exactly your garden-variety Hungarian patriots. What were we anyhow? I've been wondering about that myself. What was I? I needed my father. Once I had my father back, I was sure the feeling would go away that somehow I had lost my footing and was free-falling without knowing how to use my wings.

We found the infamous Kecskemét prison by looking for the watchtower. It was not easy. The tower barely stood ten meters above the outcropping of buildings. The main building, rectangular in shape, was surrounded by tangles of barbed wire.

We left the car out of sight by an abandoned shed not too far from the compound. Sewer Rat's information was right. Two men with submachine guns guarded the entrance to the basement. We took a closer look at the tower. No searchlight? The tower looked like it was unmanned.

Sister Ágnes and I went into action while the others watched from a ditch across the way.

The night wind had a real bite to it, but it didn't stop Sister Ágnes from unbuttoning the neck of her blouse. I stood next to her holding the half-empty bottle of wine. "Hey, soldier boys," Sister Ágnes bleated to the guards.

The searchlight came on and panned toward us. The blinding light settled on us. We were lit from head to toe, our eyes pressed shut. We heard a gasp from the ditch.

"Keep smiling," Sister Ágnes whispered. I smiled. We heard the man in the tower. His voice was booming. "Oh, no you don't," he was shouting to his comrades. "This time I'm getting in on it, too."

The two other guards laughed. The searchlight turned off. I saw a huge red disc in front of my eyes for several seconds. I rubbed my eyes, the red disc was still there.

We heard the man in the tower climb down. I counted the rungs. It was a very short tower.

Soon, the three guards were standing next to us, on the other side of the barbed wire fence. "How 'bout a kiss?" said one of the men.

Sister Ágnes smiled broadly so they could see her even teeth. "I don't think eating wire would be good for my teeth," Sister Ágnes said. "If it's all right with you boys. Are you going to crawl through or should we?"

"You're right," said the man. "What's a kiss without some cuddling. We'll walk you to the gate."

Sister Ágnes and I walked along the barbed wire fence like a couple of streetwalkers. Once we got to the gate, the guards couldn't unbolt it fast enough. One of them was all over Sister Ágnes when they were in for a rude awakening. Sewer Rat and Michelangelo had their bayonets shoved right at their throats. "Don't move! Don't make a sound!" Sewer Rat hissed.

The guards put their hands in the air. We took them outside the prison to the abandoned shed. We pumped them for information, like who was in the building.

They said it was empty. The officers had their hands full with the insurgents, they said.

"What about the key? For the main building," Sewer Rat pressed.

The man from the tower handed over a large key. We gagged them and tied them to the wheels of an old wagon inside the shed.

Sewer Rat gave his handgun to Imre Pálréti. He was to keep an eye on them. The rest of us slithered to the gate and to the basement door. Michelangelo and Sister Ágnes guarded the entrance while Sewer Rat and I went in.

Sewer Rat's flashlight zigzagged in the darkness. The smell of human waste was overwhelming. Spiders retreated from the cavernous wall. We took the ten or so steps down to ankle-deep water. Nothing inside the first cell but a rusty cot and water. We sloshed by one empty cell after another. The stench was horrible. Little squealing things ran off in all directions on the brown surface.

We heard a groan. Another cell stood far off in a corner. A man, covered from his chin to his toes with a raggedy blanket, cried out. We sprang his cell open. I rushed to him. He was coughing, licking his lips. The whites around his sunken eyes were yellow. We propped him up, and Sewer Rat gave him a sip of *pálinka* from his flask. The man coughed it back out. He was very sick. I thanked the Lord he was not my father.

When I mentioned my father's name, he got suddenly animated. He sat up, squinted, and stared for the longest time. "You're his daughter, aren't you?"

I nodded.

"You are Kitty, then. Dear God. The bouncer. Oh, your poor father," the man groaned in pain. "He didn't last long, your father. One month in this hellhole and he died of pneumonia. One month," the man said, then he coughed violently.

I broke down. Sewer Rat held me, and I sobbed like the little girl that I was. I had to let it out, otherwise I wouldn't be able to catch my breath. I felt like I had fallen from a great height, and the wind got knocked out of me. My mouth was open wide, but no sound came out. Only this awful, dry, rasping. My nose was running more than my tears. I wiped it with my sleeve.

The man motioned for me to come closer. With the last of his strength he said, "Your father refused to betray the Cardinal. Cardinal Mindszenty. It cost him his life."

"Was the Cardinal here, too?" I asked.

The man shook his head no. "Andrássy Street," he said. "Andrássy Street." Then, choking on the last word, he lost his voice and mouthed something I couldn't make out.

"It's the ÁVO's torture chamber in Budapest," Sewer Rat said.

My tears started to flow. Everything was blurry.

We had to go. We wrapped the man in his blanket and carried him out of his dungeon. The trip to the car proved too much for him. His throat gurgled like he couldn't get air. We had to put him down.

Michelangelo propped him up while Sister Ágnes patted his back so he could clear his lungs and breathe easier. The man's head wobbled around strangely, pink foam bubbled out of his mouth. His back arched. It was like a current of electricity ran through his whole body. Only for a few seconds. Then he lay still. Very still. Sister Ágnes put her ear by the man's chest, glanced up at us and shook her head. There was nothing she could do. There was nothing any of us could do.

"One month," I said to no one in particular. "My father lasted one month here. He's been dead almost a year, and I just found out about it now."

Chapter Six

6

Sewer Rat took his revolver, cocked it and handed it to me. I aimed the gun at the gagged and bound ÁVO men. The gun shook in my hand. My heart pounded in my ears. I couldn't pull the trigger. Sewer Rat snatched the gun out of my hand and aimed.

"NO!" I shouted. "We're not like them. We'll never be like them!"

Sewer Rat put the gun flush against the tall guard's forehead. He was the man on the tower, their ringleader.

Sewer Rat ripped the gag from the man's mouth and sneered, "Took three of you to guard a dying man? You should be strung up!"

The man was breathing hard. He said they weren't guarding anybody but the armory. To keep the guns from the insurgents before the Russians got here.

Sewer Rat whacked him with his gun. "You mean freedom fighters!"

"If we don't kill them, they'll be killing us the first chance they get," Imre Pálréti said.

The ÁVO man said they were not violent like his comrades. "We were just assigned this detail three days ago, I swear to God," he pleaded. "Nobody told us about a dying man down there."

Sewer Rat asked the man how to get to the guns.

The man said, "There's a truck behind the long building. The key is locked in the passenger compartment. None of us have the key."

"You better be right," Sewer Rat warned. He and Michelangelo headed for the truck, taking Imre Pálréti as a lookout and leaving Sister Ágnes and me with the prisoners.

I didn't feel like talking to them but Sister Ágnes did. "Why?" she asked. "Why would you join a group of killers that massacres its own people. How can Hungarians kill Hungarians, tell me that?"

The ÁVO man said he never thought about killing or massacring anybody. He was a regular soldier when they recruited him. His father had been a gendarme for the old regime, his brother a member of the Labor Brigade. Everybody in the family was in some kind of service. Though not always on the same side. Some were Nazis, some Communists. "I just did what I was told. Like my comrades here."

"If you were told to fire on innocent civilians, would you do it?"

"No, I would not."

After an hour, Michelangelo, Sewer Rat and Imre Pálréti were still not back. We started to get concerned. Maybe they walked into a trap. I told Sister Ágnes I was going to check on them. She said no. She'd go. After she got her gun from the car.

I was alone with the bound ÁVO men. "Have you heard the name László Barna?" I asked them. I searched their faces. "My father died in that…that dungeon." I said. "Have you even been down there? Do you know what it looks like? It's not fit for animals!"

They didn't say anything, just shook their heads.

"You mean to tell me you didn't hear a man's groans down there? Not once in the three days you're supposed to be on watch here?"

The ÁVO men said nothing. They just sat there with a hang-dog look on their faces. I had nothing more to say to them.

I heard a truck's engine fire up. I peeked outside the shed, and there it was. A canvas-top truck, with Sister Ágnes at the wheel.

They all got out and came inside. We had to decide what to do with the men.

"If you don't have it in you to shoot them, lock them in the dungeon and throw away the key," Imre Pálréti said.

"I think they deserve a promotion, don't you, Sewer Rat?" Sister Ágnes said. She tossed the car key by their feet. "There's a new

Pobeda parked outside. It's an ÁVO officer's private motorcar. All you have to do is to free yourselves and drive away."

The ÁVO men looked bewildered as did Imre Pálréti.

"Guess it's your lucky day, boys," Sewer Rat said.

Imre Pálréti was fit to be tied. "Of all the godforsaken—!" he swore under his breath.

As we were getting in the truck, Sister Ágnes showed him the wire to the distributor she tore out of the Pobeda. "They won't get too far without this," she said.

With little room in the cabin, two of us would have to go in the back. I volunteered. I wanted to be alone for a while. "You sure?" Michelangelo asked.

I was sure.

Michelangelo hopped on the back, anyway. At least he could stretch out his long legs. Actually, the back of the truck was very comfortable. The huge cache of guns was covered with straw, tarp and blankets. Michelangelo had even tossed some extra blankets on the floorboard in case someone wanted to sleep.

I wasn't very sleepy, just numb. The little window in the cabin slid open. "Are you guys all right back there?" Sewer Rat asked.

"Fine," Michelangelo said.

I lay down on the felt blanket and closed my eyes, only to open them again a few minutes later to stare at the dark canvas top. Michelangelo sat by my feet, his back leaning against the side. Sewer Rat was telling the others it was risky business driving a car like the Pobeda in daylight, no matter whose side you were on. "Now let's go and take you home to Balástya," he said to Imre Pálréti. "What's the population there? Roughly?"

"No more than a two or three hundred souls. That was seven years ago."

"Well," Sewer Rat said. "We have enough loot on the truck to arm your whole village, and then some."

"Jesus," Imre Pálréti said. "We'll have a revolution."

"We already have a Revolution," Michelangelo said. "We have an honest-to-God daughter of the Revolution right here next to me."

I was only listening with one ear. I heard enough to know Michelangelo said that for my benefit. He went out of his way to be nice. He knew I was devastated by news of my father's death. I couldn't really think about anything else.

Papa.

I saw Papa's chestnut brown hair and his warm, brown eyes. Little things. Like the way he peeled my apple with his clasp knife, going around and around the apple until the snake-shaped peel fell off in one piece. How I loved playing with it as a little girl. Something as trite as an apple peel was special to me because Papa carved it.

Long before my art teacher shared her passion for the buildings of Budapest, I was already in love with the city, thanks to Papa. When he took me along on his mail route, he was like a tour guide, pointing to ornate doorways or billowing wrought iron balconies, colored ceramic roofs, domes, copulas, towering spires. I'd get a stiff neck looking up at all the beauty.

When I was a little girl, he actually took me inside the Museum of Applied Arts, the bright green and yellow fantasy palace that I loved. He didn't teach me terms like Art Nouveau or anything like that, but he didn't have to. He'd prop me on his shoulders and let me feel the magical faces carved into the stone.

He made everything special. I felt his breath on the back of my neck when he pushed me off on the swing. I'd keep telling him to go higher and higher.

He always had trouble punishing me. When I was a baby being potty trained, my mother had no problem giving me a spanking, so I'd whisper to Papa as he walked by: "Papa, Papa, change me." He always did. He didn't spank me once. And he never told my mother about it.

I wondered what those heartless monsters wanted from my father and Cardinal Mindszenty. I had no idea how a man like my father could be connected with someone so high up in the Catholic church. Where could my father have met Cardinal Mindszenty? And when? I thought the Cardinal's trial was a long time ago. It must've been at Andrássy Street, the place Sewer Rat had referred to as the torture chamber.

Imre Pálréti told us they kept shuttling prisoners back and forth from Andrássy Street for special interrogations. I tried not to think about what they did to Papa there, how they hurt him. A fresh stream of tears burned my eyes.

My father and mother would want me to be strong, to be able to take care of the family I had left. The family I had left behind. When my mind drifted to my little sister, the poor thing, and to my aunt with her walking stick, the feeling of guilt was so intense that it bore into me to the point of nausea.

I prayed to God I could make it up to them one day. The thought that I deserted them at such a critical time on the pretext of bringing my father back made me sick.

There would be no cemetery where I could go to visit my dead. I had no mother, I had no father. I guess Michelangelo was right. I was the daughter of the Revolution now.

"We must've missed it," I heard Imre Pálréti say.

Balástya. A small town you could easily miss, especially if you're going 100 kilometers an hour. Because we missed it. Imre Pálréti was red-faced. He didn't recognize his own village. We were already in the next town when he caught on. We had to turn around.

Imre Pálréti said the poplar trees had grown so tall in seven years, they were now taller than the church steeple.

Sister Ágnes stopped the truck between the church and the town pump to get some water and to get our bearings. For me, it felt good to be out of the dark truck. The light barely touched the top of the trees, and the roosters were already at it. The air was cool and wet. You could see the dew on the bare branches. I looked up at the sky wondering about my mother and father, whether they have found one another on the other side of life. If something like that was even possible.

Imre Pálréti was looking around and scratching his head.

Sister Ágnes brought me some fresh water from the well. She was really good to me. So was Michelangelo who was paying me one compliment after another. And Sewer Rat in his gruff way tried hard to be tender. Imre Pálréti was a little unsure of me. He didn't know how to act around me. I knew he was disappointed I didn't have the stomach to kill those ÁVO guards. But I don't think it takes much to pull a trigger. I've done it many times. Too many. I was a show off and I was cocky. I was many things, but I could never be judge and executioner all rolled into one. Just didn't feel right.

Imre Pálréti was a good man. But he was an angry man. I would be, too, if I had spent seven years of my life in a cold, moldy cell in Vác. Sewer Rat had given him instructions not to tell anyone who we were. We just gave him a ride, that was all. It was okay to tell his family my father died in prison, but we were not to talk about the ÁVO men, Russians, or anything else like that.

We climbed back on the truck and took a dirt road past an old cemetery. From there he had little trouble finding his cottage-like house by the railroad tracks.

Back in Vác, the townspeople had given him some ill-fitting civilian clothes. The sleeves were too short as were his trousers. He had no socks. He was unshaven and the closer we got to his place, the more nervous he seemed to be about his appearance.

A barking scruffy dog ran alongside the truck as we pulled in. We got out and dusted off our clothes. Imre Pálréti's dog recognized his master at once. It was wagging its tail, jumping on him, pawing him, licking him. Imre Pálréti petted his dog, saying, "So, you didn't forget me, you old scoundrel, you."

A short, round woman wearing black from her head to her toes came running out of the house. She was screaming, "Imre! Imre! God be praised. It *is* you!" The poor woman was missing most of her teeth, but she was all smiles. She wiped her eyes with her skirt. Imre Pálréti, his eyes liquid, introduced us as the people who had driven him all the way from Vác.

His wife nodded toward us. "But first, let me have a look at you," she said to her husband. She backed up a little to size him up. "All you need is a little fattening and I'll take care of that."

She invited us in while she walked him in, holding his arm as if her life depended on it. A little boy about nine waited at the door. The woman said to her husband: "You remember your little nephew Péter. He was just a baby when they took you away. Give your uncle a kiss. He's been gone a long time."

The boy did as he was told, then ran off to get the neighbors and his brother. "And tell them to bring some of their good salami," the woman said.

We told her we were not hungry, but she insisted. "You've come a long way," she said. She was so excited she had to sit down, only to shoot up from her chair to disappear into another room and come back with a bottle of *pálinka*. We all toasted her husband's newfound freedom.

The family from next door arrived with a basket of food. We got up to greet them on the front porch.

I noticed the nine-year-old and another boy several years older gawking at our truck. I was afraid they'd get into the guns and walked toward them. That's when I saw him. Could it be? I couldn't believe my eyes. The other boy was Guszti Pálréti. In shorts. He hadn't changed much. Why should he? It's only been a few days. He was still his tall and lean self, and probably mean. His dark hair was curly and he had these intense black eyes. I always liked the shape of Guszti's mouth. He may have had a mouth that curved like a perfect bow, but what came out of it most of the time were poison-tipped arrows. Oh yes, he was smarter and stronger and faster and had more friends than me. And he let me know.

Once I had beat him in the 100 meters, he started to twitch and his whole world, including his Olympic hopes, came crashing down like a house of cards. The fact that I was a girl really salted his festering wound. He hadn't talked to me since then.

I went up to him. He was just as shocked to see me. We didn't shake hands or anything. He looked at the ground, put his hands into his pockets, and shifted his weight from one long leg to the other.

"We brought your uncle home," I said.

"Yes," he said. "I hear. I should go and say hello. How did you...how did you bring him home? Does your father drive? Did he get out, too?"

I shook my head. "My father never made it. He died in prison."

"You talked about him all the time," he said.

"I'm with friends. The truck is theirs."

Guszti was wide-eyed, but he checked himself. Then changed the subject. This was a habit with him. Not to hear what he didn't want to hear, and then flip to another subject, like *him*.

He recounted how he got here. His mother was taken ill and was recuperating in a hospital in Budapest. She sent him and his brother on the train to their aunt here, just till things settled down in the city. "Have you been to Budapest lately?" he said. "When I left, there was fighting in the streets. Guns. Tanks and everything. God! I got into big trouble once. Almost got killed. My friend and I—remember that idiot Lajos Vetró—Lajos Vetró and me set fire to this Russian bookstore on Lenin Boulevard. Big mistake. We could've been shot. I swear. You should've seen me run."

Yeah, I thought to myself. Guszti was good at that kind of running. "You should've timed yourself," I said. "You might have set a world record."

"Ah, you're still sore about the posters. You still think I snitched on you."

"Well, did you?"

"I had to. I had to look out for you. It was crazy what you did. Nuts. Anyway, after Lajos Vetró and me set fire to the Ruskie bookstore, my mother shipped me off to this hick village. I hate it here. I wish I could go back. What about you, Kitty?"

"Guszti!" His aunt called him from the open door. "Your uncle's here, son."

"This girl here is from Budapest. From our school. I'll be there in a minute." Guszti made a face like he didn't really want to go in. He said something about barely remembering his uncle. He was only six and he lived in Budapest, while his uncle and aunt lived here, in the middle of nowhere. He hated all this peace and quiet. Especially the sound of crickets at night.

Guszti looked me up and down and said, "I see you're wearing our teacher's tennis shoes. You never paid for it, did you?"

"I will. I got a lot of use out of them."

Sewer Rat poked his head out the door. He was glad to see I was keeping an eye on the truck. "We'll be leaving soon," he said. "We have a nice salami all packed up for you."

Guszti asked where we were headed. I told him we were taking food supplies from Szeged to Budapest. Balástya was on the way. "That's how we were able to give your uncle a ride. You really should go and see him," I said. "I know he's anxious to see you."

"I will," he said, and started to go.

All of a sudden, wild cheers erupted in the house. Even the dog barked. We walked through the door to the smell of cooked apples and cinnamon mixed with cigarette smoke and pure-grain alcohol. Everybody was up from their chairs, holding a cigarette and a shot glass of good old *pálinka*. They raised their glasses high in the air, taking turns toasting Imre Pálréti and Hungary. His wife kept saying, "Thank the Lord. Thank the Lord."

When Imre Pálréti saw his nephew, he clasped him tightly around the waist and lifted him off the ground. Guszti's face turned *paprika* red. I didn't know if it was from embarrassment or because his uncle was squeezing the life out of him.

I looked at my friends quizzically.

"Good news on the radio," Sister Ágnes said. "Radio Budapest just announced that they formed a new government, with Imre Nagy as Premier. That's what we wanted. And what's most important, he's acknowledging our Revolution. He's acknowledging our Revolution with a capital R!"

Michelangelo said: "He's still a Communist. He's still calling us Comrades. Can we trust him?"

Imre Pálréti said, "Let me tell you something about trust, my friend. Life in prison makes you suspicious. One of the things you learn real fast is not to trust anybody. To watch your back all the time. It's something you have to fight against. It's so easy to lose hope and give up. I'll tell you. On our way here, I was all messed up. I felt it. Part of me wanted to trust, another part saw an ÁVO man or an informer behind every bush. I was always on guard. Always. I don't want to live like that anymore. This is a new start for me. A new start for us all. For Hungary." He raised his glass: "To Hungary!"

"And now," he plowed on, "they're going to dissolve the ÁVO. About time, I say. I never thought it could happen. Not in a million years, no sir. And they're negotiating with the Russians to pull their troops out of the country. Now, that's really something. It's more than we could've hoped for, I tell you. The tide is changing in our favor, which means that you," he pointed toward his nephews, "both of you will have a future after all. God be praised! Mother, bring out another bottle!"

Everybody drank. Even me. The sip from the shot glass burned going down.

"You really think all those Russian tanks we saw on our way are just going to make a U-turn back to Russia?" Michelangelo said gloomily.

"Why not? Imre Nagy said he's negotiating with Mikoyan, the Soviet foreign minister," Sewer Rat said.

"You trust that Armenian? I wouldn't," Michelangelo said. "I'll believe it when I see it."

"There's always a doubting Thomas," Imre Pálréti said. "Have a drink, man! Things are looking up for us for a change."

"Hear. Hear," Sewer Rat said.

I never saw Sewer Rat like this. All the pure grain *pálinka* he was downing started to have its effect. I wished my father and mother could've shared in this moment. We were all giddy with the thought of a free Hungary. The next door neighbor raised his glass. "Here's to Hungary," he said. Then the neighbor asked about the ÁVO. What was going to happen to them?

Imre Pálréti said, "If they have blood on their hands, they're going to have to be put on trial."

"What about Party members? There's so many of them," the neighbor said.

"I don't know," Imre Pálréti said. "Just about everybody who had anything important to do in this country had to join. What are we going to do? Lock them all up, like I was locked up? I don't think we have enough prisons."

I was surprised to hear Imre Pálréti talking like that. He was sure whistling a different tune. Just today he was ready to toss those ÁVO guards into the Kecskemét dungeon and throw away the key.

Michelangelo gave me a knowing look, before he said, "So, we're going to keep letting them run the country, is that it?"

"Speak up, damn it. I can barely hear you," Sewer Rat said.

Michelangelo repeated himself.

"They're not going to run the country. For what it's worth, I'm a believer in gradual transitions. I mean, you can't take a pinko airline pilot and replace him with a non-Communist who never flew a plane. Who's going to be in the cockpit? Michelangelo?"

We laughed.

"Very funny," Michelangelo said. The beginnings of a smile tugged at the corners of his lips.

"Here's to Michelangelo!" Imre Pálréti said.

We drank some more. Toast after toast to everybody in the room.

The adults talked about Communism as if it were in the past tense. What life was like under Stalinism. Imre Pálréti asked his neighbor if the beer mugs were still chained to the counter in the town tavern. So no one stole them. The neighbor said they were. Along with a warning sign that read, "So and so got two years in prison for stealing a mug."

Imre Pálréti said, "Jesus! The first thing I'm going to do tomorrow is to rip those godforsaken chains off."

"Maybe you better not," his wife said. "You just got home."

Imre Pálréti ignored her. "I don't know about you, but for me, life's been hell since the Russians put the Communists in power."

"Hear. Hear," Sewer Rat said. "Our lives have been one big turd since 1945. Every time the doorbell rang in the middle of the night, I'd get the shits. I thought they were coming for me. And I wasn't the only one. We had rats and informers in the workplace and in every building. It was crazy. One of my neighbors was arrested for having too many shirts!"

Imre Pálréti's neighbor said they had to butcher their pig in secret for fear of being reported. You weren't allowed to own anything. Everything belonged to the state.

Michelangelo gave a brief overview about the state of Hungarian art under Stalinism in one big bold stroke by saying, "It was the art of the state." He told them about his larger-than-life portrait of Stalin. "It was like having to make Genghis Khan look like Saint Nicholas," he said.

"Bravo!" Imre Pálréti said. "Here's to Michelangelo!"

"You are a clever bastard," Sewer Rat said to Michelangelo. "Here's to Genghis Khan!"

I was glad Sister Ágnes was doing the driving. Good old Hungarian *pálinka* was making all the others slap-happy. I couldn't resist. I had to tell them I was almost shipped off to the Stalin Brigade for campaigning against compulsory Russian. "What about freedom of expression?"

"That's right," Michelangelo chimed in.

"Here's to freedom of expression!" Sister Ágnes said.

"And to freedom fighters!" Imre Pálréti said.

Guszti's little brother brought out a poem he had written about the Revolution. He called it "Freedom Fighters." His uncle read it out loud and cried. I liked it, too. Not bad for a nine-year-old.

Now Imre Pálréti raised his shot glass toward us: "To my rescuers," he said. "Thank you again, friends."

"You rescued yourself, man," Sewer Rat said.

I was afraid Imre Pálréti would start talking recklessly about things he shouldn't be talking about, like how we saved his life and all that. Anyway, I ended escaping to the veranda.

Guszti came after me. It was cool outside but better than air reeking of smoke and homemade *pálinka*. Or was it? I realized then that the air smelled of warm cow shit. Guszti said his aunt's one cow usually came home once it started to get light out. "Watch where you step."

I told Guszti I though his uncle was going to crack his ribs when he lifted him in the air."

"It felt like it. He may be thin, but he's got a grip like a python."

I tried to grin.

We talked more about school, our teachers and friends. He said he liked the way I ran. "You usually bolted from the starting block."

"I did not. I was never called for a false start."

"No. You were clever. You did it so no one noticed it. Except me. I saw it."

"You would say something like that! I would, too, if I lost a big race. To a girl!"

"Actually I like you." he said.

"You have a funny way of showing it. I always thought you hated me."

"Oh, I did," he said. "Why d'you think I turned you in?"

"At first you really fooled me, but when I really thought about it, only one rat came to mind. You! You *were* the rat."

"I was. I've changed and so have you. So—I'm a rat and you're a cat. What is it that your friends call you?"

"If you knew, you'd be my friend, wouldn't you?"

There was no follow-up. Guszti shifted to another subject. "Anyway, I've matured a lot since then. But you were right about Russian. I wanted to learn German, myself, but I was afraid to say anything about it in school." Guszti turned red and shifted again. "What do you think of my brother's poem? Pretty good, huh?"

"Better than good. I could never write like that."

Guszti said he's been listening to Radio Free Europe on the sly. "America's on our side. Totally. If you ask me, that's the real reason the tide is turning."

"What about all the freedom fighters in Budapest? Don't they count for anything?"

I don't think Guszti understood. Even if he knew, he wouldn't be able to appreciate how a rag-tag group of untrained civilians, many of them teenagers like us, could make a difference. I had in mind to ask him if he remembered how the American Revolution started. I remembered, because it was a test question in our World History class. The name Johnny Tremain still sounded exotic. No, I thought I better not ask.

We stood a few paces from each other, reminiscing about school and fantasizing about making the Olympic team one day, when I realized I had to go to the bathroom. I asked Guszti where it was.

"We only have an outhouse. Come, I'll show you." He took me out back to a ramshackle outhouse and said, "I try not to use it. I rather go behind a tree. Anyway, here it is. Good luck with the flies. Don't let them bite your butt."

"Thanks for looking out for me. I didn't know you could be so romantic."

He said, "See you," and left me there.

When I came out everybody stood outside, shaking hands, laughing. Everybody except Guszti. I said goodbye to a teary-eyed Imre Pálréti who held my hand and didn't want to let it go. He didn't say anything. He just nodded and spoke with his eyes. My eyes welled up, too. I said goodbye to his wife, their neighbors, and to Guszti's little brother who gave me his poem. He said he copied it over again, just for me. I thanked him and gave him a kiss on the cheek. I asked him where his brother was.

"Probably listening to the radio," he said. "Once he starts listening, we can't pull him away from it. Oh, yeah, another thing. He hates goodbyes."

"Well," I said. "Tell him Cheetah said goodbye."

"Cheetah?"

"He'll know what it means."

We jumped into the truck, Sister Ágnes turned on the motor, we waved and were off on our way back to Budapest. Again, I volunteered to go in the back, this time alone. I told the others I was tired. I was. I felt drained. I hated goodbyes, too.

When we got to Kecskemét, I noticed that Sister Ágnes turned off the main highway. I went to the back and opened the canvas flap above the tailgate. Early morning light flooded my face and I had to squint. I had a feeling we were heading back to the prison to see if the ÁVO men were still there trying to get the car started. I was right. I saw the shed. And the car parked at an angle alongside it. These guys were no fools. No one wants to be a target.

"Hey, Cheetah," Sister Ágnes shouted loud enough so I could hear. "The Pobeda is still there. What I tell you."

Michelangelo brought up the name of Imre Pálréti. "Did you listen to that man? Talk about a 180 degree turn! He was ready to execute those ÁVO guards himself. When? A few hours ago?"

"It was more than that," Sister Ágnes put in.

"I don't care. I want to know what made him change his mind like that. Hellbent on vengeance one minute, Saint Imre the next. I don't get it."

"Will you speak up!" Sewer Rat said.

"You're deaf, my friend."

"What?"

"I said what made Imre Pálréti change his mind?"

"Maybe he's happy to be home. Did you ever think of that? He's got his wife back, his dog and the kids. What did he have the day before yesterday? A six by six cell, a sheetless cot and next to it, a pot with a turd in it. Wouldn't you be in a better mood?"

"I just don't think we should be giving these killers amnesty. Look what they did to Cheetah's mother. And her friend. How old was she. All of fourteen?"

"What?"

"Oh, forget it."

Sister Ágnes stepped in: "No one's talking about amnesty. We're already talking about running the country. Why don't we talk about what we're going to do once we're back in Budapest."

Michelangelo said he'd like to volunteer to round up the bastards. "Flush out the rats!"

"I heard that," Sewer Rat said.

"Yeah. What you didn't hear was that they're now hiding in your sewer system. Waiting to come out like cockroaches. They invaded your territory, man."

Sewer Rat said the first thing we'd do when we got to Budapest would be to go to our headquarters in the theater and see what Mustache has to say. "If he says flush out the rats, then we'll flush out the rats."

I stuck my face by the cabin window and said, "I'd like to go home first. I need to tell my sister and aunt about my father."

They agreed. They offered to come along for moral support. But our first stop would have to be the Corvin Theater to drop off the guns.

"Hey," Sewer Rat said "We have real tank mines. No more sissy shit painted boxes."

"They were works of art," Michelangelo said indignantly. "Took me hours to get them to look like real mines."

"Yeah? And you and Cheetah almost got killed playing cat and mouse with that T-34!"

I sank back down on my blanket where I kept my father's letters. I strained my eyes reading through a dozen or so. Papa wrote how he missed carrying little Krisztina on his shoulder. I remembered how he'd carry her around, it seemed for hours. Sometimes I wished I had heart disease, too, so my father could carry me on his shoulders while we looked at all the animals in the zoo.

He wrote how happy I made him by going on his mail route with him. He said on those days, it was more play than work. Even his heavy mailbag seemed lighter.

I put Papa's letters down. For a change, it was quiet in the cabin. I guessed Sewer Rat and Michelangelo got tired of going back and forth. I heard one of them snoring. Soon they were both sound asleep.

I myself dozed off for an hour or so. An urge to go to the bathroom woke me up. I had to go, but I wasn't about to say anything. It's not as easy for girls as it is for boys. I had to squat over a hole in the floorboards and keep my balance at the same time. I missed a little when the truck hit a bump in the road. I was about to reach for some straw under the tarp to clean up when I had this idiotic thought. That Guszti had hidden himself under the tarp.

It would be awkward. I'd rather dodge Russian bullets than have him catch me with my bare butt out.

I pulled up my pants and looked under the tarp. All I saw were machine guns and tank mines neatly stacked among the straw.

Guszti was a funny kid. I think the only thing I envied about him was his ability to go to the bathroom by a tree. Otherwise he was just another loudmouth.

I asked Sister Ágnes how far we were from Budapest.

She said we just passed the city limits. "No road blocks so far. Plenty of Russians, though. If you unfasten the canvas in the back you can see a whole convoy. Were you able to get some sleep back there?"

"Some," I said.

I stumbled back and unfastened the flap again. The light seemed overly bright. A sudden gust cooled the sweat on my forehead. The afternoon sun flickered through the trees. As we passed the line of trees, I saw a Soviet convoy of tanks and trucks. The crazy thing was, they weren't moving. As the road turned, I noticed the tents. And the cannons. I had no idea what the Russians were up to. It sure looked like they were camping out for the time being.

I went back to the cabin window and asked Sister Ágnes what she thought it all meant. She wasn't sure. For some reason, the Russians didn't want to cross the city line. Sister Ágnes said one column even headed south. She passed them while we were sleeping.

We passed by the first bridge spanning the Danube between Buda and Pest. Soviet T-34's were positioned on both sides of the river. I noticed that the cannon was covered with canvas to keep it dry. I hoped it meant they were not expecting to use it.

I heard Sewer Rat's voice: "What's up?"

We told him about the Russian convoy pitching camp just outside the city. He said he wouldn't be surprised if they were the same tanks we saw on our way out. "Things are changing at a fast clip since Imre Nagy took over the reins," he said. "The Russians probably have orders to sit tight, while Mikoyan and the Supreme Soviet figure out how to withdraw their troops without losing face."

"Hey! Look at that!" Michelangelo shouted. I guess he was up now, too.

"Oh my God!" said Sister Ágnes.

Just then an open truck crammed with freedom fighters with guns and armbands roared past us, going the opposite direction. They waved to me, I waved to them. It was the best sight I've seen for a long time.

As we neared the center of the city, we saw a short column of tanks. Flying Hungarian colors! At an intersection, bands of freedom fighters with rifles on their shoulders walked briskly across the street.

Another truckload of armed Hungarians rolled past us. Then another. They were not soldiers but civilians, some in their factory clothes. People were out on the street in droves. No curfew here. Many were inspecting the damage caused by several days of fighting.

A roof was missing from one building. An entire corner of another was blown away on Kossuth Boulevard. A once-beautiful wrought-iron balcony was twisted as it dangled under a crater left by a shell. The carcass of two tanks and an armored car blocked the road.

We were forced into a detour. This section of the city was shot up, and badly, but some of the residents were already out shoveling the rubble into neat piles near the curb. None of the streetlights worked, so we had to go slow.

Eventually we got on Üllői Avenue where we had our last skirmish with the Russian tanks. In the daylight I could see what the tank shells had done to the buildings. Craters stood in place of windows, entire roofs had collapsed, ornate doorways blown to bits. And we had a part in it. The destruction. The price we had to pay to drive the Russians out of Budapest. But there was a much higher price. My mother, Mariska, the kid with the derby hat, the pretty Gypsy girl, and all the kids of Budapest who had to die in this bloody Revolution.

The shoe store, where Michelangelo and I hid out before my mad dash across the street, was completely destroyed. And so was the Russian tank near it. All you could see in place of its turret was a dark, gaping hole. The entire block lay in ruins.

Our truck came to a sudden stop. "Checkpoint?" we heard Sister Ágnes say.

My heart automatically jumped into my throat. I relaxed when I saw the two armed civilians with Hungarian armbands come up to the window. They said they were with the new Home Guard and they had to check our papers. "Identification please."

Sewer Rat did all the talking. He was short and to the point. He told the men that we were under the command of Gergely Pongrátz.

"Oh, yeah? What's his code name?"

"You mean his nickname? Mustache. I've been calling him that since our days at boot camp. Now, let us through."

They nodded, apologized, and gave us a half-hearted salute. They had to check every truck for ÁVO men, they said.

Sister Ágnes put the truck in gear and we were moving again. Further down the road we saw a blackened, battered body hanging upside down from a lamp post. We were close enough to read the letters on the sign pinned to his skin. Á-V-O. Under it, in an uneven hand, were the words: *This is what happens to traitors!*

The sight made me swallow hard. I shuddered. I just didn't think things would go this far.

Along the avenue, almost all the shops had broken storefronts, the shattered glass glistening along the curb. None of the goods were disturbed. You'd think there would be plenty of looting. A sports store still had all these soccer balls, volleyballs, soccer spikes, track shoes left untouched in the window. All you'd have to do is to reach in and grab them. They were so real and so close, I could almost smell the leather.

Our truck stopped. We parked as close as we could to the Corvin passage. The theater was riddled with bullets, the entire box-office obliterated. The building itself and the surrounding structures looked like as if they were hit by an artillery barrage.

The guards stationed by the entrance told us headquarters moved to the Killián Barracks.

We got back in the truck and took it across the street to the barracks. The thick walls were pock-marked with blasts from tank shells and bombs, the stucco blown off from around the windows, but the old fortress stood its ground. The Hungarian flag fluttered on the roof.

Sewer Rat asked the soldiers guarding the heavy doors to let us through. We had to report to the Commander and drop off much needed munitions.

The soldiers said that would not be possible. They said they couldn't. Major General Maléter's tank was parked in the entrance.

We backed up the truck into the Corvin passage and left it there in the care of a soldier Sewer Rat trusted. We walked back to the barracks where an armed guard escorted us to a second-story office.

Mustache sat behind a scratched-up desk. The heavy machine gun, mounted behind him, poked its long barrel out the window.

"Looks like you and Maléter got promoted," Sewer Rat said.

Mustache waved him off with a laugh. He got up from his chair and shook our hands firmly. He found a bottle of *pálinka* somewhere on the floor and said we were going to drink to victory.

Just then a huge explosion went off somewhere in the distance, followed by the sound of machine guns.

"As you can see, it's not complete yet, but I think we're heading there. There are isolated pockets of resistance on both sides. I think the ÁVO is desperately trying to hang on to power. Sure, the Russians are still holding key positions. But they have orders to obey the cease-fire, while Mikoyan and Maléter agree on a withdrawal timetable. The two are supposed to meet sometime this week. To victory, then!" He took a swig and passed the bottle around.

His mustache and eyebrows were bushier than usual. He was in good spirits. "Oh, yes," he said. "We're all part of the Home Guard now. Workers, soldiers. Ex-soldiers like us. And the kids. Let's not forget the kids. The city has christened them *'Pesti Srácok.'* The 'kids' of Budapest. You know what the Russians call them?" he laughed. "The Russians call them the 'Pests of Budapest.' For good reason. We wouldn't be where we are now without those kids." He raised the bottle of *pálinka*. "Here's to the kids of Budapest."

We all had a little more *pálinka*. I felt my face flush after my second gulp. I thought it was going to burst into flames.

"All right," Mustache said. "Let's get down to business."

Sewer Rat told Mustache about all the tank mines, grenades and automatic weapons we brought with us.

Mustache was delighted. "Of course, we're going to have to move them somewhere else. If the deal with Mikoyan goes sour, the Russians will be back in full force. I want you and Michelangelo to take everything to the old Casino. You know, the one across from the old University Church."

The instant Mustache mentioned the name of the church, I thought of my father. That was his favorite church. I had been inside it many times. Instead of praying I spent my time admiring the rich wood-carvings. My father said the monks themselves did most of the interior.

"Anything else?" Mustache asked.

Plenty. Sewer Rat gave a full report of our activities since we had left the Corvin Theater for Vác.

"Actually," Mustache said, "I was already made aware of some of your machinations. News travels fast around here. Especially good news. And the bad. I'm real sorry about your guide. What did he have, two days of freedom? Bad luck about your Russian prisoner. And all the weapons that were blown up with your truck."

"And the kid that acted as our interpreter," Sewer Rat said.

Mustache took another swig from the *pálinka*, sighed, ran a finger by his bushy mustache and knit his eyebrows. He got up and opened a drawer from his desk. He took out a half-melted pair of tortoise-shell glasses, looked at it and tossed it on the table. "Looks like our interpreter was an informer."

Where was this going? I had no idea what our Commander was talking about.

"What you didn't know was that he's the one who killed the Russian in Vác. And a civilian. He planted his glasses and personal effects on the scorched civilian's body. Then he blew up the truck to make it look like the townspeople set it on fire. He almost got away with it. We caught up with him early this morning. He confessed, not only to that, but to other things. Like giving away our positions to the enemy. He turned out to be an ÁVO spy who infiltrated our ranks. They recruit them pretty young these day, I guess. But then, look at us! Maléter wanted him court-marshaled, but the crowd got hold of him. You probably saw him if you came down Üllői Avenue. He's decorating one of the lamp posts. There was no way of stopping it."

We were all stunned. I know I was. I remembered the college man offering me coffee that first day in the Corvin Theater. Then he asked me all sorts of stuff. I had no idea. He had such a studious look with his glasses and all.

"All right, enough about that. Let's talk about you." Mustache riveted his eyes on me. "Did you find your father in Kecskemét?"

I told him about the basement dungeon and my father.

"You mean he died a year ago and those bastards never bothered to inform the family? All that time you didn't know if he was dead or alive?"

"We didn't know anything."

His eyes got watery. He turned from us, walked to the window and looked out, his hands behind his back. "I'm sorry, kid. I'm sorry that the Revolution has made you an orphan."

"I have my aunt and little sister. I have to go home and be with them. They don't know if I'm dead or alive either," I said, my voice faltering.

"I understand."

Mustache turned his attention to Sister Ágnes, asking her if she knew about the plan to free Cardinal Mindszenty.

She said she had heard a plan like that was afoot, but she didn't know the details. She'd been told that the Cardinal refused to leave his cell until all Hungarian political prisoners were free.

Mustache said the precise date would be October 30. He asked if Sister Ágnes would volunteer to be part of the rescue team.

"What do you think?" she said.

"It's settled then."

Sister Ágnes said she would be honored to be involved in a mission that to her was nothing less than sacred.

Sewer Rat and Michelangelo were to be involved with something less sacred. It involved the sewers. Mustache said the ÁVO was hiding out in the sewers lately, and he had reason to believe that they had plans to blow up our ammunition depots. "What we're trying to do now is to move some of our weapons and explosives to different locations."

Mustache looked at our faces and said, "Well, that about wraps it up, unless you have questions."

I had one. I asked who would have my keys, the ones we had to turn in to you once we arrived at the Corvin Theater. You know, so we remain anonymous."

"Of course," Mustache said. He went back to his desk and rummaged through a drawer. "I'm sorry, Cheetah, what is your name? I mean your real name, again?"

"Izabella Barna."

Chapter Seven

7

In spite of the rain, my comrades insisted on going along with me to my aunt's apartment. But first we went back to the Corvin passage where our truck was parked. Sewer Rat said we might as well get the pick of the litter before he and Michelangelo took all the good stuff to the Casino. He climbed in and fished around for a light submachine gun for me, similar to what I had before. He found one. I slung it around my neck, hoping I would never have to use it. But I was not about to leave my sister and aunt defenseless, either.

Sewer Rat had a new high-powered rifle for Michelangelo. Michelangelo held it and said it felt good. Each of us got a new weapon.

We ended up walking to my aunt's apartment on Sándor Bródy Street in the cold rain. I was dirty, my clothes a caked mess. The bottoms of my pants were shredded from our cat and mouse game with Michelangelo's dummy mine. I looked forward to taking a hot bath and sleeping on my couch.

With our armbands and guns in tow, we no longer stood out from the crowd. Every now and then we'd come across similar groups of gun-toting fighters. Occasionally, a Hungarian tank bristling with armed civilians would rumble by us.

It was already twilight when we got to our street. My breathing quickened and my heart pounded against my ribs. The cobblestone had been torn up. Chunks of concrete, plaster everywhere. Our neighbor's entire balcony was blown off along with a piece of wall, so you could see the inside tapestry of his room. To my horror I saw bullet holes around *our* windows.

I rushed through the entrance and up the steps, two at a time. My friends were panting right there with me.

As I stood in front of our door, my hand trembled trying the key. When I put the key in, it turned, but the door wouldn't give. I tried again and again. Michelangelo tried it. The door was jammed. I looked at the key. It was the right key. I pounded on the door as hard as I could. I shouted for my aunt and sister.

No answer.

I tried the key again. Sister Ágnes and the others checked with the neighbors. They weren't home. Our neighbor's door was battered in. The rainy wind whistled through his entire apartment. I glanced in and was shocked to see the pile of plaster and rubble in his living room. His windows were not just broken but blasted out.

An old lady I recognized as Ilona Vajda came out in a bath robe from an apartment several doors down. The first things she said was that my aunt was looking for me for days, knocking on doors at the strangest hours. "Then, yesterday," she said, "before the shooting started, I was out lining up for bread when I saw a copy of *Népszava* on the sidewalk. With your picture in it. Right on the front page. You and another girl. With guns! I rushed home and gave a copy to your aunt. She didn't say much. In fact, she slammed the door in my face. Oh, there was fighting something awful yesterday. All because of our neighbor. He was an ÁVO agent, you know. Can you believe it? An ÁVO man right here among us!"

I couldn't believe it. I saw him many times. He seemed like a nice man, except his hair was always neatly trimmed. That should have been a clue. Only the ÁVO could afford a barber. Still, I shook my head. It was all too much to take in.

The lady had no idea where my aunt and sister were. Many of the residents had fled. She complained of having no electricity or running water.

While we figured out what to do, Michelangelo ran back down to the ground floor to check on his own apartment.

Sewer Rat tried to ram the door with his shoulder, but it wouldn't budge. Why didn't they come to the door? With Kristina as sick as she was, they couldn't have gone anywhere.

Sewer Rat reached for his gun. "No," I said. Before he did something insane like pump bullets into the lock, I went to the little window between our kitchen and the breezeway landing. Straining on my toes, I tried looking in. I wasn't tall enough. Sewer Rat tried. He said it was all dark.

Michelangelo was back. He said his place was okay. No damage. He was tall enough to open the window from the outside. Locked.

I was going crazy with worry. Where could they be? I had no other choice but to tell Michelangelo to smash the window with the butt of his rifle.

The glass broke easily. He undid the latch. Then he took me by the waist and held me up so I could climb in. The first thing I did in the dark kitchen was to shout, "Krisztina! Auntie!"

They didn't answer.

I tried to flick on the lights. They didn't work. I went to the door. I still couldn't open it. In the dark, it was difficult to make out if the lock was tampered with or not. I told the others I was going to check the rooms.

"You forgot the flashlight. Go back to the window and I'll hand it to you," Sewer Rat said.

I turned on the flashlight and went into the dark living room. None of the windows had glass in them. The wind was billowing the curtains. My aunt's precious collection of figurines lay scattered and broken on the rug. Her China cabinet was smashed.

The windowless sewing room was untouched. Half-finished espresso cups and ashtrays heaped with cigarette butts were all in their place.

I went to the bathroom and turned on the spigot to see if we had water. I caught a glimpse of myself in the mirror. I didn't recognize the face. The shock of thick, dirty hair looked like it was torn out of a mattress. The hardened face was something hacked out of stone. I held the flashlight closer to the mirror. Soot covered my pores.

I turned on the spigot. No water, hot or cold. A few rust-colored drops trickled from the spigot.

In the bedroom, I saw my aunt's prized lace curtains in a heap by the shattered window. The bed was stripped bare. Her sheets, pillows and comforter were all gone.

By this time, I was frantic. I dashed back to the kitchen and looked to see if the cellar key was on its hook. I got a hammer and screwdriver and forced the lock open. A simple pull did the rest.

"I have an idea where they might be," I told the others breathlessly. "The cellar! All the bedding and the cellar key are gone. My aunt told me how they used the cellar as a bomb shelter during the war."

We scrambled down the three flights to the cellar.

I put in the key, turned it and pushed. The door creaked open. The wet smell of coal and kerosene reminded me of the dungeon in Kecskemét.

The flashlight was flickering, losing power. My aunt and sister were bundled up in a comforter among the wine barrels. A spent kerosene lamp stood on one of the barrels. I went over to them, my flashlight zigzagging weakly in the blackness. My aunt woke with a start. I forgot about the submachine gun around my neck, and when

I bent down to hug them, it was in the way. Not only was it in the way, it scared the living daylights out of my aunt.

I took off the gun and handed it to Michelangelo.

"Kitty!" my aunt said. "Dear Jesus of Mercy! Kitty!" I got on my knees and hugged them both. Krisztina woke up coughing. Her eyes were shiny. She couldn't stop kissing me.

"Where in sweet heaven did you go? Leaving us like that! Your note made no sense at all. No sense, you hear me?"

My aunt cried and kept repeating that I left them. I hugged her even as she kept pummeling me on my heavy jacket. My body couldn't feel the tiny fists of a sixty-year-old woman, but my heart did. She was kissing me and hitting me and crying all at the same time.

"She's here now, Auntie," Krisztina said softly. "And she is never going to go away again. Tell Auntie you will never go away again."

I told them I would never go away again. I promised. "I'm here for you now. I'll always be here for you. I'm sorry for making you worry. I'll take care of you, I'll fight for you. You are all I have now."

"You don't think I knew what you were up to?" my aunt scolded. She reached over to a pile of newspapers and tossed a copy of *Népszava* at me. "Ilona Vajda gave this to me yesterday. Put out by some kind of revolutionary council."

The flashlight was getting weaker and weaker, but I could still make out the picture of me and Sister Ágnes holding our guns and smiling for the camera. The caption underneath it said, "Young Freedom Fighters."

My aunt continued: "Telling me that cock and bull story that you're getting your father. While you and that woman," she pointed to Sister Ágnes, "while you and that woman were playing guns, I had to worry about getting your sister's fever down. So, don't start making any promises to me!"

I passed the newspaper to Sister Ágnes and the others. "What were you two smiling about?" Michelangelo wanted to know. Sister Ágnes said it was taken by the Corvin passage. "We thought it was a foreign journalist. He was cute. He asked us to smile."

Krisztina stopped coughing long enough to say I was famous. My aunt grunted. She put her hand on Krisztina's forehead. Then she took a cloth, soaked it in the bucket next to her and placed the wet cloth on my sister's forehead. "Hold it there, sweetheart."

Sister Ágnes told my aunt that she had a doctor friend and she would bring her by.

"But there's a war going on!" my aunt said.

"There's no war, Auntie," I said. "The lady upstairs, Ilona Vajda, says our neighbor was an ÁVO man. That's why the shoot-out. The whole street is shot up."

"They were shooting at us, I'm telling you. It's not safe up there."

"We'll take care of everything, Auntie," I said.

"You? You and what army?"

"This army." I pointed to my friends.

My friends said they were going to help and fix up the apartment so it's safe. Make sure we had plenty of food and water. And get a doctor for her and for the little girl.

My aunt sighed and sat up. I noticed she wore a winter coat under the comforter. "We could use a doctor all right," she said. "Krisztina's heart doesn't take too well to all this excitement. And I'm out of tranquilizers, and, I'm warning you, I'm very close to losing my mind. Does anyone here have a godforsaken cigarette? And could you put those guns away? They make me nervous."

Sewer Rat was more than happy to giver her a cigarette. He lit hers and put one in his mouth. "I don't have any tranquilizers, but I have a little medicine," he said as he pulled out his flask of *pálinka*.

"Oh, yes, we're out of that, too," my aunt said.

After a cigarette and a few swigs from the flask, my aunt was calm enough to let us take her and Krisztina up to the apartment. Michelangelo and I carried Krisztina, and Sewer Rat and Sister Ágnes helped my aunt up the stairs.

We sat down in the kitchen while Sister Ágnes and Michelangelo moved the mattress from the bedroom and some cushions from my couch to the sewing room. Because it had no windows, the sewing room appeared to be the safest room in the whole apartment.

We all went into the dark kitchen and sat down. My aunt had me get out the kerosene lamp from the pantry. As far as she knew, it was still working.

Once I lit the kerosene lamp, I noticed that both my aunt and sister had some kind of make-up on. It looked good on Krisztina. Her lips were red and her cheeks pink instead of blue. My aunt had missed her own lips entirely. I thought it was the flashlight in the cellar that distorted things, but that wasn't it. My aunt's lipstick was off its mark. It was like seeing double. I asked her about it. Why would she put make-up on in a dark cellar?

"Oh, that," she said matter-of-factly. "We wanted to look beautiful when they found us dead."

For some reason, Sewer Rat thought this was very funny. I gave him a look and he stopped laughing, lifted the hot glass from the lamp to light his cigarette which had been in his mouth for a while now. Both Sewer Rat and my aunt were smoking like chimneys, one cigarette after another.

"Your niece," Sewer Rat said, "is something else. A real fighter. A real alley cat."

"She's the Cheetah, isn't she? That's what I keep hearing from her little sister."

Sewer Rat jumped right in on my behalf. "There's a bit more to it."

"You mean to tell me she actually used that gun. It wasn't just for the picture? Not just a pose?"

"Sure, it was just a pose," Sewer Rat said as he winked at me. "You're a real ham, you know that?" Then he said to my aunt: "You may want to ask the Russians about that. Or the ÁVO guards at Vác."

My aunt locked her gaze on me. She took a long pull on her cigarette and let the smoke out of her mouth slowly so she could inhale it back through her nostrils. "My, my," she said. "You mean to tell me she's a hero. You know what happens to heroes in Hungary? Sooner or later, they end up in jail. If the Russians and the ÁVO stay in power, they'll know where to look for you. On the front page of the paper!"

"If it comes to that," Sewer Rat laughed, "they're going to have to put the whole city of Budapest in jail."

I wasn't laughing. I glared at my aunt and said, "Why don't you just say you're angry with me because I left. It would be a lot more honest and direct."

"*Touché.* Oh, she *is* a fighter. Well, I'm sorry if I seem angry. We were worried sick about you. Of course I'm angry. You would be, too, if you were in my shoes. So, you're just going to have to forgive me. What about you? You look like Medusa!"

I wasn't worried about how I looked, I wasn't worried about being a hero or a jailbird, I was worried about how they would take the news about Papa.

"What's wrong?" my aunt said.

I didn't say anything.

"It's all right," my aunt said. "Your sister knows about your mother."

"She's with God," Krisztina said sweetly.

"I couldn't save Papa either," I said. "I tried, but it was too late. A year too late."

"What do you mean, you couldn't save your Papa?"

I took Krisztina into my lap and pressed my face close to hers. "Oh, Krisztina," I said. "Papa is with God, too."

"Then Papa is with Mama," she said.

"That's right," I said and gave her a kiss. Then I turned to my aunt whose face was suddenly pale, even with all the make-up. Her badly painted lips trembled.

I put Krisztina down on a chair and said, "We went to Vác to try and free him. But he wasn't there. One of the inmates said Papa was in Kecskemét. We found the prison. More like a dungeon. He wasn't there either. Papa's been dead for over a year and no one told us anything. You didn't know, did you?" I was crying now.

My aunt got up and put her arms around me. "Of course I didn't know. How could I? How...how did he die?"

"Pneumonia," I said. "They put him in that horrible dungeon because he wouldn't betray Cardinal Mindszenty."

"Cardinal Mindszenty? I don't understand," my aunt said, sniffling. She took out a crumpled handkerchief and blew her nose. "I heard on the radio they were going to release some political prisoners and I started to take your note seriously."

"I'm sorry, Auntie. I didn't mean to hurt you or Krisztina. I'm no hero. I just missed Papa terribly. I thought I could help. And now I'm never going to see him again."

Krisztina started crying and coughing.

My aunt found my hand and clasped it. "I missed him, too. Do you have any idea how your sister idolizes you? It was Cheetah this and Cheetah that. When I showed her your picture, she lit up like you wouldn't believe. You are what keeps this girl and this old bag going."

Krisztina clutched at her chest. She was trying to cough but couldn't. My aunt put her head to her chest to listen to her heart. "It's galloping, all right," she said.

I jumped to the sink to get a cloth wet and put it on her chest, like we did when she got like this. But there was no water. I went to Krisztina and picked her up and took her to the bed we set up in the sewing room. She needed to lie down. I propped up her pillow so she could breathe easier. I stayed with her and stroked her arm to calm her down.

My aunt discovered she had one sedative tablet left. She crushed the last of it and sprinkled some on a teaspoonful of jam and brought it in for her.

"She had the same reaction, only worse, when I told her about your mother," my aunt said. "The poor girl is so sensitive." She held the spoon to Krisztina's mouth. "Here, take this, angel."

"I want to be with Mama and Papa," Krisztina whimpered.

"That's crazy talk," my aunt was biting her lip, trying not to cry. She tried to leave the room, but it was too late. She burst into tears before she made it to the door.

"Stop talking like that," I scolded Krisztina. "You're the reason I'm still alive. You're the reason I came back. You want to leave me all alone, with no one?"

She sat up to hug me.

I held my little sister in my arms until she fell asleep.

Sister Ágnes promised to bring the doctor by the next day.

I spent about an hour cleaning up the mess in the living room, putting my aunt's knick-knacks back into her cabinet. The pieces that were broken, I placed on the table by the telephone. I covered the busted windows with curtains by nailing the sides to the wall, but the cold wind wormed its way through the lace.

My aunt and my little sister went to sleep in the safety of the tight, little sewing room. I lifted the rest of the cushions from my couch and took them into the sewing room so I could be with them. Covering myself with a blanket and a winter coat, I lay down on the floor next to Krisztina's bed.

Though I was exhausted, I couldn't sleep. Without electricity, everything was pitch black. The rattle of sporadic machine gun fire awakened Krisztina.

"Cheetah?" she whispered. "How come there's still all this shooting?"

"I don't know," I said. "Soon it will stop."

After about ten minutes, she said: "Cheetah? What is heaven like?"

"It's a place of happiness. God is there and all the people that love you, and all the people you love, like Mama and Papa."

"But you won't be there."

"Of course I'll be there."

"What about all the dead soldiers?"

"The good will go to heaven."

"How do you know what soldiers are good and what soldiers are bad?"

"God knows. Now go to sleep."

"Cheetah?"

"What?"

"Could you open the door a little. I'm scared of the dark."

I went to the door and opened it a slit. We both had our eyes open staring up at the sewing room's high ceiling.

"You know what?" I said. "I never told anyone this, but I'm scared of the dark, too."

"Me, too."

We kept talking till we talked ourselves to sleep. I was rudely awakened early to the sound of pounding by the window. I rubbed my eyes open, saw that my aunt wasn't in the bed, got up, stumbled into the living room and closed the door behind me.

Sewer Rat and Michelangelo were boarding up the windows.

"How did you get in?"

"Your aunt let us in," Michelangelo said. "Can't you smell the coffee?"

I couldn't.

"Sister Ágnes was here at the crack of dawn with rolls and bread," he said. "There's a little butter left. A little salty, but it's real butter. When was the last time you had real butter? If I were you, I'd go into the kitchen before it's all gone."

My aunt was in the cigarette-smoke-filled kitchen, listening to the radio.

"How's Krisztina?" she asked.

"We talked a little last night. She didn't cough once."

"Thank God."

"I thought I'd let her sleep."

"If she can sleep through all that pounding," my aunt said. "Sister Ágnes said she'd be coming by later this morning with the doctor."

I nodded. I couldn't help but to notice a huge metal can, no, make that a drum, set on the table. "What's that?" I asked. "Is that the butter? That's a lot of butter," I said.

"Your friends brought it. Gift of the United States of America, it says on the drum."

My aunt had buttered several slices of bread and tried making some coffee only to realize there wasn't any water. "Using the bathroom will be wonderful," she said. "Especially with all these visitors."

I ate my bread and American butter quietly. On the radio, Tibor Déry was reciting a poem:

"On the streets of Budapest,
Rivers of blood, rivers of death."

I said I heard shooting all night.

"You should've heard what went on here the day before yesterday. I lived through the fifty-one day siege of Budapest in 1945. I'm telling you, that's what it was like. The Americans didn't come then, and they won't come now."

I told her I had run into a classmate of mine in Balástya, of all places. Guszti Pálréti. Who turned out to be the nephew of Imre Pálréti, the political prisoner we helped escape from Vác. "Anyway, according to him, Radio Free Europe keeps saying the Americans will come. It's only a matter of days. Do you get Radio Free Europe here?"

"If you can find it, be my guest. When I try, I get nothing but a bunch of static. The government is still blocking their broadcast. If

Imre Nagy is really in charge now, why doesn't he open the lines with the West?"

I went to the radio and played with the dials. Nothing but sonar sounds, beeps and whistles. Then a faint voice, like from under the ocean. A woman was saying that the United Nations has placed the Hungarian question on its agenda.

"Sure" my aunt said. "Right after they discuss the Suez Crisis for the next three weeks."

"What's that?" I asked.

"The English and the French attacked the Suez Canal," my aunt said. She said she's been listening to Radio Budapest and that's all they're talking about between bulletins. How the Western powers attacked a sovereign country. Why should the Russians do any different here? And if the Communists and their guard dogs, the ÁVO, stay in power, we're done for. Anyone who ever held a gun will be a target."

Bullseye, I thought. I knew my aunt was aiming at me. All on account of that idiotic picture in the paper. "Our Commander," I said, "is pretty sure the ÁVO will be dissolved."

"Commander? How old is your Commander," my aunt asked.

"Twenty-four," I said.

"Oh, all of twenty-four. Well, then, I rest my case." She took a bite of buttered bread and said: "The Americans better send us more than butter is all I have to say. Salty as herring."

"I like it," I said.

"You would."

Radio Free Europe was losing its signal. I turned the dial back to Radio Budapest. The radio announced that there would be a special bulletin in fifteen minutes.

"You better get your friends from the other room. They may want to hear this."

I left and came back with Michelangelo and Sewer Rat, who said they were almost done with their pounding. "If nothing else," Sewer Rat said, "it'll keep out the rain."

"Shhh," my aunt said. The bulletin was coming on:

> "This is Radio Budapest, Home service. The Ministry of the Interior states that at dawn there was peace all over the country. Although there was still some sporadic fighting, there were no riots or armed clashes…Several more foreign planes are expected to arrive in Budapest with food, blood plasma, medicines and food-stuffs…As reported earlier, the withdrawal of Soviet troops from Budapest is in progress. Units of the Hungarian Army, the police, armed workers and youth are taking over the job of maintaining order."

"Yesss!" Michelangelo, the skeptic, said.

Sewer Rat said it was damn good news.

"Thank, God!" my aunt exclaimed. "I can't believe it. Could it be?" She gave me a hug. "Your Mama and Papa did not die in vain!"

I nodded. My eyes got watery. Everybody cheered. Michelangelo said, "And to think we had a part in it. My God! Just think about that a moment. Things will be different, I just know it! Man, oh man, we did it! God bless the Hungarians!"

This was the most excited I'd seen him.

"Sewer Rat dug out his flask and took a quick gulp before passing it around. "He echoed Michelangelo's words. "My God, we did it!"

My aunt took a swig from the flask and laughed: "We may not have water but we have our good old Hungarian *pálinka*! It doesn't get better than this."

So, the Russians were actually on their way out of the country. This was great news. Really great. We kept our fingers crossed that it was true.

We checked the other radio stations to see if we could receive broadcasts from other Hungarian cities, including Győr and Miskolc. In these cities, the radio was already in the hands of the freedom fighters, and, in many ways, their information would be more reliable. Radio Free Győr came in loud and clear:

> "Russian troops have begun their withdrawal from Budapest. We call on the population and on the freedom fighters to refrain from attacking them, for by doing so they will only delay peaceful settlement."

More cheering.

"All right. Now, let's see what Radio Free Europe has to say," my aunt said.

I was told to find Radio Free Europe again. I did, and in quick order, and this time no static. Radio Free Europe confirmed that elements of the Soviet armed forces were withdrawing from Budapest on orders from the Kremlin. They had other news. They said volunteers from Western Europe were lining up along the Austro-Hungarian border. These included special forces and military units.

"My God," my aunt said. "Finally. Finally."

Michelangelo said, "This is for real, people," and with that he said he had to go. He had some tanks to paint.

"Not on canvas," Sewer Rat said. "He paints the Hungarian crest on the turrets."

"And I do a damn good job, if I say so, myself," Michelangelo said. "And one more thing. For your information, I started work on a new piece. On canvas!

Sewer Rat said a toast to the Hungarian crest. "To the red, white and green," he said.

We were cheering, celebrating, giddy with the good news when we heard a knock on the door.

Sister Ágnes and Dr. Judit Leocky and her doctor's bag were on the threshold. I brought them into the kitchen, where Sister Ágnes introduced her to my aunt. She was here to examine Krisztina.

My aunt was surprised Dr. Leocky seemed to know us. I told her Dr. Leocky worked out of the Üllői Avenue clinic. She was the one treating the wounded.

"Did you hear?" I said to Sister Ágnes. "The Russians are pulling out. Help's on the way from the West. Soldiers are lining up by the Hungarian frontier."

"When?"

"Now," I said. "They just announced it on the radio."

"Thank heavens!" she said.

"That is good news," the doctor said. "More good news! We have new medicines thanks to the Swiss. Medicines we didn't even dream of having a week ago. Planes have been landing all day. My husband Attila and Pali Szilágy spent half the day at Ferihegyi Airport standing in line. The whole world is coming to our aid. Now, let's see if we can help that little patient of ours. Can you take me to her? I have to be back at the clinic by noon. What is her problem, exactly?"

My aunt explained that Krisztina was born with heart disease. Her heart valves leaked badly, and the wall separating the left and right side of her heart had holes in them. That's why her skin was bluish and she tired easily when she exerted herself or when she got overexcited.

"Who isn't overexcited these days," the doctor said.

My aunt took her in to the sewing room. I followed.

Krisztina was still sleeping. My aunt told the doctor she had given Krisztina a tiny bit of sedative when she had the attack last night. She described Krisztina's breathlessness.

The doctor stirred Krisztina awake gently. She took out her stethoscope and listened to her chest while she looked at her watch. She nodded and said: "130 per minute." Then she listened to her back, had her cough and took her blood pressure, first one arm, then the other. When she was done she asked Krisztina how she was feeling.

"Tired," my sister replied.

"Why don't you just rest for now, dear," the doctor said. "I may have something for you that will make you feel better. Okay? Ohkay."

Krisztina smiled. I covered her up and she went back to sleep. It was still early and she needed the rest.

The doctor spoke to us privately. She told us what we already knew. She could hear her mitral valves. They weren't closing properly. The knocking sound was pretty strong, which meant the condition was severe. In cases like this, surgery offered the only hope for a cure. Of course, it was the kind of operation doctors could not perform in Hungary.

"We just don't have the technology," she said. "We can make her comfortable with sedatives, but that's about all we can do. It's not all bad news. Her heart is stronger than her symptoms suggest. She has a rather fast resting pulse, but it's strong and stable. A very good sign. I brought some new heart medicine with me. It's Swiss. I had read about in an East German medical journal not long ago. The medicine slows the heart, so it doesn't require so much oxygen. I'd like to give it a try. See if it brings her pulse down. If it does, she could tolerate a lot more activity. But, I'm afraid, it only works for the short run. Eventually, she'll need to have an operation. With time, those holes in her septum will get larger. All we can do is delay it. I'd like to give her a dose, and wait an hour or so to see if she responds."

"Kitty, dear," my aunt said, "would you please get a glass of water for Krisztina?"

"We don't have any water, remember?"

The doctor looked concerned. Krisztina may be dehydrated on top of everything. "How long have you been without water?"

"Two days."

The doctor said as soon as she gets back to the clinic, she will send over some water. For now, Krisztina could take the medicine with a little jam, so it doesn't taste so bitter.

I got a spoonful of jam and gave Krisztina the new medicine. An hour later, the doctor took her pulse. Miraculously, it was down to 100.

The doctor said she could exercise now. Not too much, but a little exercise would actually do her some good. As long as she didn't overdo it. "Now that the curfew is lifted, a little walk in the park might be nice," she said.

My aunt asked if taking her to church would be all right.

"How far is the church?"

"Not more than a few city blocks."

"I don't see why not," the doctor said. "If she gets tired," you can stop and rest a little. Take her pulse. If it's over 120, then you know she's overdoing it. Otherwise, exercise will actually strengthen her heart."

My aunt told me to make some hot coffee and bring out some rolls. "We have that wonderful American butter," she said.

"No water, remember?" I said.

"All right, then make something, anything."

I knew my aunt. She wanted me out of the way. She wanted to talk to the doctor alone. I went toward the kitchen, but only turned the corner so I could spy on them.

"Let me ask you something," I overheard my aunt ask Dr. Leocky. "I need your honest opinion. Most of the specialists her late mother and I took her to said she would not survive beyond two or three years. Now that we have this new medicine, is the prognosis still so bleak?"

I heard the doctor sigh and say, "Unfortunately, without an operation, there is little hope. Even with the new medicine. Maybe with the new regime, Hungarians will be able to travel out of the country and the little girl can have that operation. I would keep that in mind."

"Thank you, doctor," my aunt said. "How much do I owe you? Kitty, dear," she yelled as if I were in the kitchen. "Could you get me my purse, please?"

In front of company she wanted to impress, my aunt could be annoyingly polite.

"Ah, there's no charge. I'll leave you a packet of the new medicine for her. I've marked it. Once in the morning with water."

"Thank you. You are very kind."

I had known for a long time now that my sister was hopelessly ill. My mother and aunt went from specialist to specialist looking for a ray of hope. There wasn't any. Until today. Maybe Dr. Leocky was right. Maybe if the borders opened up, we could take Krisztina somewhere where she could have the operation she needs. Thank you, God.

"Kitty, do you have my purse?"

I hustled into the kitchen for her purse. Lucky for us, the doctor refused any payment whatsoever, because I found nothing in my aunt's purse except some loose change and a pair of scissors she carried around with her, no matter what.

Dr. Leocky could not stay and eat with us. She had to be back at the Üllői Clinic. The wounded were still coming in.

Sister Ágnes had to go, too. She had to go and pay a visit to a certain Cardinal, she said. If everything went well, the Cardinal ought to be in his official residence in Buda by tomorrow. Tomorrow would be the big day.

As it turned out, tomorrow would be a big day for us, too.

Chapter Eight

8

It was not a Sunday, but a Wednesday on the last day of October when we walked to go to church in our Sunday-best or the closest thing to it. We were going to Papa's church, the one they now called University Church, although it had other names in the past, like the Church of the Immaculate Conception. We were going to light a candle for Papa and for Mama.

Official church services and Catholic schools were not allowed under Communism, since the government banned a all religious orders.

I wondered if Sister Ágnes would go back to being a nun once it was legal again. I had to smile when I thought about it. I just couldn't imagine my comrade with that wild, long blond hair of hers in front of a class or staying put in a dark convent saying the Hail Mary all day. According to the radio, Cardinal Mindszenty had been freed by Hungarian freedom fighters and returned to his residence in Buda in an armored car and a tank escort. I was happy for Sister Ágnes. I wished I could've been there.

My aunt asked me what I knew about Sister Ágnes. I told her. Sister Ágnes did not like to talk about herself, but Sewer Rat eventually pried out the story of her life.

Sister Ágnes' father was a highly regarded official at one of the largest Catholic schools in the country. It was no coincidence that he was arrested and jailed for allegedly killing a Russian soldier, when everyone knew the soldier committed suicide. He was later executed in Siberia. The Communists used this as a pretext for closing all Catholic schools.

But something even more terrible happened to her during the war. Something that she shared with me in a very private moment. I told my aunt how Sister Ágnes' mother was raped and killed by Russian soldiers right in front of her. Then they raped her. She was about my age at the time. Soon after, she joined the Sisters of the Sacred Heart. A year later when she took her vows, the Communists dissolved her order. That poor woman had a lot of pain in her life. She endured more than most men, and no matter how life had hardened her, she never complained.

We all liked the soft-spoken ex-nun. Thanks to her and Dr. Leocky, Krisztina was feeling much better, and we had several liters of water now. With all the water, we could keep Krisztina from being dehydrated, and we could wash up and flush our toilet.

My aunt dressed us as if we were going to Easter Service. She found a hat for me in her closet, and for Krisztina, she took a brown beret, altered it by sewing a cute little beige flower on it. It went nicely with her brown winter coat. I wore a wool skirt and sweater, and cleaned up my tennis shoes.

My aunt nixed the tennis shoes and forced me to wear one of her pumps. She said if she could wear pumps with her arthritis, then I could wear pumps.

Krisztina was excited. Her pulse before we left was 90. For her, this was nice and low. I took it again after we had walked a good block at an intersection bustling with gun-toting freedom fighters. Her heartbeat climbed to 100. Still good. A Hungarian tank swarming with cheering students clattered by. They waved at us. With all this excitement, she should've been panting by now, but she wasn't. She smiled and waved back.

Although it was hidden on a narrow, winding street corner in the old part of the city, the baroque church was riddled with bullets. The centuries-old rose window was shot out so badly, the stucco around it crumbled. The rubble was piled into a heap on the sidewalk.

Directly across from the church stood a four-story building that was at one time an Officers' Club with a casino. Now it was simply called the Casino. This was one of the buildings where Mustache was stockpiling guns and ammunition to avoid keeping everything in one central location, like in the Killián Barracks. I guess it made sense.

We went around the rubble to the church's thick wooden doors. They were level with the sidewalk and they were wide open. We walked into the darkness and waited for our eyes to get used to the light that filtered through in streams from the bullet holes in the stained glass windows. Not a soul inside.

We walked up to the beautifully carved wood altar and knelt down. My aunt opened her purse and took out two candles, one for Mama and one for Papa. She let Krisztina light one and I the other. While we watched the flames, we said a prayer for the souls of our mother and father, asking God to have mercy on them and to have mercy on us.

My aunt fished out a rosary and stood up with the help of her walking stick. She whispered for us to sit down while she hobbled over to the side altar where she knelt down before a statue of the Virgin Mary.

We sat in the first pew where we usually sat with my father the few times we came here. Krisztina was probably too small to remember.

I said a special prayer to God to guide me, because I wasn't sure what I was going to do with my life. I knew I wanted to take care of my little sister and my aunt. The things is, I wasn't sure how. My aunt wanted me to finish school and learn to sew all at the same time. She hoped things would change in the country so people could have little businesses. She would teach me all she knew about sewing, and I could start my own sewing salon. I wasn't sure I would know how to do that, but I was willing to learn. I thanked God for my aunt and for my little sister. I asked Him for a miracle. So Krisztina could have the operation she needed. I thanked God for what was happening in our country, for blessing our people with the promise of freedom. And I asked Him to receive the souls of my fallen comrades into His heart.

My aunt finished her prayers, crossed herself and stood up with a groan. Suddenly, gunfire erupted in front of the church. Deafening bursts of machine gun fire. I shouted for everyone to get down.

My aunt crawled over to where we were hunkered down, a look of terror in her eyes. Krisztina was panting, gulping air.

My aunt was holding Krisztina tightly. I told her to give Krisztina some more medicine, maybe half a tablet. I glanced over the pew. Bullets were ripping into the cobblestone right in front of the open door. I could see the manhole covering the sewer slowly rising. A man with a machine gun jumped out of the sewer. Bullets hit the metal cover with a ping sound. The man was hit and went down. He started to crawl toward the church when he was hit again. That's when I noticed something white covering his ear. Oh, my God! It was Sewer Rat!

Without thinking, I leaped out of the pew and charged toward the door. Bullets were flying over my head. I dragged Sewer Rat and his gun into the church and pulled the door shut behind us. His jacket and shirt were soaked in blood. Sewer Rat spoke in quick gulps of air. He said the ÁVO had booby-trapped the Casino and Michelangelo was in there with a hundred other men and tons of ammunition. "They have a fuse running through the sewer to the basement," he said, his teeth clenched. "You have to stop them. You have to cut the cable!"

"Auntie!" I shouted, "Bring the scissors. In your purse."

She hurried over with the scissors. I tried to grab it from her, but she said she'd do it herself. She quickly cut away at Sewer Rat's shirt. Sewer Rat kept telling me to leave him. And go! He had a bullet hole by his ribs and one by his shoulder. My aunt and I wrapped him up.

I picked up Sewer Rat's machine gun and looked my aunt in the eye.

"Do what you have to and God be with you," my aunt said.

"Cheetah?" Krisztina said. "Don't forget Sewer Rat's flashlight.

Instead of taking the flashlight from his belt, I took off his belt, doubled it up and wrapped it around my waist. I shoved the scissors inside the belt, yanked off my shoes, and made a mad dash toward the open sewer.

As if on cue, the ÁVO snipers from the rooftop went into action. I jumped into the dark hole and flicked on the flashlight. The cold, ankle-deep water was numbing and slime was oozing between my toes.

A fierce firefight erupted above ground. I heard a truck screech to a stop not far from me. Then shouts of "ÁVO on the roof!"

I scanned the bottom of the sewer leading toward the Casino basement. The cavernous sewer smelled like Guszti's outhouse. Little squealing things were running amok in front of me. I couldn't see anything that looked like a line or a fuse.

Then I heard voices. Not one, but two. Not above, but inside the sewer.

I put out the flashlight and crouched down, listening. I heard something about prisoners in the sewers. Under one of the city squares. Then I saw a light in the distance. They kept talking as they got closer. Whoever they were, they would have to get much closer before their flashlight could spot me. The man's voice was clear now:

"What if the insurgents can hear them? They'll dig through" The other man said, "What? On a busy square like Népköztársaság Square?"

Insurgents, huh? Only the ÁVO called us that. They gave themselves away. I had a choice to make. I could shoot it out with them and risk my life and the lives of the hundred fighters inside the Casino, or I had to find the cable. Now! I started clawing at the bottom like an animal. My hands felt something under the muck. Like a rubber-coated electric cord. I had to hold the scissors with two hands and gnaw at the rubberized cord before the blades finally cut through.

Their flashlight found me. They fired a pistol in my direction without asking any questions. I fired back with a short burst from my machine gun. Their flashlight went out. I heard boots kicking up water as they ran.

A deafening explosion. A blast of air and debris. The sewer caved in on top of me, burying me in stone.

I must've blacked out. What I heard next was deadly silence followed by the sound of my own groans. Then I thought I heard someone shout my name. The voice was faint, distant: "Cheetah! Cheetah! Can you hear me?" A gun was fired, sounding like five stories above me. I felt like it was all a bad dream. "Hello! Can you hear the gun?"

"I'm here," I shouted. Something long and slimy slithered into my hair. I grabbed it and tossed it into the water. God Almighty, what was that?

After a minute I heard: "Dig there." The voice was still muffled, but closer. "Are you all right? It's me," he shouted, "Pali Szilágy! Are you all right down there?"

Pali was the student volunteer who took the wounded to the Üllői Avenue clinic. "I'm okay," I shouted back.

It took them a long time to dig me out. One end of the cable was still in my hand when they brought me up on a stretcher. Pali stood over me. A whole crowd surrounded us.

"How could the charges explode?" I asked Pali. "I cut the cable. What happened?"

"I don't know about dynamite. I just know what I was told. Only one exploded," he said. "Could've been a lot worse. We lost three men, and your friend Michelangelo is critically injured. He's asking for you."

Pali said my aunt and Krisztina went to the hospital with Sewer Rat. They were all going to be all right. The bullets went clean through Sewer Rat. My aunt's blood pressure was very high. They gave her medicine. They'll probably let her out tomorrow. Krisztina was fine. My friend was the one everyone was worried about.

"How long have I been out?" I asked.

"About two hours," Pali said.

"Two hours?! Is Michelangelo in the same hospital? The Üllői Avenue clinic?"

Pali shook his head sadly. "He's still in the Casino. We can't move him. The ceiling caved in. A rafter fell on him and he's pinned under tons of concrete. He can't feel his legs. Dr. Leocky's with him. She says if we move him, his blood pressure will crash and he'll die."

I had to go to him. Now. I stood up and felt a wave of dizziness.

"Sure you're okay?" Pali asked.

I steadied myself. "Take me to Michelangelo."

Wet, slimy, and covered in muck, I followed Pali to the Casino.

From the outside, the building didn't look any worse for wear. The inside was another story. The lobby looked like it was bombed.

A huge piece of the ceiling was gone so you could see the floor above it, and a fancy crystal chandelier dangle by a wire. We climbed over knee-high rubble to get to Dr. Leocky. Her husband Attila was with her. "Cheetah's here," I heard the doctor tell Michelangelo as we came near.

The giant cement rafter seemed to cut Michelangelo in half. He was buried from the waist down and drenched in sweat.

He spoke with great difficulty. He had something urgent he wanted to tell me. I held his hand as he groped for words. "I don't have anyone," he said. "My family. My mother and father. They died in the camps. My sister survived. She lives in Miami. In America. She writes to me—ah—all the time, but I...I'm so stupid. I hardly ever answer. Your father. He'd bring me the letters. Would you...would you write my sister and tell her. I don't want her writing, not knowing. I...don't have anything. Except my paintings. They're in my apartment. I want you to have them. You're the Cheetah," he tried laughing but didn't have the strength. His new goatee dripped with sweat. He stopped talking and licked his dry lips.

I asked for some water and held his head while he took a sip. He gritted his teeth, pressed his eyes shut with all his might: "Remember that drawing I did for you for school?" he said with his last breath. "It wasn't really that bad, was it?"

That was the last thing Michelangelo said. He died a few moments later.

I was in shock. He died so fast. Why did he have to die now? Just when things were looking up. All the things we fought for. It just wasn't fair.

I cried when Michelangelo died. I had grown to like him. Overnight, he went from being a whiner to being a warrior. He said I did it to him, but I never really believed that. He was too embarrassed to say how he loved his country. He only died for it.

Dr. Leocky and her husband drove us to the Üllői Avenue clinic so I could see my aunt and sister.

When we got to the clinic, I was surprised to see Sewer Rat on the steps smoking. He was wrapped up from his shoulder to his waist and there he was, smoking. "Shouldn't he be in bed?" I asked Dr. Leocky.

"No free beds," she said.

The first thing Sewer Rat said when he saw me was, "Thank God, you're alive!"

I went up to him and hugged him. "Ouch," he yelped. "That hurt."

I told him about Michelangelo.

He said nothing for a second. He looked up into the sky, then lowered his head, shaking it. He said he had a bad feeling about the Casino. Too many people knew it was turning into an armory. "God. Michelangelo?" he said. "You know he painted the Hungarian coat of arms on just about every tank and 84 mm cannon he could get his hands on? I had to collar him to help me move the antitank mines to the Casino. It's lousy. Just lousy."

"I cut the damn cable," I cried.

"I know you did, kid. Listen, if all the charges went off, the Casino would've blown sky high, with everybody in it."

"But why did Michelangelo have to die?"

"I don't know, kid. But you did real good. Real good."

"I don't know," I said. "When I was in the sewer, before I cut the cable and before the explosion, I heard two men talking. They said something about prisoners being held in the sewer system under Népköztársaság Square. We shot at each other. I couldn't tell what happened, it was so dark, but I think I got the better of them. Then the explosion. But I cut the cable. I showed it to Pali."

"I know you did," he patted my back. "I know."

We let go of each other. I went inside the clinic to wash up. Dr. Leocky wanted to check me over to make sure I was all right.

Other than a couple of scratches, I was just fine. The stitches on my calf were holding. No infection. "You're a very lucky girl," the doctor said.

I told her I had given Krisztina extra medicine when the shooting started. Just half a tablet. I thought she'd ball me out. Instead, she said I probably saved her life, too.

Sister Ágnes showed up. She said my family was here.

My family. I liked the sound of it. They were my family now. I got dressed in what was left of my "Sunday-best" and went to them. They were so glad to see me, and this time my aunt didn't pummel me. For all she'd been through, Krisztina looked good. The doctor said Sister Ágnes could take us home.

Sister Ágnes was out front grieving with Sewer Rat about Michelangelo. "There is never going to be another Michelangelo, she said. "He's one of a kind. I'm going to miss him terribly." We all were. I said, "He may have been a pain in the butt, but you couldn't get a better friend. He looked after me like I was his little sister. What I liked about him the most was that he treated me like his equal. He never talked down to me."

Sister Ágnes told us about how they freed Cardinal Mindszenty at the crack of dawn. She and the armed escort were lucky. When they got to Felsőpetény, the guards saw the Hungarian armored car and tank, and gave up. "Not a single shot was fired," Sister Ágnes said. "The Cardinal was incredibly brave. He was the last political prisoner to be freed. When he saw us, he said, 'You are good Hungarians."

"I was really lucky. Because I used to be a nun, I got to talk to him before they put him in the armored car. He invited me to his old residence in Buda, where we had a long chat. We got to talking, and your father's name came up. Just like that. He was telling me about being tortured at Andrássy Street. How they were trying to force a confession out of him that he was collaborating with the Americans. Just because he consulted a visiting American doctor about his heart. Turned out his heart was good. It was his thyroid. Anyway, the Cardinal refused to sign. They said they had a witness. Your father was in the cell next to him. He mentioned him by name. Laszló Barna. When the interrogators withheld bread from the Cardinal so he couldn't say Mass in his cell, your father gave him his. The trouble is, your father got caught. Then they accused your father of being part of the conspiracy. They beat both of them with a truncheon day in and day out. They wanted your father to be a witness against Cardinal Mindszenty. But your father refused."

We were already in front of our building, but we stayed in the truck to hear more.

"Eventually," Sister Ágnes said, "the Cardinal did sign a coerced confession, but after his name he put the initials C.F. When the authorities asked him what the C.F. stood for, the Cardinal said it was '*Cardinalis Foraneus*' which meant Provincial Cardinal. When your father asked him later, why the Cardinal signed a confession, the Cardinal said the initials really meant, '*Coerci Facit*' or signed under coercion. Not only did your father refuse to be a false witness, he kept his word to keep all this a secret. They couldn't beat it out of him. They shuffled him back and forth from Vác to Andrássy Street and back again, but your father stood his ground. Finally, they gave up and sent him to Kecskemét to die."

Krisztina was getting tired. Sister Ágnes said," You're sleepy aren't you, little one. Oh, one more thing, I almost forgot, and it's so important. I told the Cardinal about Krisztina. He said the American doctor who treated him for hyperthyroidism is a famous cardiologist in America, Wait. I have the paper here somewhere. He wrote it down for me to give to you. He said you could tell the doctor the Hungarian Cardinal sent you. He will help Krisztina."

Sister Ágnes handed me a piece of paper, then turned on the cabin light so I could see. It was all in English:

John Kralik, M.D.
The Cleveland Clinic
Cleveland, Ohio
U.S.A.

My aunt asked Sister Ágnes if she wanted to come up. She said she better get back to Sewer Rat. He was not very good at taking care of himself. And she said she wanted to say some prayers for Michelangelo. He was a good friend. May God rest his soul.

Before driving off, Sister Ágnes told us to keep the radio on tomorrow. Cardinal Mindszenty will be making a speech to the people.

I was tired. I think we all were. The elevator wasn't working. I picked up Krisztina and put her on my shoulder and we trudged up the dark stairs. My legs were killing me. I must've twisted something when the sewer caved in on me. I cautioned my aunt to be careful. I knew she must've hurt her knee when she fell in the church, but she didn't tell anyone. Once upstairs, we went straight to bed. Tomorrow would be another day.

I collapsed on my couch cushions on the floor again, next to Krisztina's bed. With the windows boarded up, it was darker than usual. I was listening to Krisztina's breathing. After about fifteen minutes, she said: "Cheetah? Papa was very brave, wasn't he?"

"Yes, he was."

"I think you're brave, too."

"Thanks, Kriszti. You should go to sleep. Aren't you tired?"

She didn't answer. Then, after another fifteen minutes, she said, "Cheetah? Am I brave?"

"You're very brave."

"But I'm scared of the dark, and I'm scared of having an operation."

"That's not what brave means. Brave means fighting for something you believe in."

"Like Michelangelo?"

"Yes, like Michelangelo."

"Michelangelo liked you a lot."

"I liked him a lot."

"How old was he?"

"I don't know. Twenty-two."

"But you're only fourteen."

"What is that supposed to mean?"

"I don't know."

"He was like a big brother, Kriszti."

"I wish I had a big brother."

"You have a big sister," I said.

"I love you, Cheetah."

"I love you, too, Kriszti."

It was getting late, and we were both tired. I knew I was exhausted. Michelangelo's sudden death weighed on me heavily. We had gone through so much together, and in such a short time. He was the big brother I never had. And I guess I was the sister he never got to know. I'm not sure why Michelangelo didn't answer his sister's letters. It didn't sound like him. But then, I've only known him for what? A week?

So much has happened in that week. Like life and death. Mostly death. With Michelangelo's death, I felt an emptiness that surprised me. It was like the world would be a less cheerful place without him, that things would be boring. I wished now, I would've taken his art more seriously. I made up my mind tomorrow to go over to his apartment and to try to find that drawing he did for me. The one I didn't like. I wanted to see it again.

I felt too restless to lay my head down and fall asleep. I sat up and watched Kriszti sleeping. I wanted her life to be different, for her to be healthy and happy. I was asking God for a miracle. I didn't want her to die.

I slept fitfully till eleven in the morning, when I heard the faint sound of the radio from the kitchen. I got dressed and put on my tennis shoes.

I found my aunt smoking in the kitchen, listening to the radio. She said the commentators were all new. The radio was now in the hands of the revolutionary council instead of the Communists. They confirmed the Russian withdrawal. Things were slowly returning to normal. The radio announced that shops were opening in Budapest. People were going back to work.

We talked about what Sister Ágnes said yesterday. "Your father," my aunt said, "was one of a kind. Most would be more than happy to inform on their fellow men if it meant getting ahead. Your father had integrity. He really stuck by his friends. He's a lot like someone else I know." My aunt looked at me and smiled. "The apple hasn't fallen far from the tree," she said. "You're a strong young woman, Cheetah, and that's good."

"I hope so," I said. While I was looking around for something to eat, I asked, "Did they say when the Cardinal is supposed to make his speech?"

My aunt said around noon.

I looked around for some tea.

"We're out of coffee, too," she said. "You know what I was thinking? Why don't you see if that little coffee shop is open downstairs. What do you say if we get a chocolate éclair and split it? You and Krisztina. There's some loose change on the counter." She said we were kind of low on cash. "Let's put it this way. Business has been on the slow side these last few days. Still, I think you deserve something sweet. I'm very proud of you. Your father would be very proud, too."

I thanked her for saying that. It made me feel good. "What about you, what would you like?"

"Oh, a double espresso for me."

On my way down to the sweet shop, I stopped at Michelangelo's apartment to sneak a peek at his paintings. He was so secretive about his place, I don't think anyone I know has seen it.

The key turned over easily to the smell of linseed oil and turpentine. I was surprised how nice the apartment was. Other than a thin layer of dust that covered just about everything, the apartment was very tidy, especially for a bachelor. Another surprise, maybe the biggest surprise, was how many paintings he had. I expected to see four or five. Not a hundred or more. None of his paintings were up. The walls were empty. He had all these canvases—and they were huge—many as large as a door, leaning against each other and against the walls.

They were impossible to pick up. I slid one to the window for more light and leaned the canvas against an old writing desk.

I recognized the view. From Gellért Hill overlooking Castle Hill and the Danube. The colors were vivid. The city never looked so bright. Orange leaves, olive-green buildings, rose-colored clouds, everything swimming in a sunny glow.

Another canvas, a bit smaller, was a still life of a portion of a room with a table and a window open to a street deep in snow. Inside, a bowl of fruit on a white tablecloth, draped over a polished table. It looked so homey and so warm in contrast to the winter scene outside.

I dragged three more of the larger pieces to the light. A nude sat on a bed on one. She looked sad. A lovely old chair with a curving back stood in front of the bed. A blue-gray cat lay curled under it.

The next piece was one of the largest. A gendarme in black, with a rifle slung on his shoulder, was leading a group of men and women over a snow-covered field.

I took a closer look. The people being led away had a yellow star on their coats and fear in their eyes.

At least a hundred more paintings like these leaned against the walls in the living room, in the bedroom, in the bathroom, in the kitchen, stacked against each other.

I put the paintings back where I found them. When I went back to the window, something on Michelangelo's dusty writing desk caught my eye. A stack of envelopes with canceled American stamps and, next to them, what looked like a half-finished letter by Michelangelo. I couldn't help myself. I read his unfinished letter:

My Dear Zsuzsa!

Forgive me for being such a lousy letter writer. Every time I think of what happened to our mother and father in that horrible German camp and how you had to suffer, I cringe. I feel so guilty for climbing out of that basement window in the Budapest ghetto. I want to tell you that...

Here the letter stopped. I saw the date. August 1, 1956. That was three months ago! I took the letter, determined to send it with a letter of my own to Michelangelo's sister. I looked around for the little drawing Michelangelo did for me, but I couldn't find it anywhere. Oh, Lord. I realized that I completely forgot about the espresso and the éclair.

I hurried out to the street only to find the coffee shop closed. A long line of people snaked around the corner of our building waiting for bread. I didn't want to go back up empty-handed, so I decided to stand in line. After some forty minutes of standing in line I got my loaf of bread and ran upstairs with it like an animal squirreling away food for the winter.

I smelled tea brewing. Krisztina was up, sitting around the kitchen table with my aunt, listening to the radio. I was surprised my aunt didn't yell at me. Everyone was in a good mood. The water was back on. My aunt borrowed some tea from one of our neighbors. I told them about the coffee shop being closed and about the long bread line, but I said nothing about Michelangelo's apartment. I don't know why. I guess it's because we always made fun of him and his art.

They were very happy to see the bread. My aunt cut some slices and buttered them. She spread a bit of jam on each slice. Our late breakfast tasted better than ever.

We waited all day for Cardinal Mindszenty's address to the people. Finally, at one in the afternoon, the radio announced that Cardinal Mindszenty received representatives of the Hungarian and foreign press, radio and television at his Buda residence. He said:

> "After long imprisonment, I greet all the sons and daughters of the Hungarian nation. I bear no hatred against anyone. The struggle being waged for liberty is unparalleled in world history. Our young men and women deserve all the glory. They deserve our gratitude and prayers."

A few hours later, another bulletin hit the airwaves. Imre Nagy declared Hungary's neutrality:

> "The revolutionary struggle fought by the Hungarian people and its heroes has at last carried the cause of freedom and independence to victory. The heroic struggle has made it possible to implement our fundamental national interest—neutrality."

This meant, my aunt said, that Hungary was withdrawing from the Warsaw Pact and joining the family of free nations which would recognize us as a free and independent country in our own right. As a free people we would be determining our own destiny.

"Hungarians are a hard-working lot," my aunt said. "We'll clean up this mess in no time. Soon, things will be returning to normal."

"Does that mean," Krisztina asked me, "that you'll be going back to school soon?"

"Ask her if she misses school," my aunt said.

"Do you?"

My last experience in school didn't exactly leave a good taste in my mouth. All I had to do was to think of Comrade Aczél and his Stalin Brigade. Sitting in neat rows, with our hands behind our backs. The school would have to change just like the country. Most of our textbooks touting Marxism and Leninism would have to be rewritten or thrown away. No more propaganda. "It's going to be a different school than the one I attended," I said.

"Just think," my aunt said. "You may be able to pray in school."

I made a sour face. I liked praying, but I didn't like to do it in public. I guess I didn't like compulsory anything, especially something personal like praying. I always thought of Communism as a kind of state religion anyhow, except *their* Trinity was Marx, Lenin and Stalin.

"What if you don't want to pray?"

"Then you don't," my aunt said impatiently.

Krisztina said she wanted to go to school, too. "Will I ever be able to go to school, because of my bad heart?"

I told her we were going to have her heart fixed up, so she could do anything she wanted to. Cardinal Mindszenty had a friend in America, and he was going to fix her heart.

Krisztina smiled.

"Well, what are we going to do now?" my aunt said.

"We could clean up," I said. "Kriszti could help me a little. We have running water now, don't we? Then after that, we could take turns taking a hot bath. Doesn't that sound good. I've been looking forward to a bath for a week."

My aunt said it sounded good to her.

The telephone rang in the living room.

"Look at that, we have our phone back, too," my aunt said.

It was Sister Ágnes. She said one of Sewer Rat's wounds got infected. His fever was high. He was very sick. He may need an operation. I told Sister Ágnes to wait a second.

"Sewer Rat may have to have an operation," I said to my aunt and Kriszti."

"Oh, no," my aunt said.

Sister Ágnes asked about doing something for Michelangelo. Maybe we could just have a little gathering in his apartment. A memorial kind of thing. She knew Michelangelo was not religious, but it may be nice to say a few words about him.

"I'd like that."

After I hung up, I started to clean. Krisztina helped by wiping off my aunt's figurines with a moist cloth. I swept and she held the dust pan. Then I went at the apartment with soap and a bucket of hot water. Although the water was back on, I was still afraid to splurge and made sure I didn't waste any.

Once we were done with my aunt's apartment, I took Krisztina down with me to show her Michelangelo's paintings.

She was amazed. She said it was like a museum. Her favorite was of an old Serbian church on top of a hill of narrow, winding alleys. She picked up on the sun, too. How the old steeple and the tiled rooftops were lit up with purple and orange colors.

I told Krisztina all I knew about Michelangelo. How his parents were killed in a concentration camp, and how he was probably raised in an orphanage, though he never talked about it. How they tried to make him paint propaganda for the Communists, but he refused. How he was in the air force without ever flying a plane. How he was afraid of heights, yet he fought the Russians from the rooftops. How he was brave like Papa. How he was good at everything, except letter writing. And how he wanted me to have all these paintings.

"What are you going to do with them," Kriszti asked, wide-eyed.

I told her I didn't know. Maybe his sister will come and get them and take them to America where they would be appreciated.

Krisztina went into the kitchen. "Cheetah? Come look at this."

She was sliding the tablecloth off the table. That's when I noticed it wasn't a tablecloth at all but an oil cloth.

With a fresh painting underneath it. I could smell it. The painting took up the entire table.

I propped it up.

Michelangelo painted one of our street fights, with me and him standing close to each other among the rubble. I had a flaming Molotov cocktail in one hand. He held a rifle. We looked like we were ready to ambush the tank lurking around the corner.

This painting was different than the others. The colors were gray and black with dark, angry green in the strokes. The only light colors were on the Hungarian coat of arms on Michelangelo's coat. It was so lifelike, I started to cry.

Kriszti was impressed as I was. She asked me if I was going to take it home.

I didn't think I should. There was something—I don't know how to put it—something sacred about the painting. Like it belonged in a church or a museum. I didn't feel I had the right to take it. I wondered if this was the painting he meant to give me when he was dying.

"No," I told Kriszti. "We'll just leave everything. I'm not touching anything." I decided to leave everything the way Michelangelo left it. I was afraid to touch anything.

We lay the painting back on the table and covered it with the oil cloth. Kriszti pointed to the tubes of oil paint and the palette on the counter. His brushes were soaking in turpentine.

We left the apartment and headed upstairs.

After a supper of bread and salt pork and hot tea with lemon and lots of sugar, we sat around the kitchen table talking about Michelangelo and his paintings. My aunt was surprised he had so many

pieces. When did he have the time? As far as she knew, he worked
fifty hours a week at a tire factory in Csepel.

"He could've had a future," my aunt said. "Anywhere else in the
world, he could've had a future."

Kriszti wanted to know if *she* was going to have a future.

"Of course you are, dear," my aunt said. "What would you like to
be when you grow up?"

Kriszti didn't have to think long. She wanted to be a doctor, like
Dr. Leocky.

When it came my turn, I was stumped. I didn't really know.
Kriszti kidded me about becoming an Olympic champion, to which
my aunt said I needed to think about something a little less fantastic.

Eventually, the subject of the sewing business came up again.
According to my aunt, I could become the best seamstress in all of
Budapest and make a bundle of money designing clothes for the
famous and the rich. They would flock to me because I was a hero of
the Revolution.

Kriszti said I could advertise by putting up posters.

She knew how to rib me. "Ouch," I said. "You heard about my
problems at school, I see."

We laughed. Even picked names for my sewing salon. *Kitty of
Budapest, Budapest Boutique, Parisian Salon, Fashion World, Golden
Needle, Revolutionary Fashion* and so on. Everybody came up with
something. Some suggestions were clever, like *Kitty's Wear-House.*

"I got it," I said in a flash of brilliance. "Two words. How 'bout
Cheetah's Underwearhouse?"

We all laughed like crazy. My sister laughed so hard, she had tears
in her eyes. My aunt's wheezing laugh turned into a cough.

After a late lunch the next day, Krisztina and I went to the post
office around the corner, to see if it was open. I wanted to mail my

letter and Michelangelo's half-finished letter to his sister in America. When my father was with us, all we had to do is to give him our letters. For us, he said, it was always special delivery.

Two uniformed Hungarian soldiers stood guard at the post office entrance. They said we couldn't go in, but we could drop our letter in the red metal box on the corner. We were told that service would start up again, probably the next day.

Once we dropped off the letter, we had to hurry back to the apartment, so we could be there when Sister Ágnes came.

She was already waiting for us. She brought over a case of soda, some beer, and lots of pastry. The Gerbeaud coffee shop was now open she said, and the boys pitched in for Michelangelo's wake.

My aunt kept her entertained with her horror stories from the war until Sister Ágnes excused herself by saying she had to go to Sewer Rat's apartment. He needed a change of clothes and his pajamas. She asked if I wanted to go along. Kriszti wanted to tag along, too, but I didn't want her to overdo it, especially in the cold.

When we got to Sewer Rat's street, it was a shock. His street looked like it was bombed. The entire block lay in ruins. His building was a nothing more than a shell with blown-out windows and a mountain of rubble. Across the street, a lovely baroque playhouse was severely damaged. The marquee was lying on the street. Someone had written on it, "Special Matinee: Russians Go Home" in both Hungarian and Russian.

We were crushed. "He had everything in there," Sister Ágnes cried. "His whole life was in there." We let the tears flow and held on to each other.

I told Sister Ágnes we had saved some of my father's old clothes. They were in the apartment. She could have whatever Sewer Rat needed.

On the way back, we came across a mob of people heading toward the square opening in front of us. A woman said they found victims of the ÁVO in the city sewers.

I told Sister Ágnes about what I heard in the sewer by the Casino. Before the explosion. I wondered if we were heading toward the very square. It sure looked that way.

Népköztársaság Square. That was it! "Must be a thousand people here," Sister Ágnes said.

All the commotion was around a bulldozer. Some of the square was already dug up. A handful of men were chopping at the concrete with pick axes.

When Sister Ágnes asked someone what was going on, she was told they heard voices underground since morning. Apparently the ÁVO had secret cells in this part of the sewer system. The victims were buried alive.

A soldier standing by a manhole fired his gun in the air. The crowd grew silent.

The soldier shook his head.

The man next to me said they haven't heard from them for over an hour now. He said their faint cries were horrible to listen to. They had obviously run out of air.

We started for home in silence. I forgot whether or not I told Sewer Rat about what I heard in the sewer. I thought I did. He was going to tell Mustache. But that was a while ago. Why did they start digging so late?

Every now and then we'd come across these makeshift graves with a wooden cross and a mound of flowers. The name of the victim and his or her age were written in black script. We saw one that said "Julia Boros, Age 17." Another read: Imre Fazekas, Age 15.

On a nearby wall, a sign asked for contributions to the families of the fallen heroes. A brown wicker basket was filled to the brim with bills.

Sister Ágnes tossed whatever change she had in her pocket into the basket. Her eyes got watery. I took her arm, and that's how we walked home the rest of the way.

We talked about Cardinal Mindszenty's speech on the radio, how inspirational it was. Sister Ágnes said she wanted to be at his public press conference in person, but she had to take care of Sewer Rat. He was a handful.

I asked her if she wanted to go back to being a nun. Funny, she said, the Cardinal asked her the same thing. She wasn't sure. She was thinking about going back to school to study nursing. She was getting plenty of experience lately, taking care of Sewer Rat and helping out at the clinic. She'd have to think about it long and hard. "At least," she said, "now I have choices. One thing I don't want to do is to go back and drive a trolley. What about you? Do you have any plans?"

I shrugged. One thing I didn't want to be was a seamstress, and I told her as much.

She didn't see me as a seamstress either, thank God. She asked me what I like to do. Like in my spare time.

"I don't know. I like to take long walks in the city," I said. "It's not something people would pay money for, is it?"

"Well, what do you do on your walks?"

"I just walk."

"You just walk without looking at anything."

"I look at the buildings, of course. I always liked doing that ever since I can remember. I guess it's because my father used to be an architect. That was before the war. Before the Communists made a mailman out of him. You probably know why. He refused to join the Party, that's why. My father didn't whine. He didn't mind. He was even closer to his beloved buildings."

"There you go! Why don't you do something with architecture."

"I'd have to go to a university."

"So? Study hard and you'll get there."

If something like that could be true, if study and hard work could actually get you places, then it would be all worth it. "Sounds too good to be true," I said. "I guess I'm not used to freedom yet."

"Who is?"

Once we got to my aunt's apartment, I gave Sister Ágnes a pair of my father's trousers, a couple of shirts, a turtleneck sweater and a pair of pajamas.

The following day I was out again, this time in a winter coat. I got tired of listening to the drone of the radio about how the United Nations and the Western democracies were stalling. The "Hungarian Agenda" was shelved for another week.

I told my aunt and Kriszti that I was going to visit Sewer Rat at the Üllői Avenue clinic.

I took a roundabout way, so I could check on some of my favorite buildings, to see if they were all right. The temperature had dropped several notches. My nose and ears were feeling it. I headed straight for Lenin Boulevard to see how the beautiful New York Café building fared.

Large snowflakes swirled in front of me. A white mantle started to form on ruined tanks, rubble mounds and chunks of armor. I couldn't tell whether the frozen corpses near the tanks were covered with snow or lime.

The weather suddenly got brutally cold. I had to walk the twenty-some blocks without a hat and gloves.

My heart sank when I saw workers cleaning up the rubble on Lenin Boulevard. Right in front of the New York Café. A Russian tank had rammed one of the most ornate buildings in all of Budapest. The T-34 tank was still there, out of commission, covered in rubble and snow. It was so modern, although it was built at the turn of the century. The architects added these neat geometric details to every square meter of wall, even the spire, a spectacular mix of Art Nouveau and some other style I no longer remember. I couldn't help but to think about the work, the craftsmanship that had gone into carving out those intricate designs from stone.

What I was looking at was a severely damaged work of art. First the bullet-riddled University Church with its rose window blown out, now this.

I was angry. Those bastards sure knew where to hurt us. This coffee house had been a meeting place for writers and artists since the early 1900's. My father told me once that some of our best poets and novelists started their morning here with a cup of coffee and spent the day writing until it was time to go. The place was a shrine for intellectuals.

The New York Café came up once during one of my discussions with Michelangelo at the Corvin Theater. Sewer Rat was there, too. I recall asking Michelangelo what it was like on the inside.

"Oh, I've never been inside," he had said. "Too pricey for me. I prefer to work at home."

As a tease, Sewer Rat had suggested that Michelangelo do his sketches there. "I mean, how much can a cup of coffee cost, man?"

"Thanks for calling me cheap! It's not that. I just don't care for the company. A bunch of Communists plying their propaganda art. I understand poets get paid by the line now. So you get these poems that look like vertical poles. One-word and two-word lines. Great art! No thanks!"

Poor Michelangelo would never see the inside of it now. I probably won't either. Restore something like this? Never!

By the time I got to the clinic, it stopped snowing, but the wind kept at it, blowing fine powder across the sidewalk.

As I walked through the door, two men were carrying someone in a blanket. The underside of the blanket dripped with blood. Like the last time, the clinic was filled to capacity with the wounded. Many were lying on stretchers or on the stone tiles. Some were covered with a sheet.

I spotted Pali Szilágyi and had to step over a dead body to get to him. He said Sewer Rat still had a fever. One of the bullets didn't go clean through like they thought. It was lodged in a rib and got infected. He was getting antibiotics through a vein. If he didn't respond, they might have to operate. "He's been slipping in and out consciousness for the last two hours. Sister Ágnes is with him."

I asked him if I could go up and see him. Pali took me through a long corridor of the wounded. They were lying on gurneys or stretchers, their heavy bandages smudged with rust-colored blood.

Sewer Rat lay motionless on a gurney. A tube ran into his arm. He didn't know we were there. But when Sister Ágnes pressed his hand, his eyelids fluttered. That was the only response. Dr. Leocky, who saw him earlier, told Sister Ágnes it was a good sign.

I said hello to Sewer Rat. Sister Ágnes encouraged me to touch his hand. I did. No fluttering of the eyelids this time. Sister Ágnes touched him again. Sewer Rat's eyelids responded.

"Maybe it's just with you," I said to Sister Ágnes.

"Maybe."

We heard the sound of boots behind us. I turned around. Mustache came directly toward Sewer Rat's bed. He took a good look at Sewer Rat, then asked Sister Ágnes how he was doing.

"He could be better," she said with a sigh. "If only he wouldn't be such a stubborn mule, the doctors could've given him antibiotics right away. He's going to need surgery. He had to play the tough guy and refuse a bed. He said others needed a bed more than he did."

"Sounds like him," Mustache said. "I hate to sound selfish, but we may need him. He's a damned good soldier."

Then Mustache dropped a bomb. He said Major General Maléter hadn't returned from his meeting with the Soviet High Command. A rumor floated around that Maléter had been arrested. That he walked into a trap. "Anyway," Mustache said, "we lost all contact with him. In the meantime, we're getting reports of Soviet troop movements across the Soviet-Hungarian frontier. Russian military trains have been spotted in the border town of Záhony. Although they're sketchy, some of the reports say that as many as 5,000 tanks are advancing toward Budapest from the east and the south. The Russians are planning an all-out assault."

"Lord God," Sister Ágnes said. She shut her eyes and put a hand to her forehead.

Mustache said he hoped it wasn't going to happen. It was difficult to separate fact from speculation. One rumor had it that the Americans were moving an entire tank battalion from West Germany to the Hungarian border.

"Oh, my God! It's going to be World War III!" Sister Ágnes said.

It may come to that, Mustache said. "Right now it may look like a waiting game, but we can't afford to wait. We need every available fighter to prepare for the Russian attack. The last thing we need is the element of surprise. If Stalingrad could make a stand till reinforcements arrived, we can make a stand. But we need to be ready. Every building needs to be ready."

"What should we do?" I asked.

He said the best thing we could do is to make sure we have enough ammunition, water and food. "If," he said, "and it's a pretty big *if.* If we fight them building by building, street by street, like they did in Stalingrad, we have a chance. Not much of one but a chance. We have an advantage. This is our home. We know every nook and cranny of our city. We need to arm as many civilians as we can. If we had enough weapons, every building in the city could be a fortress."

"What should *I* do?" I asked.

Mustache looked at me with those warm, brown eyes of his. "If I were really selfish, I would ask you to stay. To make a last stand to the last drop of blood. But I can't do that. This is no longer a battle. This is war. It's not for kids. I feel bad enough about the kids I lost. I'm not about to have the last one of them become cannon fodder. Listen to me a second. Can you listen? The borders are open. Right now they're open. Who knows about the next day or the day after that. The best thing you can do for yourself right now is to leave the country. Who knows, you may run into the Americans."

"Leave Hungary? Leave my country? I have a sick sister and a frail aunt to think of. I have already lost so many here. Why should my life be any more important than theirs?" I was almost on the verge of tears.

Sister Ágnes said: "Do it for your sister, Cheetah. So she can live."

"How?" I asked. "How do I get over to the border?"

"We'll help you," Mustache said. "Sister Ágnes has the truck. You can leave tomorrow. I'll send an armed escort along."

Suddenly, I was in a daze. I didn't know what to think or do.

"You need to prepare tonight," Mustache said. "Dress warm."

"And if I decide not to go?"

"Then you should stay in a shelter. Your building's basement or cellar. Take your family down there with enough food and water for a week. Don't come out till all the shooting is over."

"And make sure you have enough medicine for your sister and your aunt," Sister Ágnes said.

"We were just celebrating yesterday," I said.

None of this was making any sense. But, then, what did? Michelangelo just died. I suddenly realized I might not see Sewer Rat again. I ran my hand by his unshaven cheek and said goodbye.

I tried saying goodbye to Mustache, but he wouldn't let me. "I'll see you yet," he said.

Sister Ágnes took me down to the kitchen and packed bread and a big slab of salt pork. She told us to fill up every available container with water and take it down to the cellar. But, most important, make sure we had plenty of blankets and warm clothes so we didn't freeze. And if I changed my mind and decided to escape with my aunt and sister, she and her truck would be in front of my aunt's apartment at exactly midnight tomorrow. "Dr. Leocky starts her shift at 11:30 p.m.," Sister Ágnes said.

She disappeared to find Dr. Leocky to get some more heart medicine for Krisztina and sedatives for my aunt. When she couldn't find her, she handed me the bag of food and told me to go ahead. She'd take the medicine over around midnight, if not today, then tomorrow.

"Looks like the wake for Michelangelo is postponed for the time being," I said

"Maybe not. We'll just have to wait and see."

On the way home, I gave up the idea of checking on my most favorite building of all. Although it was close by, I just didn't have it in me to go to the Museum of Applied Arts building. I wanted to remember it the way it was. Bright green and yellow, with the fantasy copula reaching high into a blue sky.

I trudged home the rest of the way, carrying the heavy bag Sister Ágnes gave me. I felt more lonely than I have in a long time. But instead of feeling sorry for myself, I worked myself up into a rage. Why should we let our enemies kill our people and destroy our city? What was more barbaric than killing innocent civilians and attacking things closest to our hearts? Were they trying to break our spirit, too? It was not going to happen. I was determined more than ever to make a stand. I had to stay and defend my city against the Russian offensive, and if and when it comes, I had to be ready.

My steps speeded up, and I no longer felt the stinging cold. In no time at all, I found myself standing in front of our elevator. The red elevator light was on. The elevator in our building was working.

As I turned the key to our apartment, I heard voices inside.

I was shocked that Guszti came to the door. Guszti said they had come up from Balástya only to find they had been burnt out of their apartment. It was close to the Corvin Theater.

His mother and brother were in the kitchen with my aunt.

Guszti's mother was a thin woman with thick hair like her sons. Her skin was a little yellow and she had brown bags under her eyes. She cried her way through a list of things they had lost.

I let them know about Sewer Rat's place.

"It's terrible what they've done to the city. Where will all the people go whose homes were destroyed? The street? I just got out of the hospital. I don't need this. I don't know what we'll do."

My aunt said they could stay with us till they find something. "We have plenty of room. And running water. You and the boys will be fine here."

Guszti's mother nodded and said thank you in a tiny voice. "Just for a while." Then she started crying again. My aunt gave her a handkerchief.

"Everything we ever had was in that apartment."

"They're just things," my aunt said. "The main thing is you have your boys."

Guszti's mother hugged her sons.

"How did you get up here? The trains must be running," I said.

"No, they're not. A friend of a friend drove us up from Balástya."

"You should've seen the car," Guszti's little brother said. "A brand new Pobeda."

I thought for a moment, then said, "Was it light brown?"

"How did you know?"

"Just a guess."

My aunt pointed to all the food on the table and said the Pálrétis brought all this from Balástya.

Guszti's mother said her brother-in-law, Imre Pálréti, sent these provisions to thank us for bringing him home.

On the kitchen table lay a large baked goose wrapped in newspapers, two sticks of salami, and the largest jar of homemade plum jelly I have ever seen. She also brought a bottle of *pálinka*. It was already opened. What I brought from the clinic were meager rations in comparison.

I had to tell them what I heard from our Commander. That the Russians were planning to attack the city.

"You're telling me," Guszti's mother said. "We saw nothing but tanks on the National Highway. And they're coming this way. What are we going to do?"

My aunt was nervous. She was out of sedatives and she was out of cigarettes. "What can we do?" she said. "We'll do what we did in

1945. Sit on our rumps in the cellar and wait. There's nothing else to do." She took a sip from her espresso cup. Something told me it wasn't filled with coffee.

Guszti's mother wiped her eyes and told us to sit down and eat.

I noticed that Guszti's mother still cut up the food for these big kids. Couldn't they do it for themselves? Was she going to feed them, too? God Almighty!

I wasn't very hungry and forced myself to chew on a piece of bread and plum jam. I was happy about all the extra provisions, but sorry Guszti came with them.

"If the Russians plan to attack the city, they will attack at dawn." Guszti announced.

There he goes again, I thought. Guszti's know-it-all antics started to grate on my nerves, but I kept my mouth shut. My aunt said, "How do you know that? I don't think it's something they're going to pin on our noses, you can bet on that."

"They usually attack at dawn," Guszti said.

I ignored him. I thought we should start to make preparations. Like right now. "Then we better get ready. We don't want to get caught off guard," I said. "Guszti and me will get the cellar ready. Sister Ágnes will be by later tonight with medicine for Krisztina. Where is she?" I asked.

"She got a little tired and she's lying down," my aunt said.

"Sister Ágnes has some medicine for you, too, so you can sleep."

"God bless that woman," my aunt said.

After complaining about having to do woman's work, Guszti grudgingly gave me a hand. We carried half the kitchen down to the cellar, including all those bottles of soda and beer Sister Ágnes had brought over.

We filled every empty bottle and jar with water and took it down. It seemed to take forever, then I got an idea. Why not fill up a wine barrel with water?

Guszti was upset that he hadn't thought of it at first, because he just glared at me and said, "You should've thought of that sooner. We could've saved a lot of time. Girls. They don't think!"

"If you're so smart why didn't you think of it?" The more I tried to be nice, the more he rubbed me the wrong way "I'm really glad you and your mother brought all that food, but it's not going to be enough to feed *all* of us." It meant, go home, big baby." If the stores closed anytime soon, we'll starve."

He didn't say anything.

"Let's go over to Michelangelo's," I said.

When we opened Michelangelo's pantry, boy, were we surprised. He had enough stuff in there for an army. Everything from potatoes to peach preserves. Ham, salt pork and sticks of smoked sausage hung from the rafters. I had no idea how he had managed to squirrel away so much stuff, but I was glad he had.

We took all of it, including his bedding and some felt army blankets, which we could put to use right away for Guszti's brother and mother.

We found some kerosene and a lamp, which would come in handy in the cellar. It was always good to have a back up. I already had Sewer Rat's flashlight.

Guszti said nothing about all the paintings. Instead, he wanted to talk strategy.

Strategy, huh? I asked him how he planned to fight tanks.

"Grenades or *panzerfaust*."

"What's that German word?"

"You don't know, do you?"

"Look, I don't care what it means. We don't have grenades and we don't have whatever that other thing is. What we have are bottles. All we need now is gasoline. To make a Molotov cocktail. Do you know what a Molotov cocktail is?"

He rolled his eyes.

"Okay, I'll show you."

First we needed an empty bottle. We quickly drank a liter of orange soda. I filled the empty bottle with kerosene to about three quarters, then I stuffed it with a rag from Michelangelo's kitchen counter, leaving a long fuse. I corked it and presented it to Guszti. "Best served when hot," I added. "The only problem is kerosene won't explode like gasoline. We need gasoline."

Guszti thought for a minute, then said he had it: "I know where we can get our hands on some gasoline. I'd seen a bunch of motorcycles parked in the courtyard. What if we siphon out the gas? We could do it with the rubber hose by the wine barrels. It looks long enough."

"Finally," I said, "a brilliant idea."

We spent the next hour sneaking around, stealing gas. I unscrewed the gas caps, and Guszti sucked on the hose till the gasoline tinkled into the bottles.

We ended up preparing no less then fifteen Molotov cocktails following the Russian recipe.

I looked at all of Michelangelo's pots and pans, and added: "I've got a brilliant idea of my own. Mines!"

We took the pots and pans out by the armfuls and placed them face down on the snow-covered street. In the dark, the Russian would mistake them for tank mines. We heard Guszti's mother calling from an upstairs window. My first thought was that maybe she saw us siphoning gas in the courtyard. "Find out what she wants," I said to Guszti. "If she says anything, tell her we need the gas for the kerosene lamps. I'll be up in a bit."

Guszti raced upstairs.

I had barely closed Michelangelo's door behind me when I heard the sound of a truck pull up in front of our gate. Sister Ágnes? Here so early?

I went out front. The truck's headlights lit up the swirling snow. She turned off the engine and it was pitch black again.

I went around the driver's side to get the medicine. I figured she wanted to get back to Sewer Rat as quickly as possible. But she opened the door and jumped down. "I have a delivery for you," she said. "Compliments of our esteemed Commander. Oh, here, before I forget it." She handed to me two packets of medicine. One thing I liked about Sister Ágnes was that she treated me like an equal.

She said the doctors took out the bullet from Sewer Rat's rib and sewed him up. His fever dropped. He's wide awake now and raring to go. Dr. Leocky told him he was out of his mind.

We went to the rear of the truck. Sister Ágnes looked around the street before undoing the latch to the tailgate. What I saw next was something else. I was looking into the funnel-like barrel of the machine gun I saw at Mustache's, dipod and all. It had a circular magazine, a kind of pan on top of the barrel. Sister Ágnes said, "Ready?"

We lifted the heavy gun off the truck and rushed it inside the gate. The elevator stood in front of us. The stairs spiraled down to the cellar. The first apartment on the left was Michelangelo's. Without giving it a second thought, we took the gun into Michelangelo's apartment where I was given a crash course on how to work it.

We rolled down the window shutters and set up the gun so it faced the window. Sister Ágnes said it was called a Degtyarev. The

Soviet-made machine gun could fire 500 rounds per minute. The pan held only 47 rounds, which meant I had to reload a lot. The good news was the Degtyarev seldom overheated. She showed me how the dipod extended. I told her she sounded like she invented the gun herself. She said, "Don't let me fool you. I'm just a novice." When I didn't laugh, she said, "It was a joke. You know, *novice*, like in nun? Nevermind."

We went back to the truck for three heavy boxes of ammunition.

She said Michelangelo himself painted the Hungarian coat of arms on the magazine. Maybe it will bring me good luck. In case I decided to stick around for the battle of all battles.

We moved Michelangelo's paintings as far as possible away from the window.

I told Sister Ágnes our cellar was ready. That it even passed my aunt's inspection. She spent weeks down there during the war, I said.

"But are *you* ready?"

"Guszti's mother and brother are here. They came today. With their building gone, they have nowhere else to stay."

"Does Guszti know how to shoot a gun?"

"I guess I'll find out. I showed him a few things, but it wasn't exactly target practice. We made a few Molotov cocktails and fake mines, but who knows?"

"Let's hope it won't get to that. Listen, Cheetah, I'll be here tomorrow around midnight with enough gas to get you and your family to the border. Just in case." She gave me a hug and said she had to get back to the clinic.

Upstairs, I handed the medicine over to my aunt. She asked me how I was doing. I said, "Everything is almost ready."

"Not the preparations, I meant you. Come here, dear," she said, and gave me a kiss.

Everybody went to bed early. I gave my couch to Guszti's mother. Me, Guszti and Guszti's brother, Péter, slept on the floor. I wondered if Guszti would be able to fall asleep. If he missed the sound of the crickets in Balástya. As usual, I couldn't sleep. I kept thinking about the Russians. Would they really attack? Maybe the reports were inaccurate. 5,000 tanks? If they did attack, how long could we hold out? Were there American forces lining up along the border or was that just another rumor? There was nothing to do but to wait and see.

As I told my aunt, we were as ready as we could be. Then I thought about the open border. Starting a new life. Starting all over in a foreign country. How? My aunt had no money to speak of. The only language we spoke was Hungarian. What in the world would we do if we didn't speak the language? How would we get by? My aunt was old. She could still sew, but I couldn't expect her to hold down a regular job? What could I do? I was just a kid. No schooling, no skills, nothing. And my little sister was sick. Where would we go for help if she got very sick?

It was insane. You couldn't just pick up and leave. We had a furnished apartment here. My school was here. What was left of my life was here.

What were the Pálrétis going to do, now that they had no place to live? Go back to Balástya? Please, God, help us get through this, I kept praying till I fell asleep.

I slept with my clothes on, maybe an hour at the most.

Chapter
Nine

9

I woke up to the sound of heavy cannons. Our building shook. The Russians were shelling the city. Each explosion felt like an earthquake.

I scrambled out of bed. Everybody else was getting up. My aunt rushed into the living room. She still had her night cream on her face. Krisztina was right behind her.

"My God," my aunt said. "1945 all over again. It can't be."

I turned on the light so I could find my tennis shoes.

"Turn it off," my aunt ordered. "We have to keep the lights off. Everybody! Down into the cellar! She went into the kitchen and was back with a kerosene lamp. Cheetah, unplug the radio and bring it down with you."

Another explosion rocked our building. This one was closer than the last. "Hurry up, let's go," my aunt said.

No one dawdled. Guszti and his brother grabbed some cushions off the couch to bring them down. My aunt had her bedding and the medicines. I helped bundle up Krisztina. In under five minutes, we were out the door.

The kerosene lamp threw jittery shadows on the wall as we hurried down the steps to the cellar. It was musty and cold and smelled of coal and the sewer, but it was safe.

I locked the heavy cast-iron door behind us.

We tried to get as comfortable as possible. I should've gotten the cushions from Michelangelo's couch. Maybe when there's a lull in the shelling, because for now, the Russian cannons were pouring it on.

We plugged an extension cord from an outlet in the ceiling, the same fixture for the light bulb and ran it down the cellar. My aunt plugged the radio into the extension cord and set it down in front of her. Who knew how long we'd have electricity? The radio was our only connection to what went on in the city. She couldn't find the station and gave up. The dial must've moved when we brought it down. All we heard was a bunch of static. She fooled with the dials again but had no luck. "With our luck, the Russians knocked the radio off the air?" she said.

"Let Guszti try," I said.

"Be my guest," she said.

Krisztina was coughing again. I thought she could be sensitive to the dust and the mold in the cellar. Péter was trying to keep her busy by taking turns drawing on a sketch pad I had brought down from Michelangelo's place.

Guszti couldn't get anything either other than a faint garbled voice. We weren't sure what the language was. To me it sounded Russian. Guszti tried moving the position of the radio to see if he could get a better reception. Finally, he moved it to the top of one of the barrels. The sound was loud and clear now, and in Hungarian.

The announcer on Kossuth Radio Budapest sounded urgent:

"Attention! Attention! Premier Imre Nagy will address the Hungarian people:

This is Imre Nagy speaking. Today at daybreak Soviet troops attacked our capital with the obvious intent of overthrowing the legal democratic Hungarian government. Our troops are in combat. The government is at its post. I notify the people of our country and the entire world of this fact."

The announcement was repeated in English, Russian, Hungarian, and French.

The shelling intensified, joined by the rattle of machine gun fire.

"God Almighty!" Guszti's mother said. "How long will this go on?"

"God knows," my aunt said.

Guszti's mother asked my aunt if she had an extra sedative. She said she was so nervous, her heart was in her throat.

My aunt gave her one of her pills. She said during the siege, the 51-day siege of Budapest in 1945, the Russians broke into the building looking for Germans who were out of ammunition and hiding out in the ground-floor apartments. "The Russians killed so many, they had to stack the bodies in the elevator shaft. Imagine! Frozen corpses piled up to the second floor."

"Did you lose your husband to the war?" Guszti's mother asked.

My aunt nodded.

"Mine died somewhere in Russia. I hate war. God, how I hate war. So many women were raped. They didn't care about age. They didn't care about anything. They'd just say, "*Davay!* Hurry, take off your clothes. Oh, it was awful."

Three hours had gone by and the Russian artillery was still at it. What were they trying to do? Level the city to rubble? Then we heard the drone of bombers overhead, a terrible whistling sound then an ear-piercing explosion.

One explosion caused dust to sift through the ceiling. Krisztina had an immediate coughing fit, a reaction to the dust. I didn't think she would be able to stay down here without getting sick. She was already wheezing.

I had to do something. After a while I felt so restless, I could almost scream. Suddenly, I was aware of silence. Then the heavy cannons would start up again.

It went on like this the whole day. During a lull, I heard the familiar sound of tanks rumbling down the street. The sporadic gunfire was now constant. I thought I heard shouts. In Russian.

I asked my aunt if the gate was locked. What if the gate wasn't locked?

My aunt shot me a frightened look.

"I better make sure it's locked," I said. I motioned to Guszti to come with me.

I told my aunt to lock the door behind us.

"Why?" my aunt said.

"We have to defend the building," I answered.

Before my aunt and Guszti's mother could figure out what that meant, we were out the door, running up the stairs.

I had known all along that the gate was locked. I just had to get out of the cellar to see what all the shooting was about.

We went straight to Michelangelo's apartment. Guszti was stunned by the sight of the Degtyarev by the window.

"Where did you get this?"

"Sister Ágnes brought it over last night. The Commander wanted me to have it."

"Why did he give it to you?"

"I don't know. Maybe he likes me."

"Who doesn't like you?"

I rolled up the blinds. Amazingly, a gun battle was unfolding in the snow right in front of our eyes. Three Russian soldiers were running and firing into a doorway under a hail of bullets from the building across the street.

"*They* don't like me," I said and pointed to the Russians. "I don't think they like you either."

I finally got a laugh out of him.

A Soviet tank at the end of the street was angling its barrel at a window with a sniper. Its cannon fired. The shell exploded in a smoking flash on the side of the building, leaving behind a crater.

It was time to get to work. We opened the window and lined up the gun. Guszti wanted to work the Degtyarev, while I "fed" him.

"I'm not your mother," I said. "No one's going to feed anybody. You've seen too many films. Can't you see the magazine here on top? You're better off with my submachine gun for now."

He took my submachine and pretended he knew what he was doing.

I loaded the Degtyarev as Guszti watched me. I could tell he was nervous, but he held the submachine gun at the ready. I positioned the dipod and swiveled the machine gun into position.

"How fast can this thing fire?"

"500 rounds a minute." I took aim and pulled the trigger. Two of the three Russians went down, splattering blood on the snow. The third soldier spotted us and returned fire.

Guszti gave off a burst from his submachine gun. The Russian dove for cover.

The tank came forward.

Once it was within range, I waited till the last possible second before I opened up with this monster of a gun. I must've emptied the entire magazine. I hit the fuel tank or something, because after a loud blast, flames shot in the air. The tank was burning. Only one man made it out of the hatch. I glanced at Guszti. He pulled the trigger without hesitation. A long burst riddled the man with bullets.

I looked at Guszti's face, trying to gauge what he was feeling. No reaction. There was no time to feel or to think. If we stopped to feel, we would break down. If we stopped to think, we would be paralyzed. And if that happened, we would be killed. Everything was happening too fast. All we knew is that we had to stay with it. We had to stay the course. There was no time to talk. We spoke to each other in snippets.

"Got him."

"Good."

We noticed the long barrel of another tank lurking around the corner. I didn't know if they saw us or not, but I didn't want to take a chance. Once they got wise to our position, we wouldn't last long. We had to keep them guessing. "Quick," I said to Guszti. "Upstairs! We'll hit them from there."

We left just in time. A volley ripped into the roll-up blinds. We hit the floor and crawled on our bellies, dragging the Degtyarev and a box of ammo with us. From the inner courtyard, we hustled into the elevator. I punched the button for our floor and in two minutes we had the gun in the apartment.

We pried off the boards from the window. I reloaded the pan and set up the Degtyarev. We had a good shot at the Russian who worked the machine gun from the turret. This time Guszti wanted to try it. We changed places. He pulled the trigger and unleashed a burst.

He took out the gunner along with a stone statue of Atlas holding up a doorway. Two Russian soldiers raced out of the doorway, one bleeding by the shoulder.

My submachine gun kept them pinned down in the snow.

Another tank swiveled around the corner and opened fire on the building across the street. Hungarian snipers were firing at them from the rooftop. A shell exploded between the top floor and the roof. A large portion of the roof and debris rained onto the sidewalk.

Thick smoke fanned by flames billowed out of the windows. Soon, what was left of the snow-covered roof was engulfed in flames.

The building's top floors were burning fast and furious. There were no sirens. No fire trucks. Only shrieks and the rattle of gunfire.

More Russian infantry poured into the street, taking cover behind the tank and scurrying into doorways.

Guszti and I looked at each other. Our eyes met, and, in that instant, we knew we couldn't hold out much longer.

Gritting his teeth, Guszti aimed his weapon and fired off a salvo at the unsuspecting Russians. Bullets glanced off the tank's armor. The machine gunner returned fire and shattered the windows overhead.

I reloaded the pan of the Degytarev and fired off several rounds at the Russian gunner. The gunner slipped back into his turret and closed the hatch.

I told Guszti to take over the Degytarev. I was going down to Michelangelo's and surprise them in the darkness.

The plan worked. I took out two soldiers in a doorway. They had been firing directly into our apartment in an effort to silence Guszti's gun.

The tank advanced toward me.

I reached for a Molotov cocktail, one of many Guszti and I prepared the night before. We had enough cocktails for a real big party.

I served it hot by heaving the flaming bottle at the armor. It sailed through the air like a comet. But then it fizzled.

Guszti kept firing upstairs.

A blinding flash. Then a hot gust of wind blew through the window. I was hurled back by the blast. When I recovered myself, I saw that Guszti must've ignited the gasoline. The whole side of the tank including the wheels were on fire.

What followed was an intense bright light. Suddenly it looked like a night game at the People's Stadium. Except this wasn't a game. I quickly realized the Russians had fired a flare. Probably from the Soviet armored car around the corner.

The armored car saw me and opened fire. I hit the floor. I heard the screeching of tires. I got up and looked out. The armored car hadn't moved. It was now shooting in another direction.

I looked to the right. An army truck bristling with Hungarian freedom fighters arrived on the scene. They bounded off the truck, keeping their heads low, trying to find cover along the walls.

In the afterglow of the flare, I made out Peg Leg and his famous cannon. He didn't waste any time. A single shell from the 84mm cannon blew the armored car off the street. All I could see were fiery fragments left in its wake.

The shoot out between the Russian troops and the freedom fighters was intense.

I heard Guszti's Degtyarev rattling upstairs at a good clip. I got back into the action with my submachine gun.

The street had become jammed with burning vehicles. Now, a Soviet T-34 entered the fray at high rate of speed. It sideswiped what was left of their armored car as it headed straight for Peg Leg and his cannon.

I managed to lob a gasoline bomb in front of the speeding caterpillar treads. The explosion rocked the tank and caused its tread to snap off in a blast of smoke, but the momentum was enough to crush Peg Leg under its cast-iron wheels

I tossed another bomb.

This time the turret burst into flames and spewed thick oily smoke into the sky. As the Russian crew clambered out, they were met by a barrage of fire.

Five or six Russian soldiers raced from the burning building to our side of the street. They went from doorway to doorway and were closing in on us.

Another Hungarian truck rolled in, this one with a canvas cover. It stopped right by our doorway. Sister Ágnes and Sewer Rat jumped out with high-powered guns. The Russians fired at them.

I ran like crazy to unlock the gate.

They rushed in. There was no time for words. They planted themselves by Michelangelo's window, taking aim and firing at the Russians before they got into our building.

The high-powered rifles found their mark. The Russians were dropping, one after another. But we had to keep hitting the floor and crawling away from the window. Michelangelo's ceiling was riddled with bullets. One hit his light fixture which exploded on impact, spraying glass all over the place. Then we heard a blast, like a hand grenade. Guszti let out a blood-curdling scream upstairs.

I raced up to the apartment. Guszti's hand and face were covered in blood. He was trying to get the Degtyarev to work. I pulled him away from the window and looked at him. The blood on his face was just splatter.

I looked at his hand. A fragment had torn into the web between his thumb and forefinger. The finger was raw and mangled like he had stuck it into a meat grinder. The Degtyarev took a hit, he mumbled. I wrapped up his hand and took him downstairs. Sister Ágnes and Sewer Rat stood by the window looking for targets. For a moment, the Russian guns were silenced. We were gaining the upper hand, and, for now, took control of Sándor Bródy Street.

I told them Guszti got hit in the hand. Sister Ágnes looked him over. Then her eyes went to Sewer Rat. Something was wrong with

Sewer Rat. He was white as Michelangelo's walls, and he had trouble standing up. "Open your coat," she ordered.

Sewer Rat unbuttoned his coat. A blood stain covered his entire belly and more. Sister Ágnes opened his shirt. "You broke the stitches, you idiot."

She leaned out the window and yelled for Pali Szilágyi. "He's out there somewhere," she said. "I just saw him a moment ago. He's wearing a white-band around his head. He and someone else were rushing a man on a stretcher to a waiting truck. There he is! Pali! In here!"

Pali and Attila, Dr. Leocky's husband, charged into the apartment with a stretcher.

Pali checked Sewer Rat. When Sewer Rat removed his hand from his wound, blood gushed out. "You're going to need a another sewing job, my friend," Pali said.

In the meantime, Attila stitched and wrapped up Guszti's hand. He said it should heal on its own. The good news was that he'd have a nice scar to show the girls.

Sewer Rat was breaking out in a cold sweat.

Pali said, "We have to take him to the clinic. We have to take him now."

Sewer Rat resisted. Sister Ágnes cussed at him. That was the only way to calm him down, she said.

I said goodbye to Sewer Rat. We kissed each other, one kiss on each cheek. Then we hugged. I told him I was going to miss him.

Pali and Attila placed Sewer Rat on the stretcher, just as the Russians started up their artillery barrage again. The building shook.

"You people better get out of here," Sewer Rat said. "I don't want to be the only one left alive."

Sister Ágnes kissed him and called him an idiot. After the stretcher left with Sewer Rat, Sister Ágnes turned to me and said, "He's right, you know. Get your things. We haven't got much time. No matter what you decide, you have to get out of here."

I made my decision. Right then. Right on the spot where I was standing. "I made my choice," I told Sister Ágnes. "I want my sister to live. And I want her to live as a free woman. Take us to the border!"

"Get everyone ready! Hurry!"

We headed straight for the cellar. The light bulb had gone out.

My aunt, and everybody else, was wild-eyed when they saw us and our weapons in the flickering light of the kerosene lamp. Guszti had a submachine gun around his shoulder.

His mother said, "Guszti, your hand!"

"It's nothing," Guszti said.

"What do you mean it's nothing? Let me see it."

"There's nothing to see," Guszti said. "I told you it was nothing."

Guszti's mother knitted her eyebrows and looked at my aunt, who said, "What happened?"

Guszti said, "We put up a good fight. Cheetah showed me how."

Sister Ágnes came through the door. She said we were running out of time. I told everybody to put on some warm clothes, an extra sweater, winter coats, gloves. We were not going to take anything.

"What?!" my aunt demanded.

"We're leaving," I said. "Now! The building won't make it through the night. The one across the street is burning down. We're going to be pulverized if we stay."

Sister Ágnes said Cardinal Mindszenty escaped to the American Embassy. There was no time to waste. We had to leave the country if life meant anything to us.

The radio was on full blast with the same pleading message:

"Help Hungary! Help the Hungarian people!
We cannot hold on any longer!
They are shooting at the radio!
Help! Help! Help!
SOS! SOS! SOS!"

Then silence. That was the last transmission of Free Radio Budapest.

I made sure my aunt had her cane and the medicine. My aunt cried that she had no money. I helped Krisztina get dressed as I talked. I told my aunt that Hungarian money won't mean anything where we were going.

"What does that mean?"

"I'll tell you on the truck, Auntie. All I know is that we have to get out of here."

"What about the Pálrétis?"

"They're coming with us."

"What about my sewing machine? And my China?"

A large explosion rocked the building. The kerosene lamp fell over and started a small fire on top of the barrel. I doused the flames and stood the lamp upright.

The closeness of the explosion was enough to convince my aunt that we had to get out immediately.

With everyone bundled up, we shuffled up to the ground floor. That's when I noticed that Michelangelo's door was blown wide open by the blast we heard down in the cellar. His paintings lay hel-ter-skelter in the courtyard. The closest one to me was partially burned and shredded. I couldn't recognize it. I gave it a parting glance when Sister Ágnes tugged on my arm. "We have to go," she said. "There's no time."

We were whisked through the gate to the waiting truck, its engine running. The air was filled with smoke from the fire across the street which was still raging. The pavement was covered with the bodies of the dead. I glanced back at our doorway to see if old Medusa was still there. The stucco had been blown off around her, but she was still there in all her glory and coiling snakes.

Krisztina, my aunt and Guszti's mother were helped onto the truck by the freedom fighters. One by one, we all piled in. Sister Ágnes jumped behind the wheel with one of the soldiers, the other two stayed in the back with us.

Sister Ágnes put the truck in gear and floored it. We hung on to the rope running along the side panels to keep from being bounced around. The truck jerked us around like an amusement park ride, but no one was squealing with delight. We had no idea which route Sister Ágnes was taking. All we knew was that she was doing her utmost to get us the hell out of a war zone.

I saw nothing in the dark of the truck, but heard plenty. Russian heavy artillery sounded even closer as we headed out of the city they surrounded. Another half an hour of breakneck speeds, gun fire, and wild careening each time we heard a mortar land close to us.

Finally, the heavy Russian guns sounded more like distant thunder, and the road evened out, but Sister Ágnes was not about to slow down. While the going was good, she kept the accelerator close to the floor.

The pace slowed once we got on uneven country roads. We were quiet most of the way, I guess out of sheer terror. My aunt got nauseous and had to vomit into a hole in the floorboards. Krisztina had to pee, and as she squatted over the hole, I draped my long winter coat around her like a tent.

My aunt was the first one to speak. "Where are we going?" she asked me.

"Austria," I said. "And then, maybe America."

"I see," my aunt said. "Just like that."

"It's over. I want you and Krisztina to be free. She can have an operation in America. I have the doctor's address. At least she'll have a chance at life. What waits for us here? Death? Destruction? Torture? Dungeons?"

Sister Ágnes spoke up from the cabin: "The Russians may not know who Cheetah is, but the ÁVO won't forget. And they'll be back in power. And with a vengeance. Any persons taking part in the Revolution will be arrested."

"Even if they don't catch up with us," I said, "we have no future here. Guszti's an excellent student and Péter has great promise as a poet, but they'll never have a chance to go to a university, because of their uncle's anticommunist activities. All you have to be is a relative of a political prisoner and you're blackballed for life. Let's face it. There is nothing left for us here. Guszti's apartment has been leveled, ours will be, too, before morning, no matter how many Hungarian lives are lost to save it. There are 5,000 Soviet tanks in Budapest. If we destroy them all, they'll send 10,000 more. Don't you see? There is no way we can win. As far as we know, the borders in western Hungary are still open. Which means we can cross over to freedom and start a new life."

"What about the Americans? Radio Free Europe—" my aunt said.

"They lied to us. Nobody's coming," I said.

My aunt chewed on that for a while. Then she said, "But I'm so old, darling."

"All the more reason for you to live the rest of your days as a free person. No matter how many years God has given you."

"What about money? Have you thought about that?"

"The Red Cross will help us. After that we'll go to work and we'll go to school."

"Doing what?"

"Whatever it takes," I said.

"I see. What does Guszti's mother think about all this?"

"I'm still in shock," Guszti's mother said. "That we live in a country where children have to do our fighting. Something is wrong here. Something is very wrong, when young people are ready to die so easily."

It was quiet for a long time. What Guszti's mother said had sunk in.

My aunt broke the silence again: "Does anyone have a cigarette on this godforsaken truck?" She meant the soldiers, of course.

One of them said, no smoking on the truck. Smoke could give us away. We were carrying human cargo. Sorry.

After what must've been an hour of agonizing silence, the truck came to a stop. We heard the cabin door open and close, then, footsteps crunching in the snow.

Sister Ágnes unfastened the canvas at the rear. She told us we were at a safe house. It was all right to get down.

We filed into a modest peasant house in the middle of nowhere. Apparently, Mustache knew the people here. An old man and his wife received us. The woman brought out some *pogácsa*, ham and a bottle of *pálinka*. The soldier who did not let my aunt smoke offered her a cigarette. She nodded gratefully.

We sat around a table, poring over a map of the border area. Sister Ágnes drew an *x* to indicate where we were now and how far we were from the border. Maybe twenty kilometers. On these roads it meant another half hour of driving. She'd let us out near no-man's land, a stretch of about seven kilometers that was neither Hungary nor Austria.

A canal on the map wound its way to the Austrian border. All we would have to do was to follow the canal. It was impossible for the truck to go over that terrain, because it was filled with frozen lakes and snow-covered ditches. Some patches were even mined. Sticking close to the canal was our best and safest bet. The border should be open. No border guards. No Russian patrols.

Even so, the woman said, it was better if we didn't take any chances. She took some white bed sheets and cut them up to fit over our winter coats as a kind of camouflage in the snow. Krisztina didn't like hers. Guszti told her she looked cute in her white cape. Little White Ridinghood instead of Little Red Ridinghood. That seemed to satisfy her.

My aunt seemed fidgety. The woman of the house offered her a thick sweater and an extra shawl, but she refused.

"You need something to cover your heads. It's cold out there in open country," the old man said. His white, yellowish mustache was curled up at the ends. "With the wind thrown in, it'll feel like Siberia."

My aunt was on her second cigarette. She took a long pull and exhaled through her nose. "I've never been to Siberia," she said.

"I have," the old man said.

My aunt was trumped again. I felt sorry for her. She was sixty, with a bad knee and brittle bones. She was nervous and worried, and she hated the cold. I knew she was more worried about Krisztina and me than herself. That's why I never told her about my other life. If I had, I'd see myself through her eyes, and I'd feel like a kid again, helpless and vulnerable. What she had witnessed in front of the church and the Casino was bad enough. If she really knew of all the scrapes I had gotten myself into she'd have a stroke.

I had second thoughts, myself. What kind of patriot was I anyhow? A patriot doesn't leave her country. A Hungarian poet said that a true Hungarian would never do what I was doing now. I couldn't recall his name, but a verse burned in my memory.

> "From the cradle to the grave,
>
> This is thy dear country.
>
> Thou must live and die here.
>
> There is no other place for thee
>
> Outside of Hungary."

The old peasant woman tried to give me a pair of warm mittens. I told her I was fine with my knit gloves.

Guszti said he had these fur-lined gloves he could give me. They were his uncle's. I didn't need them and said so.

Guszti and I got to talking in a corner. We rehashed the firefight on our street. We both wondered how long the freedom fighters could hold out. He said it would take more than sheer guts. Like luck, the kind we had on Sándor Bródy Street today. And it would take the intervention of a world power like the United States.

I didn't know what to say to that.

We talked a little about ourselves. I asked him why he didn't say goodbye to me in Balástya.

"I don't know," he said. "I guess I was jealous. Like I was when you beat me in the 100 meters. Then you came to Balástya with these friends. They treated you like you were one of them. You seemed so much more independent than me. I guess I was jealous of that, too. You seemed stronger than the girl I knew in school. You seemed…stronger than me."

I told him it was because I went through a lot in a short time. I opened up to him about what happened to my mother the first night of the demonstrations. And about our schoolmate Mariska.

He said he didn't know. He was sorry.

I gave Guszti an idea of what my life was like on the streets of Budapest after October 23rd. How I almost got myself killed because of my stupid grandstanding during a firefight.

"But you were brave as hell to join up in the first place," he said.

"It's not that I was brave. I was just too scared to go home."

Sister Ágnes said it was three in the morning and time to get going. We thanked our hosts and boarded the truck.

This time I sat with Sister Ágnes for the last leg of our journey. She gave me a flare gun. She said the seven kilometer trek, even if we were plodding, should not take longer than an hour. She and the soldiers were willing to wait it out. If anything went wrong, I was to shoot up the flare, and they would come to our aid. She had something else for me. An American twenty-dollar bill. Just to help us get started. "And when you get to America, don't forget to write."

I told her I was going to miss her. She's been so good to me and my family. "Why don't you come with us, Sister Ágnes? They have your picture, too."

"I can't. I have to look after Sewer Rat. He's a little better, but he's not out of the woods. He's counting on me. You can write to both of us in care of the Üllői Street Clinic. Or the Kecskemét Dungeon. I really don't know which it will be. And then, you never know, we may decide to fly the coop ourselves one day. But right now, Sewer Rat has to get his health back. I've kind of grown fond of him, you know…Hey, wait a minute. What's this?" Sister Ágnes checked her side mirror. "Someone's following us. Now?? We're almost there! *Jézus Mária!*"

I glanced into the mirror on my side. Sure enough a headlight was closing in behind us. Looked to me more like a motorcycle than a car, and I said as much to Sister Ágnes.

"You're probably right. I'm not worried. We have the boys in the back. We have another kilometer to go and then we're there. I bet the cyclist will pass us up."

Once we got to the kilometer marker she was looking for, Sister Ágnes stopped the truck and put it in park. She waited for whoever was behind us to pass. But instead of passing us, the motorcycle pulled right up behind us, so close we couldn't see it.

I opened my window. I thought I heard my name. It was weird, like the time I was buried in the sewer and Pali Szilágy was yelling for me.

We jumped off the truck and went toward the rear. True enough. Someone was asking for Izabella Barna.

The soldiers unfastened the canvas and aimed their weapons at the stranger who stood by his motorbike, the lights still on.

"It's only me," the stranger said, taking off his goggles.

"Mustache?" said one of the soldiers.

We didn't recognize him because of his enormous goggles. With his fur hat and fur mittens, he could've easily passed for an Eskimo. The mustache that had given him his name was white with frost.

It was Mustache who came after us on his motorcycle. But why?

He said he wanted to say goodbye to me. Me! And there in front of everybody, he took off his mittens and gave me the biggest hug. Then he backed up a few paces and said: "Izabella Barna, I didn't want you to leave Hungary without knowing that you have served your country with honor. It has been a privilege to serve as your Commander." He clicked his heels together and saluted me.

Chapter Ten

10

We started our seven-kilometer march through no-man's land, an icy field, as flat and as bare as sheet-iron. A biting wind blew smudge-like clouds in front of the moon and snow into our faces. The few stars in the dark sky seemed cold and distant. My breath was thick smoke in front of my face.

We walked in single file along the frozen canal. Guszti was up front, followed by his brother and mother. My aunt was next. Krisztina and I were last. I held on to Krisztina's hand. The going was rough in the open field. Not only were we exposed to the wind, but the ground was uneven. The deep furrows were already frozen. Stalks had turned into icicles.

The wind whistled as we stumbled over snow mounds and frozen corn stubble. My aunt's cane didn't do her any good. She almost fell when her boots hit something in the snow.

I told everybody to stop. It would be better if we walked in the canal. The frozen surface was a lot smoother there.

The canal at least gave us some cover from the wind. Snow had drifted along the side. We were making better time in the canal. The moon came out from behind the clouds, and the smooth drifts glistened in the moonlight. No other light anywhere, in the sky or on the horizon. Where the wind had blown away the snow, the tips of frozen stalks crunched under our feet.

I was warm enough except for my fingers. I was hoping Krisztina was warm. Under all her layers of clothes, she wore long flannel pajamas. And she had fur-lined mittens.

I should've taken the mittens from the old peasant woman. I worked my fingers out of the glove and made a fist, pressing my cold fingers to the warm cushion of my palm.

We had walked maybe five kilometers, when Guszti said, "Tank tracks!" He spotted tank tracks alongside the canal. I looked. They were tank treads all right.

Krisztina said she saw a shooting star high up in the sky. But it was shooting upward. Then it opened. An eerie phosphorescent green light lit up the sky and the watchtower ahead.

A flare!

"Everybody, hit the ground," I said. It was more like an order.

Snow was burning my face, but I didn't move. I held Krisztina close to me. She didn't say a word. When I fell down, my knee crashed through the ice. Nothing under the ice, only air. It was like glass breaking under my knee.

Then came the afterglow. The snow around us suddenly turned green. My heart raced deep inside all the layers of clothes. I wondered if Sister Ágnes and the others saw the flare. I was hoping they did. Please, God, let them see it. Unless they were gone. We were trudging in the canal over an hour, I was sure.

Krisztina and I hugged the ground together. She coughed. Loudly.

"Shhh," I whispered.

Then we heard gunfire. Close. Too close. From the watchtower.

I held Krisztina down. "Shhh. It's almost over."

It wasn't.

What we heard next was the sound of a mad man ranting at the top of his lungs. I looked in the direction of the tower. A man stood behind a heavy machine gun. He was yelling and cussing non-stop. "Traitors! Cowards! Fascists! Reactionary bastards!" After his barrage of words, he let go a salvo from his machine gun. He kept screaming and shooting in our direction.

Until the flare went out.

Darkness covered us once again. I don't think the man saw us, but I couldn't take that chance. I told the others to stay down. I had to do something. "Auntie, hold Krisztina down," I whispered to my aunt.

I crawled on my belly to the tower. I was careful not to crack any ice. The smallest noise would give me away.

The wooden watchtower was not very high. I counted maybe forty rungs to the latter. I climbed up the latter slowly, quietly. I was armed with only a flare gun. When I got to the top, I waited. The man's back was less than a meter from me. He was smoking and taking long swigs from a bottle. He shot up another flare, and, without waiting for the light, starting cursing again like a maniac and shooting off his gun.

"Shut the hell up!" I shouted.

When he spun around, I fired the flare gun into his gaping mouth.

The man clutched his burning face. The skin around his mouth was peeling off in a greenish halo of fire.

He pitched backwards and crashed through the wooden railing. He made a last ditch effort to hold on before he tumbled down onto the icy ground.

I clambered down and checked on him. He was dead. I went through his pockets, carefully keeping Sewer Rat's flashlight low to the ground, so one could see the light. The dead man's official *Személyi* papers said he was a member of the Communist Party since 1947.

I hurried back to the others.

My aunt asked, "Is he...?"

"Yes, he's dead."

"Who was he? ÁVO?"

"No," I said. "Just a die-hard Stalinist. And a drunk."

Without bothering to brush the snow off our white camouflage, which probably saved our butts, we plowed on.

Krisztina looked like she was gasping for breath. I picked her up and put her on my shoulders. I told her we were going on the longest horsie ride of her life. Even longer than when Papa took her around on his shoulders in the amusement park.

She started whimpering.

I gave her mitten a squeeze. "We'll be there soon."

We must've gone another kilometer or two when my aunt took a tumble. Guszti and Péter were there to help her up. She was all right, but from then on, they held on to her.

The first sign of the sun cast a reddish glow over the snow. With the first light of dawn, we were no longer invisible, and we were no longer in single file.

The powdery snow was still blowing around our feet. My pants were frozen and stiff all the way to the knee. Our boots were caked with snow.

I asked Guszti's mother how she was doing.

"I'm doing," she said.

Her face was scrubbed raw from the wind.

We trudged along like this a good ways when I had this terrifying thought that we were going in the wrong direction. What if the map was wrong? What if I had made a mistake, and we were going around in circles? I was ungodly tired, but it was Krisztina who was breathing hard. I could check her pulse, but what good would it do? My fingers were numb.

A tall watchtower loomed ahead of us. This one had a flag on the top of it. It looked red to me.

Which meant that Russians were manning the tower. God! What did I get my family into?

Guszti said he recognized the flag. There was white in it, too. They were Austrians. Their colors were red, white and red.

We suddenly had this burst of energy. Our steps quickened. I told Krisztina we made it. We were there.

We crossed a path through a stretch of rusty barbed wire to get to the tower. As we got closer we noticed the tower was deserted. Not a soul anywhere. Strange. I scanned the horizon. Other than a snow-covered haystack that looked like an igloo there was nothing out there but a cold wind. No Red Cross. No ambulances. No American tank battalion.

Our little group plowed on in the face of the brutal wind.

Then something strange happened as we neared the first haystack. I thought I heard the neighing of a horse. Out here? In the middle of nowhere? I thought I was going crazy. But the others heard it, too.

A little brown horse and an old, rickety wagon appeared from behind the haystack. A man in a gray coat and hat sat on the wagon. They were coming straight at us. He looked like an Austrian peasant dressed in oversized city clothes. The man greeted us with a wave of his hand, as if we were long-lost friends.

He was an older man with a red face and a friendly smile that showed the gap between his teeth. "*Vie gehen Sie,*" he said in German. He also spoke bits of broken Hungarian. "*Willkommen* to my country." He held up blankets. He wanted us to get on the wagon.

I told him in Hungarian that my little sister was sick. I put my hand by my heart to show him there was something wrong with my sister's heart.

"Ah," he said. "*Krank, ja?*"

With great care, he lifted Krisztina from my shoulder and put her in the wagon, covering her up to the neck with a thick blanket.

I fished out all the money I had in the world. Twenty American dollars. I held it out to our rescuer.

He shook his head violently. He wouldn't hear of it, the man said in broken Hungarian. "You are our guest now. Austria. We help you. *Ja?* How you say, the Austrian people open hand to our Hungarian neighbors? *Willkommen.* I take you to the first town, *ja?* Thirty *minuten.* Not far. They have Red Cross bus there and doctor. Come, I help you get on my wagon. The lady next."

He helped my aunt get into the wagon.

"*Danke schön*," my aunt thanked him. That may have been the extent of my aunt's knowledge of German.

"*Bitte schön*," the man said with a smile.

Once we were all on, he gave us a wicker basket filled with oranges and chocolates. He handed a thermos to us. Hot tea with a little rum.

We were so excited, we thanked our good Samaritan over and over in both German and Hungarian.

"Ah," he said, "Very good. From town, bus take you to Sankt Pölten and Salzburg. Very nice, *ja?* Mozartplatz. *Schön.*"

The man kept turning around to talk us. We didn't understand much, but we listened eagerly. He had such warm blue eyes, with so much kindness in them. His eyes reminded me of Sister Ágnes. She followed us after all.

The air seemed to be warming up. We shed off our frosted, white camouflage. By the shoulders, my hair was still matted with ice.

Up ahead, we could see the church steeple of his little village. From the back of the wagon, I glanced back at no-man's land and the endless stretch of white beyond, at what had been my country, my home, for the first fourteen years of my life. The red disc of the sun was already climbing over the eastern horizon, lighting up the low-hanging clouds. I wished that one day my Hungarian people could feel what I felt now. A great surge of freedom they had known for only a few fleeting days.

A MONUMENT
TO A KID OF BUDAPEST,
50 YEARS LATER

You

lie there,

a statue unto yourself,

a girl of fourteen,

a submachine gun

frozen to your heart,

a monument

to death and resurrection.

You lie there,

by the Church of the Immaculate Conception,

riddled with bullets,

sprayed with blood, all innocence deceived.

Hungarian schoolgirl turned

woman warrior,

it is you, and the likes of you,

the Revolution conceived.

Freedom fighter,

with no one to fight for her.

A small body,

with nobody to bury her,

sprinkled with lime,

covered by snow, by time,
unseeing doll's eyes raging
against Soviet armor,
against tyranny.
You lie there, a relic
on a hill of bone,
frozen in grotesque geometry,
a monument to a people's bravery.
A monument to man's inhumanity.

—Peter Hargitai

Acknowledgements

I would like to thank Izabella Barna for allowing me to use her name and for her suggestions regarding the text; the American Hungarian Federation for its support, and Bryan Dawson for the photographs from the 1956 Hungarian Revolution Portal on his AHF's website. I would also like to thank the late Tamás Aczél, co-author with Tibor Méray of *The Revolt of the Mind*. Professor Aczél had been an inspiration in renewing my interest in the 1956 Hungarian Revolution when he was my mentor at the University of Massachusetts at Amherst; and I wish to acknowledge Dr. Paul Szilágyi, who was more than an eyewitness during those turbulent days in 1956, and who first came up with the idea for a book that commemorates the Revolution's fiftieth anniversary; and Dr. Sanford J. Smoller for his timely and vigilant proofreading of the manuscript; I want to express my special appreciation to my brother, István Hargitai, for salvaging my childhood poem about the Revolution, which my father carried in his wallet until the day he died; and I want to thank Thomas P. Muhl for his suggestion of including a map to help readers become familiar with the streets of Budapest; and my eleven-year-old granddaughter, Katie Leatherbury, for being my juvenile reader; and last but not least, my wife, Dianne Marlene Hargitai, for designing the book's cover and for being my first reader.

978-0-595-41444-4
0-595-41444-3

CPSIA information can be obtained
at www.ICGtesting.com
Printed in the USA
BVOW08s0232131216

470623BV00001B/57/P